"Do you do a lot of work for my mother?" Erik asked

No way were they getting into a conversation about Camille. "Oh, a bit. But it's against my policy to discuss one client with another, even if it is a relative. I hope you understand."

He squinted at her and cocked his head, his dark hair falling boyishly onto his forehead. "Don't you work at Community Memorial?"

Her stomach flopped in panic. "Oh, no," Nora said brightly, trying to act unconcerned even though her heart was beating like a jackhammer. "You're probably thinking of my sister. We're twins. She's Nora, I'm Suzanne, but most people can't tell us apart." She noticed her voice was high and chirpy.

"Oh, yeah, that's it." He pointed a finger at her. "You really look a lot alike...."

Dear Reader,

I've really enjoyed writing this, the second book in Harlequin Superromance's new series, SINGLES...WITH KIDS. It's been fun working with other writers, incorporating their characters into *The Sister Switch,* knowing those characters' full stories will be told in other books.

While all of the stories have to do with a single parent finding love again, I chose to look at starting over through the eyes of a woman whose husband had died. Nora, the heroine, experienced the profound pain and loss that comes with the death of a loved one. Though she wants to love again, her fear of getting hurt has prevented her from letting go of the past and moving forward.

Then she meets Erik, a man who has succeeded in everything, except finding the place he belongs. Of course, their journey, like life, is filled with emotion and humor and chaos. And ultimately, each must decide—is the promise of love worth the risk to their hearts?

I hope you enjoy Nora and Erik's story, and I would love to hear what you think. Please visit my Web site at www.pamelaford.net or drop me an e-mail at pamelaford@pamelaford.net.

Sincerely,

Pamela Ford

THE SISTER SWITCH
Pamela Ford

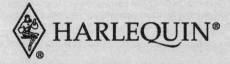

HARLEQUIN®

TORONTO • NEW YORK • LONDON
AMSTERDAM • PARIS • SYDNEY • HAMBURG
STOCKHOLM • ATHENS • TOKYO • MILAN • MADRID
PRAGUE • WARSAW • BUDAPEST • AUCKLAND

ISBN-13: 978-0-373-78149-2
ISBN-10:   0-373-78149-0

THE SISTER SWITCH

ABOUT THE AUTHOR

Pamela Ford spent many years writing for advertising agencies and corporations before setting off on her own as a freelance writer. She happily wrote brochures, catalogs, video scripts and promotional materials for a variety of clients.

All that changed with the birth of her first child. It might have been the combination of changing diapers, working from the house and writing a video script about motors and drives—or it might have been because she's a hopeless romantic—but whatever the reason, one afternoon when the baby was asleep she started writing a novel. That first book, while it holds a special place in her heart, is buried deep in her attic, never to see the light of day.

Pamela currently lives in Wisconsin with her three daughters and a frisky Malti-Poo.

Books by Pamela Ford

HARLEQUIN SUPERROMANCE
1247—OH BABY!
1291—DEAR CORDELIA

To my children, Margaux, Ella and Laurel who
know that life well lived is filled with laughter.
And to my editor, Johanna Raisanen,
for believing in me.

Acknowledgments

My thanks to

Bob Corby
who not only taught me everything I now know
about physical therapy, but was also
pretty good at brainstorming a romance novel.

Finn Gunderson at USSA; Terry Miller,
Teri Wagner, Jay Rakowski, Paul Stollenwerk,
Donna Blacker, Margo Billmeyer, John Lesko
and John Armbruster for answering even the
dumbest questions without laughing.

CHAPTER ONE

"THE SOLUTION IS OBVIOUS," Suzanne said. "You just have to be me."

Nora Clark knew she was in trouble the moment she heard her twin sister utter those words. She tightened her grip on the phone and paced across her small kitchen. "Tell me I just misheard you. Tell me this cell phone connection is so bad you didn't really say what I think I just heard."

"You have to do this, Nora. You've gotta take my place."

Irritation rolled through Nora. She'd been supporting her sister for two years as she tried to build a personal shopping business. Now Suzanne wanted her to *be* the personal shopper? Enough was enough. "Your biggest client wants you to do a rush job for her son. The correct answer is—you get off that cruise and come home."

"I'm on the Inside Passage, remember?

Alaska? Open water. Icebergs. You don't just *jump off* cruise ships up here." Suzanne's voice turned pleading. "Please…I can't afford to lose this account."

Nora gritted her teeth. "I know you need this job. I know Camille Lamont is a famous author and is connected enough to launch your business—"

"Then do the job for me. Think about it. If I keep Camille as a client, it could get me out of your hair—not to mention your house." Suzanne paused. "Maybe then you'd have time to date."

"Suzanne!"

"Nora!" Her sister mimicked her annoyed tone.

"How about if I go to the appointment as myself…and explain that you're on a seventeen-day cruise—"

"No! What will his mother think when she learns I sent someone who knows *next to nothing* about personal shopping to meet with her son?" Suzanne groaned. "I can see this account waving goodbye already."

"Then, you just have to come back to San Francisco and meet with her yourself," Nora said as evenly as possible.

"We're practically in grizzly territory up here. Probably polar bear, too."

Nora snorted. "I doubt the bear populations

will be attacking you at the next port of call—
or the airport, for that matter."

"Nora." Suzanne's voice dropped low. "When
Keegan called off our wedding, I thought I would
die. I need this cruise. Even *you* said it was a good
idea. The Lamont account is important to me, but
I'm just not up to it yet. I've only been on the ship
one day. What kind of a respite is that?"

Nora dropped into a kitchen chair as she tried
to reason everything out. Suzanne had really hit
bottom when Keegan dumped her. And though
Nora had never been able to understand her
sister's devastation over losing that idiot, she
had agreed time away might help Suzanne heal.

Still, that didn't mean Nora taking her place
was a good idea. "Suzanne, we may look the
same but that's where the similarity ends. I'm
a physical therapist. You're a personal shopper.
You're loose and carefree. I'm…not."

"I'll say."

"What?"

"Sorry. Sorry."

"Anyway, pretending to be you, even for one
meeting, is like…expecting apples to be
oranges."

"You didn't used to be an apple. You just
became one over the years."

"I did not." Indignation rose up inside her.

"Then why do you keep staying in that hospital P.T. job when you hate it? Come on, I know your complaints by heart." Suzanne's voice took on a singsong quality. "Once people have surgery, all you do is make sure they can use a walker and get out of a chair, and then—boom!—they're gone. Discharged. You never get to see rehab through to the end."

"It's important work," Nora said.

Suzanne just kept talking. "And what about that new sports medicine rehab center the hospital's opening? They have to hire someone—and you haven't even applied yet, have you?"

The truth in her words irritated Nora more than the know-it-all tone in her voice. "Suzanne, when you grow up you discover you can't have everything. You become—"

"Dull. But you don't have to."

Nora slowly counted to ten in her head. "Whatever. My pretending to be you is still a dumb idea. Switching places is something you do when you're seventeen."

"Or something you do when your sister really needs your help. This isn't about Erik Lamont—and you know it. It's about keeping his mother happy. If she wants me to do a quick job for her son, I can't *not* do it." She sighed. "Nora—she'll hire someone else."

"Couldn't you just call her and explain that—"

"Nora? You there? You're breaking up."

"Suzanne? Hello? Can you hear me?" She looked up at the ceiling in frustration. Dammit, they'd lost the connection. Hitting redial, she kicked into her spiel again as soon as Suzanne answered. "Just tell Camille you're on a long cruise in Alaska. Surely she'll understand that people take vacations." She pressed the fingers of one hand to her forehead.

"I can't risk it—she's too new a client. How hard could it be to take my place just this once?" Suzanne laughed. "You never know, he could be cute...."

"Not even funny." Nora stood, unable to stay still for long with the conversation twisting the way that it was.

"Why do you always discount the possibility of meeting another man? Kevin died five years ago—"

"How did we get from me impersonating you to my getting hooked up with some guy we don't even know, and for all we know is an unemployed loser living off his mother or still in high school or something? Suzanne, sometimes you're like a broken record."

"So will you take my place?"

She huffed. "New song. Same broken record.

No. How could I? What if his mom notices the difference?"

"Why would his mom be there? You're shopping for him."

"Well, his mom made the call. Really, Suzanne, I'd help you if I could." She felt a tugging at her shirt and looked down.

"Mama," Danny said. "I think I found a new daddy—the right one. Come." He pulled her with him toward the living room.

Suzanne kept talking into her ear. "Yeah, well, what happens if I tell his mother I can't do it—"

"Hold on a minute, Suz." She looked at Danny. "What?"

"I found a new daddy on my video." His brown eyes shone with earnestness.

"You can't just find a daddy on a video, honey. It's not that easy."

"But you said if I found one to let you know."

Nora sighed. Whatever possessed her to say such a thing to him?

"He's really nice." Danny pointed at the television where Mr. Rogers was cutting construction paper with scissors and talking in his perfectly calm voice.

"Mr. Rogers? Oh, Danny, Mr. Rogers is—" *Dead*. "Uh—married already. Tell you what, sweetie, why don't you go get a cookie and

I'll be off in a minute." She watched him dash into the kitchen, then turned her attention back to the phone.

"Something wrong?" Suzanne asked.

"He's just looking for a daddy again. Found one on TV that he thinks is just right. *Mr. Rogers.*"

"Jeez, he's really getting determined about that. Maybe you should sign up for some online dating—"

"Suzanne. Don't be dumb."

Danny hopped back into the room munching on a cookie and she went back into the kitchen.

"Okay," Suzanne said. "So I was saying, what happens if I turn this job down and Camille finds some other personal shopper who is ready and willing to help. Now she thinks, *golly, I like this new on-the-ball shopper girl who's available just when I need her. I think I'll give her all my business.* Now I've just lost my biggest account—all because I didn't meet with—"

Suddenly silence was all Nora heard and she knew the connection had been dropped again. "I hate cell phones!" she muttered. She set her phone on the counter and stared at the cupboard for a moment, suddenly noticing the dried milk spatters on the doors. How did all this milk splash up here? And how could she not have seen it before? She grabbed the dishrag from the sink and began to wipe the spatters off the black doors as she debated whether to call her sister back or not.

Her head felt like it was going to burst. She knew this account was crucial to Suzanne's success, to having Suzanne make enough money to support herself, *to Suzanne ever moving out of Nora's house*. She exhaled. Which meant, keeping this account was as important to her as it was to Suzanne.

She picked up the phone and punched redial. Her sister answered on the first ring, saying, "I don't know how much longer I'll be able to get a signal out here."

"Look," Nora said. "There's not much I wouldn't do for you, but this...this...I wouldn't know the first thing about what I'm doing."

"It's not that hard."

Nora could hear the hope in Suzanne's voice. She looked down at her T-shirt and sweatpants and felt ill. "For God's sake, I don't know anything about style, let alone being a personal shopper."

"I'll talk you through it—"

"You're on a cruise ship with crummy cell phone connections." Kneeling now, she attacked the spatters on the lower cupboard doors as if the forcefulness of her effort would erase her frustration.

"There's always ship-to-shore radio."

Nora groaned and sat back on her heels. "I'm sure that's a reasonable price per minute. Let's just stop and look at this realistically. What if he figures out I'm not you? What if his mother comes along on the spur of the moment? What if I do a really bad job and you lose the account anyway—"

"Nora! We don't have any other choices."

We? She pushed herself to standing and went into the front hall to inspect her reflection in the full-length mirror. She pulled her dark hair out of its ponytail and shook it loose around her face. Yeah, she could still pass for Suzanne without a problem.

The thought made her stomach do a nervous flop. She wasn't actually considering this ridiculous idea, was she?

Absolutely not.

"One meeting," she said calmly.

"Right. Two at the most."

"Two? When did this happen?"

"If you have to buy him something, you're going to have to deliver it," Suzanne said. "No biggie. He tries it on, you say it looks great, you're outta there in, like, twenty minutes."

"Okay. Two meetings at the most." Nora felt the room begin to spin.

"Right."

"You'll talk me through everything?"

"Everything."

Light-headed, Nora sank down into her brown chenille couch. Across the room, Danny sat cross-legged on the rug in front of the TV, still enthralled by Mr. Rogers.

"What if he *is* cute?" Nora said. "And he wants me to buy him—" her voice dropped lower "—pants. I don't have to measure his inseam or anything, do I?"

Suzanne burst out laughing. "No. He should know what size he wears. If in doubt, get a couple of sizes and have him keep the one that fits best."

"I have to tell him which pants fit him best? Some guy I don't even know? What if he's cute? What if he's, ahem, *built*."

Suzanne laughed harder. "You just say they look *fabu* and get the heck out of the house before he takes them off and asks you how his briefs fit."

"No way. I can't do it. I can't. Really, Suzanne, I am not ready for this—"

Suzanne's laughter reached hysterical proportions before she pulled herself together.

"I'm kidding. You really do need to get out more. Clients *do not* come on to the personal shopper. It just isn't done."

"Right. I know that." Nora let her head fall back against the couch.

"So, will you do it? Just this once…just switch places one more time."

She knew better. She really did. "Oh, Suzanne, how many times did we switch places and have it backfire—"

"And think of all the times it didn't… Nora?"

She hesitated even though she knew she didn't have a choice. Not really. Not if Suzanne was going to get what she wanted so that Nora could get what she wanted. She hesitated, even though she knew she was going to say yes.

She drew a breath. "You have to promise—"

"Anything. Anything you want."

"*Never* to ask me to do this again."

"Never?" Suzanne sounded shocked.

"Never."

"Never is really an absolute. I mean, what if it's mutually beneficial? Because there are times when—"

"No." Nora made sure her voice was firm and strong.

"Wow. Okay. But, just in case you're wondering, I'll still be you sometime if you want me to—"

"No, no, no. After this time, *never again*. Never."

"Okay. I think I got that," Suzanne said.

Nora closed her eyes for a moment and hoped she wasn't about to create yet another massive complication in her life. "Now what do I have to do to be a personal shopper? You're going to have tell me more than just what questions to ask the guy—you're going to have to dress me, too."

As Suzanne's laughter came across the airwaves, the phone cut out again. Nora hit redial but this time the call didn't connect. She tried again and got Suzanne's voice mail.

"Oh, just great," she muttered. "I'd better not have to make this up as I go along or we're both in big trouble."

"I'm NOT MEETING with a personal shopper." Erik Morgan scowled at his mother, who was working on a computer at her large mahogany desk.

"Why not?" She slowly spun her leather desk chair around to face him.

"I don't have the time. I don't have the inclination. I don't want some strange woman that involved in my life."

"She doesn't get involved in your life. She

just shops for you. Or with you." His mother smiled calmly and he knew manipulation was running rampant beneath her perfectly coiffed blond hair. "Whichever you prefer."

Erik rolled his eyes. "Is this why you asked me to come over today? To talk about personal shopping? Not to check your knee?"

"I want you to check my knee, too. This replacement they put in doesn't seem to work that well yet." She rubbed her knee.

He knelt by her chair and checked her leg for swelling, then straightened her knee with his hands and made it bend again. "Your range of motion is still limited. Let me see you go up the stairs." He stood and took her hand to help her up. "Are you doing the exercises? And walking, like you're supposed to?"

They moved slowly toward the wide curving stairway in the marble-floored foyer. This house was way too formal for his taste; he was glad he hadn't grown up here.

"It's hard to find so much time to exercise," his mother said. "I've got a deadline. I've just got to get this next book written and the words aren't coming easily. Maybe it's from going under the anesthetic. Doesn't that have some sort of effect on brain neuron connections?"

For a bestselling author, sometimes his mother was really a ditz. "Maybe on you."

She gasped and he held in a grin. "Really? Is it permanent? How will I ever finish this book?"

"Mom! No—"

"It's not permanent then?"

"It doesn't happen at all! I just said that because you're driving me nuts." He frowned as he looked at her left leg. "A knee replacement isn't going to finish healing unless you help it along. I know it's been five weeks, but you've got to get up and walk."

"Honey, isn't there some other way—"

"No." He tried to stay patient. "That knee is going to freeze up if you don't work it. If all you wanted for a leg was a bent stick, we could have given you one in the first place and it would have cost less." He gestured at the stairs. "Let me see you climb."

"Now, Erik, there's no reason to get testy." She took hold of the banister and started up the stairs, one step at a time. "I'm doing most of my exercises. I just wanted to double-check because I really have to get this book finished."

Patience, patience. "Some isn't good enough. Look at you on the stairs—you don't have the strength to go step over step yet."

"What are you going to wear to the party?" she asked over her shoulder.

He watched her knee. "Promise me you'll do all your exercises even if you have writing to do."

"We'll talk about it. Now, what are you wearing to the party?"

"What party?" he asked irritably.

His mother sighed. "And you wonder why I want you to use a personal shopper?" Halfway up the stairs she turned around. "The one my publisher is throwing—"

"Oh, yeah. Fifteenth straight book on the *New York Times* list."

"And you have an outfit to wear?" She continued down the stairs, her eyes never leaving his face.

"An outfit? Sounds so…matching."

"Erik—"

"Mom—"

"Don't 'Mom' me. You spend all day in scrubs and the rest of the time in jeans. It's time you start dressing like the grown-up you are."

He folded his arms across his chest. "I have other clothes, trust me—"

"I don't trust you. Not since you showed up for dinner at Cavanaugh's dressed like you were going to the ski hill." She stepped off the bottom stair and took the hand he held out to her.

"That's because I was coming *from* the ski hill. I just overestimated how long we'd be out there."

"Well, you had the appearance of someone from the wrong side of the tracks."

He snorted. "Mom, I'm a doctor. Everyone knows I can buy clothes if I want them. Who the hell cares what I wear as long as I can fix their bodies up good as new—or almost good as new."

His mother started back toward her office. "Well, Mary Jean's niece cared. She wasn't impressed at all, even if you were once on the Olympic ski team."

Oh, wait a minute. He'd thought she was manipulating something. His mother was matchmaking again. "Mom, I don't want to meet anyone at this party."

Her eyes widened. "I wasn't going to introduce you to anyone."

"Don't invite anyone who might want to introduce themselves to me, either."

"Erik, I wouldn't dream of interfering in your love life."

Ha! He held up a hand. "Just so we're clear. No more daughters of friends, friends of friends, acquaintances of friends... I'm tired of meeting plastic women who just want to land themselves a rich husband."

A pensive expression crossed his mother's face as she lowered herself into her office chair.

"Now what?" he asked against his better judgment, knowing full well that the master manipulator was just getting started.

His mother rubbed her knee.

"Does your knee hurt?"

"Only when I get into disagreements."

Erik laughed.

"Now, sweetheart," she said. "About that promise to do my exercises… I think I would feel so much more inclined to do them if I could remove the worry that you had something appropriate to wear to the party."

"Fine, put your mind to rest. I do." *Khakis and a polo.*

"What?"

"What do you mean, 'what'?" He shoved his hands in his jeans pockets.

"What are you going to wear?" she asked calmly. "Not your old khakis and a worn polo."

"I'll buy something."

"When?"

"Soon."

"I've heard this before. And it's not good enough. My shopper can take care of everything. Then I can do my exercises in peace knowing that your outfit is taken care of…and my brain neurons can reconnect so I can write the rest of this book."

If his mother hadn't succeeded as a novelist, she would have made a great lawyer. Juries wouldn't even know what hit them.

"Mom! I don't need a personal shopper. What's next? Should I have my nails buffed? My chest hair waxed?" He held up both hands. "Okay, I'll go shopping. I'll even ask the clerk for help—if I need it."

"Don't be silly. This is the same shopper I use. You'll like her. First, she'll interview you." She rummaged through the papers and notebooks on her desk. "I have an extra card here somewhere," she said. "Then she'll shop and bring back what she bought. You try it all on and keep what you want. Or in your case, you keep what she recommends so your clothes match. It's jolly fun."

"Jolly fun? Are you going British?" he asked grumpily.

His mother chortled. "So, what do think? I will force myself to get up and walk. That will make you happy. And you will force yourself to meet with my personal shopper. That will make me happy. Have we an agreement?"

At least this was better than her playing matchmaker and trying to set him up with one of her friends' daughters. "Fine. What's her number? I'll give her a call."

She waved a hand at him. "No need to call. It's all set up. She'll be at your house tomorrow night at seven."

"You already made the appointment? Mom, what are you doing?" No wonder his sister moved halfway across the country. He'd been the stupid one to move back when he finished his residency.

"I thought about having her meet you here since I know her already, but she'll probably want to take a peek at what you've got in your closet."

"She's going to go through my clothes?" he asked, appalled.

"Well, how else do you think she'll help you?"

"Mom! Why do you do these things?"

"I checked your schedule at work—"

"The Giants game is on tomorrow night. I'm not—"

"Talk fast then and the meeting will be over sooner. Now where is that business card." She shuffled through her papers again. "The party is Saturday. In order for her to have time to shop, you have to meet tomorrow night."

"Oh, well, we wouldn't have wanted to miss out on the opportunity."

"Now, Erik, that sounded a bit like an arrogant orthopedic surgeon talking."

Arrogant orthopedic surgeon? Hell, he felt like a fifteen-year-old kid right now. "But, Mom, really, she's going to go through my clothes?"

"Have you got something to hide?"

He almost choked. "No. But it's sort of personal."

"That's why she's called a *personal shopper.* Now, sweetie, I've got writing to do and, you know, knee exercises. I hate to push you off like this, but I don't have time to chitchat the night away even if you do." She turned back to her computer and poised her fingers at the keyboard. "If there isn't anything else, you really should get on your way."

He really should get on his way? That's what he'd been trying to do when he left work and got an urgent call from his mother insisting he come over immediately. "Great idea. By the way, they say blueberries are good for brain development and neuron connections."

"Really? I'll be sure I get some."

He waited a long moment, but his mother didn't offer the information he needed. "Okay. I give up. Who am I expecting at seven tomorrow night?"

"Suzanne. Suzanne Carlisle. Her company is called The Shopping Goddess. You'll like her."

CHAPTER TWO

THIS WAS ABSOLUTELY ridiculous. And the worst of it was, she'd agreed to take part in it. Nora inspected herself in the bureau mirror, her dark brown hair now cut to shoulder-length and highlighted with natural-looking streaks of red like Suzanne's. Thank goodness her sister's hairdresser had been able to squeeze her in over the lunch hour. Although, in order to get the appointment, she'd had to lie, saying she needed the same style as Suzanne because the two of them wanted to play a prank on some old friends. She shook her head. This was the whole problem with taking each other's places—it always ended up accompanied by a string of lies.

She went into the hall and peeked down the stairs to make sure her son and the babysitter were occupied, then quickly dialed her friend Margo Evans—the only other person besides Suzanne who knew what she was about to do.

"I feel like a fraud," she whispered into the phone as soon as Margo answered.

"Well, technically, you are."

"Thanks. I feel so much better about doing this now." Nora frowned at her reflection in the hall mirror. She tugged up on the white camisole she was wearing under Suzanne's form-fitting black jacket. Her legs looked long and lean in the matching flared black slacks. All she needed was to put on Suzanne's stilettos and she would be completely transformed. She only hoped she'd be able to balance on those toothpick heels. "You should see me. I'm wearing Suzanne's clothes—"

"I bet you look incredible! Like something out of a fashion magazine."

Margo had such a knack for being reassuring. "Actually, I may be a bit overexposed on top." She closed the center button at the front of the jacket and pulled up on the camisole again. Way too much skin showing. "Too bad I'm not an actress because I could probably win an Oscar for the performance I'm going to give tonight."

"Just remember what we talked about. Get in there, find out what the guy needs and get out. Say as little as possible, don't talk about yourself and, rule number one, *don't talk about his mother.* The shorter the meeting, the better."

"Right." Nora glanced at her watch. "I better finish getting ready or I'll be late. Wish me luck."

"Good luck. You'll do great. You're coming for coffee group tonight, aren't you?"

"Yeah—unless this interview takes too long. And if that happens, you'll be able to find me at the nearest corner tavern drowning my sorrows!" She hung up the phone and didn't move for a long minute, wondering for the thousandth time how she'd let herself get roped into doing a sister switch. And even worse, how she'd agreed to a meeting on the one night of the week she actually had something fun to do.

She thought back to how their group had evolved. First, it had just been her and Margo— two friends, both single mothers. Then, Nora had gotten to know Selena, another single mom, and brought her along, and Margo had invited Rosie DeWitt, an old high school friend who was raising a son alone. When Selena dubbed them Singles with Kids, they decided to make it official and meet at Margo's Bistro every Thursday night for coffee and coversation.

She went into her bedroom, looked in the mirror and made a face at the image of her sister she saw there. Thank goodness Erik Lamont had never met Suzanne, because that was really the only thing that would save them.

She closed her eyes for a moment and tried to quash her fears. A little *saving* might not be the worst thing right now, if only she had any idea who to ask for help. Her grandmother would have pulled out the name of some obscure saint qualified to assist in this particular situation. There were hundreds of saints, each one with a different specialty. But who could possibly be the patron saint of people trying to pull a fast one?

If only she'd paid better attention during her parochial grade school days. Then again, maybe one of the more well-known saints would be willing to pinch-hit just this once. Like, oh…how about Saint Christopher? She grimaced. Not really a good match—or choice. Didn't they de-saint him in the '80s anyway?

She knew she had to get going, but stalled longer. Who was that saint, the one her grandmother always said answered her prayers?

St. Jude.

"Oh, yeah," she said aloud. "The patron saint of desperate causes. Rather a good fit if I do say so myself." She ran a brush through her hair and muttered under her breath, "Please, Saint Jude…get me through this meeting and I promise, promise never to do this again."

She stopped with the brush halfway down the back of her head and raised her eyes skyward. "And, if by chance you happen to be hanging out with any other saintly types up there whose area of expertise might better match my situation, feel free to ask their assistance."

She was really losing it now.

It was all Suzanne's fault. She'd tried to reach her sister several more times last night, but only one call connected—and then only long enough for Suzanne to tell her to conduct an initial client assessment. So, at ten-thirty she'd gone digging into her sister's files and found a client assessment form to fill out and a half page of handwritten notes about personal shopping. That was it—the sum total of her knowledge about personal shopping. Everything else she had to ad-lib.

No wonder her stomach was knotted and nauseous. She opened the leather briefcase on her bed and checked to make sure she had a pad of paper and the client assessment form. One could never be too sure. She may stumble through their meeting tonight, but at least she'd have something to write on.

She slipped on Suzanne's stilettos and her confidence wavered even more. She didn't feel like a personal shopper; she didn't feel like Suzanne. What she felt like was Nora in Suzanne's clothing, like the wolf wearing only a partial sheepskin, like the emperor in the nude.

Well, not quite that.

Maybe what she needed to boost her self-esteem were some affirmations—lots of affirmations. "I am Suzanne," she said to her reflection. She wobbled across the room on her stilettos, smiling and nodding at nonexistent people. "I *am* Suzanne. I *am* a personal shopper. I love to help people fix their wardrobes. I love to shop. How can I help you? I *love* to shop. You look *fabulous* in that. Want to try on something else?"

Suddenly she felt like a talking Barbie doll. The heels didn't help, either—they were exactly like something Barbie would wear. Poor Barbie—she never got to enjoy wearing flats.

Nora checked her watch. It really was time to go. As long as she didn't have to walk too far, she should be all right in these shoes. Her stomach churned with anticipation and she stared at herself in the mirror a moment longer, wishing she was just coming home from the meeting instead of just leaving for it.

Finally she drew a long slow breath and let

it out, then went into the living room where Danny and the babysitter were mesmerized by some television program. She bent to kiss her son on the forehead. "You go to bed when Ashley tells you, and I'll come in and kiss you again when I get home, okay?"

He nodded. "You look like Auntie Suzanne."

Oh, boy. "That's because we're twins. See you later, sweetie." She ran out the door before Danny could take his thought process one step further and ask in front of the sitter why she was wearing Suzanne's clothes.

A half hour later she pulled up in front of a gorgeous old Colonial Revival rowhouse in Russian Hill, with curved windows and a columned portico in front. The guy had good taste, she had to hand it to him.

And money, obviously.

All from his mother, she bet. He was probably a freeloader living off Mom's royalties. Camille Lamont probably bought him the house and paid all the utilities. No doubt that was it because, truly, how many adult men allowed their mothers to hire a personal shopper to work with them?

Very few. *Or none.*

So he was a momma's boy.

The very thought gave her self-confidence a

boost and propelled her out of Suzanne's BMW and up the walk. Probably a geeky momma's boy at that. Nothing she couldn't handle.

She carefully climbed the steps to the front door, holding tight to the rail so she didn't fall off her shoes. Then she pressed the doorbell and waited for Erik Lamont to answer. A soft breeze slid over her bare arms and she looked down the street to a view of San Francisco Bay in the distance.

She tried to control her nervous anticipation and concentrate on the weather. She really did love May. The rains were past, the summer coolness and fog had yet to arrive and the hydrangeas and tulips and rhododendrons were nearly at their peak. She closed her eyes and turned her face toward the sun. A wave of exhaustion rolled over her: she'd been up half the night worrying about this meeting. The thought caused her nervousness to return in full measure, eroding her confidence once again.

This was no good. She had to be self-assured in front of this guy. After all, Suzanne certainly wouldn't be nervous—not with her experience level. Nora drew a breath to calm herself. Maybe she could employ the same strategy they tell you to use when you give a speech—picture the audience in their underwear. That might work.

The moment Erik Lamont opened the door, she would simply envision him in his underwear. That should clear out any nervous energy—

"Something going on down the block?" A man's voice jerked her back to reality. She spun round. *Remember, picture him in—* "Ah, no, just looking at—" *his underwear* "—the Bay." *Dr. Erik Morgan. Orthopedic surgeon at her hospital. Former Olympic freestyle skier. Dark brown hair. Gorgeous blue eyes. In...his... briefs.* Her cheeks began to burn. This was not turning out to be a good plan at all.

"Ah—ah—" She looked at him, dazed, then glanced at the house numbers in confusion as she tried to force the vision of Erik Morgan in his underwear out of her mind. Somehow, she'd come to the wrong place—*or something.* "I— I'm not sure I'm at the right house. I'm supposed to meet Erik Lamont." *You know, that geeky momma's boy.*

"That would be me. Although I go by Erik Morgan." He grinned. "You must be my personal shopper."

Him? Her heart plummeted into her stomach. She tried not to gape as she attempted to comprehend this latest revelation. *She had to dress Erik Morgan?* A picture of him in his briefs, like an undressed paper doll, flashed into her mind and she shoved it away as hard as she could.

"Lamont is my stepdad's last name. Come on in." He stepped back to let her into the house.

Nora could only nod. Erik Morgan. Dr. Erik Morgan. He worked out of the same hospital as she did. The minute he recognized her, this whole thing would be over.

"You want something to drink?" he asked.

"Water would be fine." She tried to swallow but her mouth was totally dry. *Water would be incredible.*

He disappeared toward the back of the house and returned a minute later, handing her a bottle of Ice Mountain. "I have to admit, I've never used a personal shopper before," he said. Barefoot, and in shorts that showed enough of the legs that once made him a world-class skier, he led her into the living room, which was casually decorated with a mix of antique and new furnishings. A big blue and gold patterned oriental rug covered the hardwood floor.

"Oh, well, lots of people haven't." She perched on the edge of the tweed sofa and tried not to notice the muscles in his legs. Opening her bottle of water, she took a big drink while he dropped down into a comfortably worn leather club chair.

"Do you do a lot of work for my mother?" he asked.

No way were they getting into a conversation about Camille. "Oh, a bit. But, it's against my policy to discuss one client with another, even if it is a relative. I hope you understand."

He squinted at her and cocked his head, his dark hair falling boyishly onto his forehead. "Don't you work at Community Memorial?"

Her stomach flopped in panic. "Oh, no," she said brightly, trying to act unconcerned even though her heart was beating like a jackhammer. "You're probably thinking of my sister. We're twins. She's Nora, I'm Suzanne, but most people can't tell us apart." She mentally cringed at how high and chirpy her voice sounded.

"Oh, yeah, that's it. Physical therapy." He pointed a finger at her. "You really look a lot alike, but her hair's different than yours…."

Not anymore. Who would have guessed when she got her hair done like Suzanne that the client would be someone she would see at work? She decided to sidestep future questions before any arose. "Our hair used to be different, but now I—Nora—got her hair done like mine, so I guess we're pretty much identical."

"Hmm, maybe I'll stop down in P.T. and razz her about it." He smiled.

What? Ohmigod, she couldn't possibly interact with him as both Suzanne *and* Nora. How would she keep anything straight? Leave it to her sister to drag her into the worst possible situation ever. She could feel a world-class headache kicking in. It was time to get this show on the road. "I guess we should get started…." *And over with.*

She bent to her briefcase and quickly pulled out the interview form and a clipboard. Her hair slipped forward into her face, blocking her vision, and she shoved it behind her ears. She missed her ponytail—it did such a nice job of keeping her hair out of the way. "First of all, I have to ask a few questions about your needs, preferences for style and color, that sort of thing."

He settled back into his chair as if he were enjoying himself immensely.

"All right?" she asked, somewhat disconcerted by the playfulness she saw in his eyes.

"Ask away."

"Let's begin with why you're hiring me. Is this a general wardrobe overhaul or do you just need something for a special occasion?"

"Hmm." He looked at her for a moment. "Why I'm hiring you, huh? Well, this meeting is the result of a bargain I struck with my mother so she would do her rehab exercises for the knee replacement surgery she had a month ago."

"Oh." Nora scribbled a few words on the paper just to look like she knew what she was doing.

"She's afraid I'm going to wear something to an upcoming function that will embarrass her."

"Really?" *Interesting.* "What kinds of clothes do you…lean toward wearing?"

"You don't have to go through my closet, do you?"

She hoped she didn't blanch. The paperwork in Suzanne's files had mentioned something about checking out the client's existing wardrobe. Imagine going through Erik Morgan's drawers…ah, dresser. She felt heat start up her cheeks again. *No way.* Besides, she knew far too little about this business to get in that deep.

"Oh, no, I don't think that's necessary," she said quickly. "Not when you just need help for one specific occasion."

He seemed as relieved by her answer as she was. "So, what type of event is it?" she asked.

"A party." He kicked his bare feet up on the footstool. "My mom's hit the *New York Times* bestseller list for the fifteenth time. Her publisher is throwing a big bash to celebrate."

"Wow! That sounds exciting. But, wouldn't

you just wear a suit?" He'd look good in one, but, personally, she liked the shorts and T-shirt ensemble he had going on right now.

He frowned. "Suits I've got."

She restrained the urge to ask, *then what do you need me for?* and instead said, "So…did you need help choosing a new one?"

"The party's at Corinthian Yacht Club—it's not really a formal event. I think the invitation says *casual chic*. Whatever the hell that is."

She remembered hearing Suzanne talk about dress codes in the past. The problem was Nora hadn't paid a lot of attention. Working as a P.T., she pretty much adhered to one dress code— comfortable—so Suzanne's ramblings had gone in one ear and out the other.

Nora wrote *casual chic* on the paper and under-lined it three times. She'd heard of office casual, white tie, black tie, semiformal, dressy casual… She wracked her brain. Casual chic didn't ring a bell. When she agreed to do this meeting, she'd sort of assumed the client would be giving her more direction than simply *casual chic*.

Erik was watching her as if he expected her to say something, so she opened her mouth and began to speak, hoping beyond hope that even a part of what she was saying was correct. Or at least appeared to make some sort of sense, since this guy didn't know what casual chic was, either. She sat back and crossed her legs, confidently gesturing with her pen.

"Well…casual chic is really not as complicated as it seems. Not a bit. We all know what casual is…well, weekend kind of casual…blue jeans and…such." She could feel prickling all over her body where she was breaking out in a sweat.

"And of course, there's business casual which is a step or two above that. Khakis, polo shirts, the like. Then you see, casual chic is… is…simply a few more steps above that. More *chic* kind of clothes, dressier… but still casual. In the casual family, that is." She splayed a hand across her chest in an effort to present a confidence she didn't feel.

"Okay, as long as *you* know what you're doing," he said. "What kind of clothes do you recomm—"

The ringing of the doorbell cut short his sentence and he excused himself to get the door. Nora let out a sigh of relief. *Casual chic?* She had a vague idea of what *she* thought casual chic was, but until she talked to her sister she didn't want to take any chances with the definition. She needed to get out of here and on the phone with Suzanne as soon as possible.

The door opened even before Erik reached it,

and a blonde, impeccably dressed older woman limped into the room using a cane. "Sorry to drop by without calling, honey, but I was just in the neighborhood and thought, why not stop and say hi to Suzanne?"

Nora's blood ran cold. *Not Camille Lamont.* Please God, this couldn't be Camille Lamont. The woman *knew* Suzanne. She'd never fool her with this charade. Oh, help, what did Suzanne call her? Ms. Lamont? Mrs. Lamont? Camille? Goddess?

Nora stood and the woman hobbled over.

"Suzanne! I'm so glad you could fit Erik into your schedule."

Nora frantically tried to think of something personal shopperish to say, finally settling on the only thing that came to mind. "I'm happy to be able to help."

"So now you've met Erik. He lives in blue jeans. And shorts. How is he going to catch the right woman when he's always wearing T-shirts that have writing on the front?"

"Suzanne, do you have a problem with what I'm wearing?" Erik asked.

Nora gave him a quick once-over, as if she hadn't already. He looked pretty darn good— more than pretty good actually. And what was wrong with T-shirts with writing on them anyway, especially when they had muscles the likes of his underneath? She shook her head. "But, I'm sure we can come up with something else for the party."

Erik took a step toward his mother. "Okay, Mom, it was nice of you to stop over. Good to see you up and about on that leg—"

Camille didn't move and Nora could tell the woman was giving her a serious appraisal. Oh, God, could she tell the difference?

"Suzanne," she said. "I do hope you're feeling better now that some time has passed… since your engagement ended."

Nora struggled with how to respond. Who would have guessed the woman would bring up something so personal here. *What would Suzanne say?* "Oh, I'm fine," she said brightly. "We just weren't…compatible. The breakup was a good thing."

"Well, remember what I told you…."

Nora nodded and tried not to have a blank expression on her face. *What? What did you tell Suzanne?*

"Sometimes the right person is standing in front of you and you don't even know it until you clear away the other debris." Camille patted her on the arm.

"Oh, right. I do remember that."

"Mom." Erik's voice held a note of warning. He glanced out the window. "Thomas still has the car running outside."

"Yes, I know, he always leaves it running—"

"I thought you were distraught over the price of gas—"

"Not for me, sweetheart. I worry about those sorts of things for you. As your mother, it's my job to worry. I've just always been relieved you gave up skiing and got into medicine—that took quite a load off my mind."

Erik gave a noncommittal grunt and Suzanne looked at him curiously. What was that supposed to mean?

"Suzanne, thank you so much for squeezing Erik in on short notice," Camille was saying. "Please, just dress him well."

From behind his mother, Erik grinned at Nora and shook his head. As his eyes met hers, she felt the connection of a shared understanding, and a shiver of attraction slipped up her spine.

"Mom."

"Just one more thing, Erik, and I'll be on my way. What I really stopped by for was to see if Suzanne could come to the garden club meeting Tuesday night and give a little talk about what she does." She turned her attention to Nora. "Suzanne?"

Nora felt her breathing get shallow. "How nice of you to think of me."

"I've told some of the women about your services and I think you may be able to get some new clients that very night."

"I—I'll have to check my calendar—" *Nope. Speaking to the garden club was never going to happen unless, by some miracle, Suzanne got off her cruise ship and back to San Francisco before then.*

Camille touched the back of her perfectly coiffed hair. "The scheduled speaker just canceled. So I do need to alert the chairperson right away so she can put together the program," Camille said. "This really is a wonderful opportunity, you know."

Yes, it was. *For Suzanne.* Nora reached into her briefcase, took out Suzanne's day planner and flipped the pages until she reached Tuesday. Of course it was wide-open; Suzanne was on a seventeen-day cruise…while her sister tried to hold her life together for her. "Oh," she said in a disappointed voice. "I do have something at that time…but I'll check to see if it can be rescheduled." She thought she might be sick.

"Please do. I really need to know as soon as possible."

Erik touched his mother on the arm. "You're

really inhibiting the progress here, Mom. Suzanne and I were—"

He winked at Nora and she caught her breath. "Just getting started," she finished, almost breathlessly. *Get a grip,* she told herself.

Camille looked from Erik to Nora and back again. "I suppose I should get going." She kissed her son on the cheek and patted Nora on the arm again. "Do your best with him. He can be stubborn. It's quite the affair we'll be having and Erik, well, he doesn't put a lot of stock in what he wears."

Nora nodded. *Go. Please go. Before you think of some other way to torture me.*

Camille drew her brows together. "You seem quiet tonight, Suzanne. Are you feeling all right?"

Before she could answer, Erik began to gently push his mother toward the door. "Mom, nice of you to stop by. Suzanne and I were well into this and neither of us has a lot of time."

Once he had her out the door, he sat in his chair again. "Sorry. But then, you already know what she's like."

No she didn't, but she wasn't going to admit that. "Oh, we all have our quirks. I enjoy your mother. Now, should we get back to work?" *So I can get out of here before some other disaster takes place.*

Over the course of the next half hour she interviewed Erik and completed a questionnaire detailing his lifestyle (laid-back), his personal preferences as to style and color (casual and blue), his favorite designers or retailers (none in particular) and his budget (pretty much wide-open, which meant, pretty much her entire year's salary and more, if necessary).

When she filled in the final blank on the sheet, she sat back in her chair, immensely pleased with her progress. She'd come here tonight knowing next to nothing about what she was doing—and she'd done all right. Better than all right—she'd done great. This personal shopping thing wasn't nearly as hard as she'd expected. And, she'd be out of here in time to get to her coffee group.

"What's next?" Erik asked.

"Shopping," she said with confidence, feeling more relaxed than she had all night. She knew Suzanne always offered clients the opportunity to come along, but few, if any, actually took her up on it. "You can come with me, or I can pick out several items and bring them back for a private fitting." She met his eyes…and for a moment, the image of him in his briefs jumped back into her head. The heat of a blush started to rise on her cheeks. Oh, God, that little confidence builder had been her dumbest idea yet.

"It's up to me?" He rubbed a hand across the day's growth on his jaw.

She bent over her briefcase to put the clipboard and papers away. "Don't feel bad if you don't want to come shopping. I know you're busy and—"

"No, I'll come."

"Great, so I'll pick out— What?" *What did he just say?*

"I'll come along. It seems like it would be easier than making you haul clothes around—"

"Oh, but I do it all the time." Her heart pounded. One trip to the men's department with her and he was going to know she knew nothing about personal shopping.

"Can we shop once I'm off work?"

"Ah—" Nora felt her brain try to shut down and she forced it back into action. A thin layer of perspiration broke out on her forehead. *I need to go home,* she wanted to scream. *I need to track down my sister and kill her.* "Actually, my schedule is pretty tight."

"The party is Saturday. That pretty much leaves tomorrow night."

Suzanne, I really hate you. She couldn't think of one good reason to tell the client he couldn't come with her—without making it sound as if she didn't want him along. And, if she was honest about this, under other circumstances she might just enjoy having him with her—him and those eyes—but not like this. "Okay, then why don't I meet you at—" *Where? She and Suzanne hadn't gotten this far.* In desperation she named the only place that came to mind. "Um, how about Neiman Marcus on Union Square. At six-thirty? That will give us a couple of hours…."

Five minutes later she was out the door and back in Suzanne's car. By the time she had gotten two blocks away, her heart was pounding and she was so light-headed, she had to pull over to the curb and breathe. She leaned her head against the steering wheel.

This wasn't just a bad dream—it was nightmare. *Erik Morgan.* She worked with Erik Morgan. She'd been in meetings with Erik Morgan. Jeez, every now and then she actually looked at Erik Morgan as a—*man. An attractive man. Okay, an attractive, gorgeous, single man…in his briefs.*

Ohmigod. How could she ever face him in the hospital again now that she'd pictured him in his underwear?

No question about it, she was in very definite trouble.

CHAPTER THREE

ERIK KICKED BACK into his leather chair and paged through the latest issue of *Outside Magazine.* Though he tried to concentrate on an article about backcountry skiing in Montana, he realized after a few minutes that he was reading the same paragraph over and over—and not retaining any of it. He flipped to a story on mountain climbing in Tibet and found he did no better with that. His mind just wasn't on skiing or climbing—it was on Suzanne Carlisle.

He tossed the magazine onto the footstool and thought about the pretty, dark-haired woman who had just interviewed him. She must be fairly new to the personal shopping business; she'd seemed a little hesitant…not real clear on what casual chic was. Though, to be fair, he had no idea, either.

She seemed too unaffected to be the personal shopper type, someone into clothes and looks. And she'd wobbled on her high heels a couple of times. He'd almost told her to take the damn things off and put up her feet, but figured it might make her more ill at ease than she already was.

Still, she'd handled Camille pretty well. And anybody who could take on his mother and survive was all right in his book. More than all right, actually.

The phone jangled and he looked at the caller ID before picking it up. His mother. *What a surprise.* "Hi, Mom," he said into the receiver. "Don't you want to call my sister—you know, Jenny—the child you never get to talk to because she lives across the country?"

She ignored him. "How did it go with Suzanne?"

"Great. Nice girl. Seems to know her stuff." He let his head drop against the leather cushion.

"She *is* a cute girl, isn't she?"

Matchmaker Mom hot on the trail. "Ah, yeah."

"And she'll have an outfit pulled together for you to wear on Saturday?"

"She said I was hopeless."

"She did?"

He let out a laugh at her obvious panic. "No. We're going shopping tomorrow night."

There was a long pause before his mother spoke again.

"You're going along?" she asked, shock evident in her voice.

"That surprises you?"

"Well, you did just give me a speech about how I wasn't supposed to introduce you to daughters of friends, friends of friends, acquaintances of friends, so naturally—"

"We're going shopping—not on a date."

"Whatever you want to call it, dear, I'm just glad you're going."

Erik rolled his eyes. "*It's a shopping trip.* And just so you don't start thinking I'm about to get involved here, I'm not. There's no way. You might as well know—I'm talking to USSA about coaching the ski team."

"Erik!"

"Easy. Now, keep this to yourself. We just started talking and if it happens, I don't want my partners to hear it through the grapevine before I tell them."

Silence hung on the line. Finally his mother spoke. "You'd give up your practice? And the new rehab clinic you've been working on?"

Yeah, those were the kickers. He'd been pushing the hospital to open a sports medicine rehab clinic for several years. And as soon as they'd finally agreed, USSA had come knocking at his door. Why was it that when it rained, it always poured? "Coaching the *A* team has always been a dream of mine."

"But—"

"Yeah, yeah, I know. Don't worry. I'm thinking about all the ramifications. Listen, Mom, I've got an early surgery tomorrow morning. I've got to get some sleep. Go do your knee exercises."

He shut off the phone and picked up *Outside Magazine* again, but didn't open it. He'd been coaching juniors out at Squaw Valley for several years now, which kept him pretty well connected with USSA. When he'd heard the rumors that they wanted to take the team in a different direction, he hadn't been surprised at all. It was their way of cutting loose one of the coaches, an arrogant jerk who was hard to communicate with and had alienated most of the team.

He'd toyed with the idea of putting his name in for the job. But before he'd decided whether to go for it or not, the alpine director had called him wanting to talk. The whole thing renewed a dream that had been at the back of his mind for a long time—to coach the U.S. ski team to the Olympics.

Problem was, if he chased down that dream, it meant a four-year commitment—and major life changes. He'd probably be traveling most of the year, would have to leave his partnership and take a big pay cut. None of which was out of the question.

Not really anyway.

He shut off the lamp on the table next to his chair and sat in the darkness. He thought of Suzanne and how wide her eyes had opened and how pink her cheeks had burned when he had asked if she was going to look through the clothes in his closet. His mom was right—she was cute. Maybe if he found her as intriguing tomorrow as she'd seemed tonight, he'd ask her out for a drink when they finished shopping.

NORA PULLED OPEN the door to Margo's Bistro and hurried toward the annex room with its green-cushioned rattan furniture and large potted plants. Smiling at the others already there, she dropped into a chair, pulled off Suzanne's stilettos and began talking. "You aren't even going to believe what's happened to me now. My sister—"

"That should tell you everything you need to know," Margo said to the other two women. She shook her head, her silky blond hair slipping from side to side with the movement.

"Your regular chai latte?" she asked as she headed out to the counter.

"Make it a double," Nora said. "It's been a rough night already." She leaned back into the soft cushions and felt herself start to relax beneath the gentle glow of the candles flickering in the wall sconces.

"Nice outfit," Selena Milano said. "Kind of funky, fashionable. And new streaked hair, too? Did you have a makeover?" She combed her fingers through her own short, chocolate curls. "Plain brown wasn't good enough for you anymore?" she teased.

Leave it to the free-spirited artist in the group to appreciate the change. Nora grimaced. "I am my sister."

At the puzzled expressions on the two women's faces, she held up a hand. "I'll tell all as soon as Margo gets back. Some of it she already knows…but why repeat myself on the rest?"

Moments later, Margo set a hot cup on the table in front of Nora and took the opposite seat. "So how did tonight go? Did you fill the girls in?"

"I wanted to wait until you were here." Nora quickly recounted the past day's events, finishing up with the grand finale about who her new client really was.

"You've got to be kidding me!" Margo said. "Erik Morgan, the Olympic skier who got on the Wheaties box?"

"And you work with him at the hospital?" Rosie DeWitt shoved her long black hair behind one ear. "You'd better get out of this before you get in too deep. This is how careers get ruined."

Nora nodded. Rosie's background in politics gave her a unique perspective—she knew all about how dangerous lies and rumors were. "I'd love to," Nora said. "All I have to do is get one lousy outfit picked out and I'm done. Then, never again. Even if it is the only way to get Suzanne on her feet."

They all murmured agreement. Nora sipped her chai and sat back, listening as the conversation jumped from one topic to another. When Selena mentioned how much better her seventh-grade son was doing, Nora sat forward. Small for his age, Drew had become moody and withdrawn as he struggled with the usual growing pains issues.

"What do you think has changed things for him?" she asked.

Selena gave a wry smile. "The dog. Or, I should say, the incredibly exuberant eating machine. Now officially named Axel."

"Still growing, is he?" Margo asked.

"Bigger every minute. But Drew is so happy—and so much dirtier than he's ever been, I might add. And his clothes…" She shook her head. "His clothes are full of chew marks. But he's come out of himself, he's happy, so you won't hear me complaining about any of it."

"Maybe a dog would help Danny," Nora said. "Something's really going on with him. He's obsessed with getting a dad. He drags me through the grocery store to see stock boys in baseball caps. Yesterday he zeroed in on Mr. Rogers."

"Oh, Nora," Rosie said. "That has to be hard."

Nora sighed. "I know boys need a dad—all kids need a dad. What makes it worse is that he's never had one."

"You *could* consider dating again." Rosie put her elbows on the table and leaned forward.

Nora drew a slow breath and exhaled. "Yeah. I thought of that. And, if the goal was finding a dad for Danny instead of falling in love, maybe I could. But I don't think I'll ever love someone again. Lightning never strikes twice."

"Never say never," Margo said.

"Easy for you to say. You just got engaged to the man of your dreams," Nora said.

"All I'm saying is that closing your mind to possibilities closes your heart. And why would you want to close everything off like that?"

Nora stared at her. "Because, at the risk of sounding trite, love hurts."

"So does not loving. So does being alone. When my husband left me, it hurt, yes, but to play it safe for the rest of my life—" Margo shook her head. "It would be like...half-living."

Nora felt a familiar ache in her chest. She was so tired of being alone. Sometimes she really did want to try again...and Margo made it seem so possible.

"Okay, enough of this maudlin conversation," Selena said dryly. "We're supposed to have fun on Thursday nights."

"And we're going to! I have an idea." Margo jumped up and left the room, returning a few moments later with a pencil and sheet of paper. She scrawled *Perfect Dad* across the top of the page. "Let's list the qualities of the perfect dad. Once Nora sees what she's missing, she might be more open to dating again."

Nora could only stare at her friend. Had Margo lost her mind?

"I may not want to get married, but this I can play," Selena said. "The perfect father, in my mind anyway, is tall, dark and handsome—"

Margo laughed. "Are we off track already? Likes kids. Patient." She wrote the words down. "Kind. And tender."

"To both kids and mother," Selena added.

"Athletic," Rosie said. "Oh, and has a good income."

"Willing to change diapers," Margo said, writing. "And read bedtime stories. Nora, anything to add?"

Stand up against the world for them, Nora thought. *And tell them he loves them no matter what they do.* "I'm not playing. What's wrong with all of you tonight?" She sipped her chai.

"Oh, come on, lighten up." Rosie touched her on the arm. "We're just having fun."

"Hey! On the left, we'll list the single men we know and see how they stack up." Selena grabbed the pencil and paper. "The title is now Perfect Dad *Possibilities,*" she said as she wrote. "And, of course, the first candidate can only be Erik Morgan."

"Oh, please," Nora said.

"My tax accountant is single. Put him down—Pete Jackson," Rosie said.

The women threw out a few more names before Nora decided she'd had enough. She snatched the paper out from under Selena's pencil. "Party's over," she said in a light voice.

"We're not doing this anymore." She shoved the sheet in her purse to get it away from her friends. Once she got home tonight she'd tear it into a thousand tiny pieces. "Next subject."

"Nora, we didn't do this to torment you," Margo said. "You need to start thinking about letting go. Even if it is only for Danny."

"Letting go of what?"

Margo's lips turned in that soft understanding smile of hers. "Of your anger. Your guilt. Your regrets. Of the past. It's not a betrayal, you know."

Fear kicked into Nora's gut. The same feeling she got every time she had a conversation like this.

Selena caught her eye, then set her cup on the table and cleared her throat. "Hey, did I tell you guys about the new idea I have for a live art exhibition?"

Nora looked at her, grateful for the change of topic. She took a drink of her chai and relaxed as the conversation veered in a whole new direction.

NORA KISSED HER sleeping son on the forehead and ran a hand over his feathery brown hair. His breath came soft and slow and she tucked his Spider-Man comforter around him, remembering the day she'd brought him home from the hospital…alone, with no husband at her side. She watched him for a moment longer before quietly leaving his room. She was glad he was asleep because she needed some time to think. Everything that could go wrong today, had.

Stripping out of Suzanne's clothes, she pulled on a T-shirt and some baggy sweatpants, letting out a satisfied groan as the soft fabrics touched her skin. Then she went downstairs, poured herself a glass of wine and plopped down into her favorite overstuffed chair. She looked around the living room. Last year, when Suzanne didn't have any real clients, she turned her attention to redoing the room in blues and browns. Now, Nora supposed, one could call the decor casual chic.

Casual chic. Cripes. She'd forgotten about the garden club speech.

She couldn't do it—she just couldn't give a talk to Camille Lamont's garden club. It was bad enough that she had to shop for Erik Morgan, especially since, somehow, she was feeling an attraction to the man. Probably just a regressive adolescent syndrome or some such thing.

But make a speech to his mother's garden club? No way. This was more than she'd ever signed on to do, which meant it was time for her dear sister to come home—or come clean with her client.

She took a swallow of wine and let its warmth slide down the back of her throat, relaxing her. Then she picked up the phone and dialed Suzanne's number, waiting while it rang. Great, she wasn't going to get a connection again.

Just when she expected it to kick into voice mail, Suzanne answered, giggling. In the background, the sounds of music and lively conversation mingled in a happy buzz. Nora fought the sense of annoyance that Suzanne was at a party on a cruise while Nora was struggling to hold her sister's life together.

"Hi, Nora! Hold on a second, honey. Yes, thank you, I'll have another glass of champagne," Suzanne called to someone in the background. "How'd it go?" she said into the phone.

Champagne. Nora wanted someone to bring her champagne and maybe some big strawberries, too.

"Nora?"

She let out a sharp laugh. "Sorry. *How did it go?* Depends on what part of the evening you're talking about. I actually was quite good if I do say so. But there were moments that it was more of a Murphy's Law kind of night. You know your new client, Erik Lamont? His name is really Erik Morgan. Sound familiar?" She sipped her wine.

"No…"

"The skier, the orthopedic surgeon—"

"The cute one?"

Nora sat up straight. "When have you seen him? He's not that cute."

"Oh, please. I saw him on TV during the Olympics, you know, like ten or fifteen years ago. He's cute incarnate and if you can't see that, then it's no wonder… Never mind."

"Yeah, I know." Nora almost sighed. She dropped back into the chair again. "His eyes are so blue they almost pierce you."

"I can't believe Camille's son is Erik Morgan. Boy did you luck out—"

"No, I didn't luck out, you idiot. I work with him at the hospital. Now I've got to make sure he doesn't figure out I'm me and not you." Nora took another swallow of wine to calm herself before this convoluted conversation put her completely over the edge.

"Well, if you ask me, working with Erik Morgan is not a Murphy's Law phenomenon. More like an 'all good things come to those who wait' phenomenon." Her voice grew a little distant. "Oh, thanks. Could I get one with a strawberry in the glass?"

Nora gritted her teeth. "I didn't know I was waiting for anything."

"Sure you are. True love to come again. A knight in shining armor. A hero to complete you—"

"God, what is with everyone these days?"

"What? Can you talk a little louder? It's kind of noisy here," Suzanne said.

Nora raised her voice. "Nothing. Anyway, so I was meeting with Erik when his mother showed up—"

"Camille?" Suzanne sputtered on the other end of the phone.

"That would be her."

Suzanne gasped and Nora smiled knowing Suzanne was finally beginning to see what Nora had dealt with tonight.

"Ohmigod, Murphy's Law!" Suzanne said. "Did she realize you weren't me?"

"I don't think so. But—"

"Thank God. My heart was beginning to pound. That had the makings of a disaster." Suzanne's words poured out of her. "I can't believe she showed up—"

"Suzanne, she—"

"I mean if she ever thought I was trying to

pull a fast one, like maybe I was shopping to *get* her son instead of shopping *for* her son. Well, you know what I mean—"

"Suzanne, let…me…finish. She invited me—you—to speak to her garden club. About what you do. Said something like she thought you might get some new clients at the meeting."

Suzanne screeched into the phone. "Oh, Nora! This is the break I've been looking for."

"Yes, well, you'd better get off that ship and onto a plane, because she wants you there Tuesday."

"Tuesday? Like in four days?"

"Right." Nora realized she was getting a certain amount of enjoyment out of shocking her sister. Payback for all the champagne Suzanne was drinking and Nora wasn't.

"How can I do that? I'm on a cruise. Why didn't you schedule it for when I'm back?" Suzanne was incredulous.

"I tried. I told her I had something scheduled and would see if it could be changed. But she really wants you next week and I wasn't going to alienate the big client who, I might add, is the reason I'm pretending I'm you in the first place."

"So you're okay with doing it again?"

"Doing what again?" Nora couldn't believe she was hearing this.

"Being me next week."

"No! I'm calling to tell you to get off that boat and get home."

"We're in the middle of nowhere," Suzanne said as though she were giving a geography lesson. "You know, glaciers, fjords, wilderness…*emphasis on wilderness.* I'll remind you we're lucky we even have a phone connection right now."

"You're not fooling me. I know there are airports in Alaska—"

"Not out here on the water."

Nora set down her wineglass and began to massage the back of her neck with one hand. She tried to stay patient, to keep her voice calm. "Suzanne, I nearly had a nervous breakdown being you tonight. I was lying almost every time I opened my mouth. Imagine what I'll be like when I'm with Camille Lamont, *who knows you,* who will notice little things like how I don't seem exactly like I used to be, or that I seem to have forgotten all sorts of details about her that I should know… She already mentioned tonight how quiet I was."

"Oh, just laugh a lot. That's what I do." In the background, Nora could hear the clink of crystal glasses touching one another.

"You laugh a lot?" How could her sister be so cavalier about this?

"Yeah, it makes every conversation so much more friendlier—"

"Friendly."

"Whatever. Like, I'll say 'Isn't it a lovely day,' laugh, laugh, light and airy. Or maybe Camille will try on an outfit I got her and I'll say 'That looks absolutely fabulous on you,' and then she'll laugh because she's so flattered and then I'll laugh, ha-ha-ha, like a wind chime, you know, tinkle tinkle."

Nora moved her hand to massage her forehead. "Tinkle tinkle?"

"Light, easy, friendly laughter."

"Suzanne, there is no 'tinkle tinkle' going on around here. Every muscle in my body is tense and getting tenser. The only thing I'm ready to do is cry. So get off that boat and get home. Take back your job before I blow it."

"I…don't think I can. Anyway, think of what I've spent to go on this cruise—"

"And think of what you'll lose if you miss the chance to meet these clients." Nora didn't even try to hide her irritation.

"Mommy? Why are you talking so loud?"

Nora turned at the sound of her son's voice. He stood next to her in his Superman pajamas.

"Danny…what are you doing up? Suzanne, let me call you back."

She shut off the phone and reached out to let her son crawl into her lap. His warm little body curled into her arms and tenderness swept through her. "What's the matter, honey?"

"Are you fighting with Auntie Suzanne?"

"No. Sometimes we just talk loud."

"Oh." He gazed up at her. "I saw the perfect daddy tonight."

Nora's heart sank. "You did? On TV again?"

"Yeah. His name is Ronald. He works at McDonald's."

Despite herself, Nora started to laugh. "Gee, honey, I'm just not sure Ronald and I would be a good match."

"But he'd be lots of fun. He likes kids." He looked at her with wide eyes, *his father's eyes*. "You wouldn't have to cook dinner anymore. And we could go to the playland whenever we want."

Nora nodded thoughtfully as an ache worked its way up from her chest to the back of her throat and tears tried to force themselves into her eyes. She blinked hard. "Those are some really good reasons, but I think Ronald isn't available. Guys like him are always taken already—"

"I never saw a Mrs. Ronald."

Nora sighed. "That's because she's in the kitchen making all those fries."

"Are you sure?"

"Yeah." She gave her son a squeeze and kissed the top of his head. A knot pressed hard in her throat and she gritted her teeth together. "I'm sure your daddy is watching you from heaven and loving you right now. And I know he would be here if he could."

"But he died."

She nodded.

"Mama?"

"Hmm?"

"Do you think I'll ever have a daddy that's here?"

Her heart shattered then and the tears escaped her eyes. "Yeah, I do." She stood, still holding her son wrapped in her arms so he couldn't see that she was crying. "Come on, honey, it's late. You've got to get back to bed. Morning comes early."

She laid him in his bed, drew his quilt up to his shoulders and kissed him again. "I love you," she whispered. She rested a hand on his back, could feel his breathing even out into a soft rhythmic movement as he fell asleep. In the corner, a tiny Micky Mouse nightlight shone, keeping all manner of fearsome monsters away. *All except those in your head.*

She closed his bedroom door behind her and returned to the living room where she finished off her glass of wine before calling her sister back. "Hi, Suzanne."

"Is Danny okay?"

"It's that daddy thing again." She sighed. "Maybe I should take him to a counselor."

"Nora, I've been thinking… I'll talk to the ship's director and find out if there's any way I can get off the cruise." Suzanne paused. "If I can't, I'll call Camille and tell her I'm sick or something. Since she already commented that you were quiet tonight, I can say I'm feeling under the weather. I'm sure she'll let me come another time."

Nora looked at the framed picture hanging on the wall opposite her, a cozy cottage at the end of a country lane, the trees ablaze in autumn colors of orange and red. She wanted to escape there right now, just run away from all of this. "I don't know about that," she said. "I think this was a one-time deal. Camille said the speaker canceled."

"Oh. Well, I'll see what I can do. But, Nora, if I can't…" Her voice dropped low. "Will you do it?"

Nora waited a long moment. "I'm not going to answer that. You need to find a way off that ship and come home to take care of your business."

"I'll try. I really will."

"Good. Then before this call gets dropped, I need to ask you some questions. Erik said the event is *casual chic*. What the heck is that? I mean, I have some idea but you'd better make it clear."

"Oh, it's the same as, you know, country club."

"Country club? A little clearer please." She willed herself to escape into the picture on the wall.

"Resort casual—"

"Suzanne."

"Come on, Nora, you have to know some of this. It's pretty much what you'd wear to a private country club for dinner. Dress slacks, sport shirt, even a dress shirt. If it's cool, add a sweater. Sport jacket if he wants to wear one. Nice leather shoes and belt—got the idea?"

"Uh, yeah. Maybe he owns some of this stuff already."

"He probably does. Didn't you check?"

She didn't answer.

"Nora, once you knew what he needed the clothes for, didn't you look to see what he already had?"

"No. I just wanted to get out of there." *You have no idea what it was like picturing him in his briefs and then looking him in the face.*

Suzanne let out a long-suffering sigh. "Okay. Then you'll have to buy everything you think he needs and take back whatever he doesn't want."

"He's shopping with me."

"Erik Morgan's going clothes shopping with you?"

"Uh-huh." Nora went into the kitchen to put another splash of wine in her glass.

"Well, well, well. This changes *everything.*"

"What's that supposed to mean?"

"Nothing. Just that you can talk to him about what he already has while you're shopping."

Nora felt anxiety set in. "I don't know. What if he says he has shoes already and I can't even tell if they go with what we're buying him or not?"

"You'll do fine. It's not that hard."

"Easy for you to say. You're not the one who has to look into those eyes of his." She shut off the phone with Suzanne's laughter tinkling over the distance.

CHAPTER FOUR

LATE THE NEXT AFTERNOON, Erik Morgan leaned forward, elbows on the dark cherry conference table and watched the hospital administrator use red and blue markers on a whiteboard to list and reiterate each of the points he was making. Good thing his topic was interesting, because his monotone could put caffeine-filled two-year-olds to sleep.

"As we've discussed," the man was saying, "the addition of a sports medicine rehab clinic will be a big benefit to the hospital. Obviously, we'll have the advantage of increased surgeries, but also a whole new clientele. That being the outpatients currently getting care at other clinics around the city. And we get onboard with the aging boomer trend—a growth area if there ever was one."

Man, this guy was dull. How did people like him get put in charge of things? Erik glanced at his partners to gauge their reactions. Tim

O'Connell sat back in his chair, his face totally unreadable. Andy Chapman, as usual, cut right to the chase. "We've been through all this before. What's different?"

The administrator wrote the word partnership on the whiteboard. "The board decided that if we're going to do this, our clinic has to be steps above every other in the city. So what we want from you is a working partnership. We'd like to see you three move your offices out of the professional building and into the space that we're renovating into the new center."

He gestured wide with his hands. "You'll still be a private orthopedic practice with one another, but you'll be located right here next to the best sports medicine rehab center in the city. Let's face it, you three have the experience as surgeons for the Giants, the Raiders, team physicians for Stanford football..." He looked at Erik. "The U.S. ski team and snowboard team..."

Erik nodded. Hell, if the guy only knew what Erik was working on right now, he might not be proposing this deal to them.

"Anyway, the way we see it, we'll feature you three in our advertising for the clinic— your reputations and expertise will bring in patients, making this an ideal partnership. As you know, our goal is to attract elite athletes.

Their use of this facility will, in turn, attract others to it."

Andy raised his brows at Erik and gave him a half grin. "Are we still looking at the same time line?" he asked the administrator.

"Yes. Up and running in six months—"

"And equipment? Have you considered the equipment we talked about the last time?" Andy never wasted words.

The administrator handed each of them a sheet of paper containing an extensive list. "I think you'll be pleased with what's been approved. All the usual things, plus a state-of-the-art gym with high level P.T. equipment, whirlpools, underwater treadmills, weight-lifting equipment of the same caliber professional teams use... And, because we know you're ultraconcerned with preventing postoperative infection, the hospital will set up a brand-new operating suite dedicated solely to clean orthopedic surgeries."

"That all sounds well and good, but you guys did a piss-poor job with the women's center you opened last year," Tim said, speaking for the first time in the entire meeting. "Why would we think you'd do a better job with this?"

The administrator winced. "We learned our lesson there. So the board is proposing..."

He paused for effect. "That you three take this over—"

"Complete control?" Andy asked.

"Yes. We're early enough in the planning process that we want your fingerprints all over this place."

"Complete control?" Andy sounded positively gleeful.

Erik sat back in his chair, stunned. They'd gotten everything they asked for, and then some. Complete control of the center was a dream come true that he'd never even allowed himself to have.

"We're going to want X-ray equipment and on-site technicians," Tim said, getting into it. "And for staff, I'd like to see physical therapists, sports psychologists, athletic trainers, physiologists and nutritionists." He ticked the list off on his fingers.

"Don't forget occupational and massage therapists," Andy added.

Erik could only stare. This was suddenly moving really fast and getting way too big. It may be what the other guys wanted, what he once thought he wanted, but now he wasn't so sure. He had the USSA iron in the fire and he needed time to follow up on it before making any extensive, long-range commitments.

If he and his partners got involved in this new rehab center to the level the hospital was expecting, his quitting partway into it would really create a hole, maybe damage the entire concept by turning it into a repeat of the under-staffed women's center fiasco. His years as a skier and his expertise in knee reconstruction brought a lot of patients into their practice. If he left, that draw would be gone. Plus, there was no way his two partners could do this without bringing in another surgeon—and that would take time to put together, too.

"So, Erik, what do you think?"

He started. Tim was looking at him curiously.

Hell, it sounded great—if he knew he was staying here. But the pull from the ski team was strong, a chance to return to the sense of community and camaraderie that he'd experienced fifteen years ago when he'd been on the team.

"Yeah…" he said hesitantly. "It sounds pretty good."

"You'll do all the hiring." The administrator's voice was almost cajoling.

"You okay?" Tim prodded Erik on the shoulder, turned his back to the administrator and lowered his voice. "This is what we've been wanting all along."

Erik forced his enthusiasm forward. "Yeah, I know."

Andy leaned toward him. "I've been thinking about what you said the other day. You're right, a P.T. is the way to go to run the center. What do you think about bringing one on board right away to help out with planning, ordering equipment, you know, general decisions—"

"Right." Erik glanced at his watch. He was supposed to meet Suzanne for shopping in another hour. And he still had a pile of paperwork on his desk that he needed to finish.

The administrator was talking again. "The board strongly believes the success of this center depends on having the support of a high-level orthopedic group. If it isn't you three, then…" He shrugged and they all got the message. If they turned it down, this opportunity would be offered to another group—and they all knew there would be many willing to step in to a sweet deal like this.

"No, no. We're in," Andy said. "Right, guys?"

"Absolutely," Tim said.

Erik felt caught. He shoved a hand through his hair. "Yeah, we're in." *Shit, this was getting worse by the minute.*

"One last thing… The architect who will be

working this up for us happens to be in the building right now for another meeting." He set his marker on the table. "I asked him to join us. Can you spare a little more time?"

"Good by me," Andy said. Tim nodded.

Erik checked his watch again. Any longer in this meeting and he'd never be able to finish his paperwork and still be on time to meet Suzanne for the shopping trip.

"Whatever it is, cancel it," Andy said.

Right. Far be it for him to say that meeting with his *personal shopper* was more important than business. What the hell had he been thinking when he agreed to shop with her anyway? Oh, yeah, he'd been intrigued. Her personality seemed almost in conflict with her career choice. And she had the biggest hazel green eyes....

He shook his head to get rid of the image. "Let's take a few minutes break, so I can make a quick call," he said. "Then I'll have all the time we need."

Five minutes later he was headed down the corridor, cell phone in hand, trying to figure out how to reach Suzanne. He'd left her business card at home, his mother wasn't answering any of her numbers and directory information didn't have a listing for Suzanne Carlisle.

Oh, wait. *Nora.* Her sister worked here. She

had to know how to reach Suzanne. He stopped midstride and turned back in the direction of the physical therapy department.

NORA HAD JUST FINISHED with her last patient of the day and was about to head to the desk to deal with her pile of charting when she spotted Erik Morgan walking into the treatment area. Panic surged through her. She bent her head and slid around the corner into one of the storage rooms, where she began to organize a shelf of supplies that was perfectly well-organized already. Whatever the man wanted right now could be handled by someone else.

After a few minutes, she peeked her head out the door to make sure he was gone. She didn't need him to see her as Nora an hour and a half before he saw her as Suzanne. The resemblance between the two of them might become a bit too obvious.

Not seeing Erik, she headed toward the front desk, only to have one of her colleagues call across the room, "Nora, Dr. Morgan is looking for you."

Her throat constricted. "He is?" she squeaked. "Why?"

"I don't know. Said he'd be back in a couple minutes."

At least that gave her a couple of minutes to get out of there. "I can't really wait around—I've got plans tonight." So much for finishing those charts...she'd have to come in early tomorrow.

She grabbed her purse and pushed through the doors to the hallway, head down as she silently begged St. Jude for help. *Please, please get me out of here without seeing Erik Morgan. I really do promise never to do this—*

"Nora?"

Her brain locked down and she raised her head to find Erik not three feet away. Unable to speak, she just stared, exactly the way she had stupidly stared at him on his front porch last night. She purposely avoided meeting his eyes.

"Hi," he said.

She stood there, mute.

"I'm Erik Morgan," he said.

Well, of course, she knew that. She forced her brain into gear and her mouth to engage before he decided Suzanne had a moron for a sister. "Oh, sure, sure, I know that. I know you. We've met before.... On some patient...something. I was just a little distracted and, so, I heard you were trying to find me, but I was just leaving—" *Shut. Up.* "Is there something about one of the patients?"

He shook his head and looked a little

sheepish. "No. It's about your sister." He narrowed his eyes. "You know, you two really do look a lot alike. Are you sure one of you isn't living a double life of some kind?" A smile lit up his face.

She reached up to tuck a few loose strands of hair back into her ponytail and forced a laugh that came out sounding like a bark. "Double life?" Her voice sounded high and loud and she hoped he didn't notice. She cleared her throat. "I think I'd pick something more exciting than being a personal shopper if I was going to lead a double life."

"You even sound alike," he said, as though he wasn't entirely convinced there really were two sisters.

Once again she lost her ability to speak, which was just as well because she had that tendency toward nervous babbling—and she was sounding too much like her sister, which only made sense since she was her sister. Oh, boy.

"Anyway. I'm supposed to be meeting with Suzanne tonight to—" he looked a little sheepish "—shop."

"That…sounds like something Suzanne would be doing."

"Right. I've got to cancel. An important meeting's come up… I have to go to it."

Relief surged through her. Ohmigosh her grandma was right, that St. Jude guy really delivered. "Don't worry about it—I'm sure she won't mind."

"Problem is, I left her card at home. I don't know how to let her know I won't be there."

"Oh, I'll tell her." Nora held herself back from doing a little dance. "We live together so I'll see her when I get home."

"Thanks. Can you ask her to call me about getting together tomorrow morning?"

"Tomorrow morning?" she squawked. "To shop?"

"No, to show me the stuff she's bought. I need it for a party tomorrow night."

Oh, right. She forgot about that part. "Okay." Giddiness bubbled through her. *Freedom!* She didn't have to go shopping with Erik Morgan. She could figure out what to get and bring it to his house and this whole thing would be over before she knew it. She started down the corridor again, a spring in her step. "I'll have Suzanne call if she's got any questions," she said glibly.

"Tell her I have another project I'd like her to handle. We can talk about that tomorrow, too," he called after her.

She stopped walking and turned to face him. *What?* "Another job? I'm sure she'll be thrilled."

TWO HOURS LATER, Nora stood in the men's department of Neiman Marcus and turned a circle. Racks of clothing stretched out in every direction as far as she could see. Well, okay, maybe not as far as she could see, but far enough to be overwhelming. This could be a long night. Good thing Margo's son, Peter, had invited Danny to sleep over because this shopping trip might last until the store closed.

She'd worn one of Suzanne's outfits so she looked professional in case she ran into anyone—like Camille—which would be just her luck. She'd worn Suzanne's shoes, too, which she was already regretting because, even though they were identical twins, her sister's feet were a full size smaller. Her toes were killing her already and she hadn't even been in the store ten minutes yet.

She'd just better be able find everything she needed here. She didn't have the inclination, or time or comfortable enough shoes to be running around shopping at a bunch of different stores. Call her lazy—or smart, more like it—but, no way was she going to be returning things all over town.

Pants. She'd start with pants. She took a step, then stopped in indecision. There were trillions of pants, with every possible label, designer or otherwise. Cuffed, uncuffed, pleated, plain front, khaki, cotton, gabardine… Her brain was knotting just thinking about the choices.

"Why couldn't the guy just need blue jeans?" she muttered. "Levi's. Life could be so simple."

She spotted a middle-aged, balding male clerk organizing a display and hurried to his side. "Excuse me. I need some pants for my—" She couldn't bring herself to say *client*. No way could she ask for help and then admit she was a personal shopper. Suzanne certainly wouldn't—and if Nora did it in her place, it would undoubtedly backfire on Suzanne somehow, someday, in the future. Because that was just the way things seemed to be going lately. "—for—my boyfriend—and I was wondering if you could give me a hand."

The clerk raised his eyebrows; his name tag said *William*. Couldn't go by *Bill* in Neiman Marcus, now could we?

"Of course. What specifically are you looking for?" he said in the kindest possible voice.

Suddenly she felt like a shrew for her snotty thought. "Casual chic."

He blinked. "There are so many different designations these days. Do you have some idea what they might be referring to?" He bent toward her and whispered, "This is only my second day."

Oh, great, so now she had to teach *him* about fashion. This escapade was heading for a bust. "I think it's what you wear to the country club for lunch or dinner."

William nodded but made no move to show her anything.

"Nice pants, shirt, pullover sweater, blazer, you know, that *style.*" She tried to keep desperation out of her voice. Maybe she didn't need his help after all. "I think I'll just browse—"

"How about something from over here?" He went to a nearby rack and held up a pair of smart tan-colored slacks. "A very natty dresser bought a pair of these yesterday."

"Natty, huh? That does sound country-clubish." She came closer and felt the fabric. Nice. And they looked well-made, too. But the real test was the price. She checked the tag. *Yep, more than nice.* "These might work. I'm actually going to be bringing home several things for him to try. So let's find another pair of pants before we move on to shirts."

William frowned. "Maybe it would be easier if he came into the store."

If he only knew the truth. "Probably, but he

has so little time. His job keeps him really busy."

William flipped through the pants on a couple of display racks. "What does he do?"

Her heart missed a beat and, for a moment, she thought it might stop entirely. *Don't tell the truth,* she said to herself. She could still hear Suzanne harping, *the client's privacy must always be protected.*

Still, she could make it sort of close to the truth, so the lie wasn't as bad. "Oh…he's a writer," she said. "He has so many deadlines, he puts off shopping and now we have a big event to attend with his publisher and, well, here I am, trying to get him dressed."

"I always wanted to be a writer," William said brightly. "What does he write?"

Nora waved a hand as though the answer were inconsequential. "Books, magazine articles."

"Really?" Now William was even more impressed. "Can I ask who he is?"

"Oh…he hates it when I talk about him. Let's just find the rest of what he needs and I'll be on my way." She thought to herself that she sure was playing fast and loose with the lies these days. For someone who abhorred dishonesty, she sure was sliding down a slippery slope.

Over the next hour, she and William chose

several shirts that they agreed fit the *casual chic* designation, a blazer and another pair of pants. By the time she purchased the clothes and William had bagged them for her, she was exhausted from verbally tap dancing to keep discussion about her writer boyfriend to a minimum.

She couldn't wait to escape to the shoe department without William. "Thank you so much for your—"

"Suzanne! Hey, Suzanne!" A familiar male voice rolled across the department and sent a chill skidding through her. *No, no, no.*

It could not possibly be— She turned.

No.

Erik Morgan.

What was he doing here? She forced a welcoming smile onto her face. "Hi. I thought you couldn't make it."

As he came closer, she met his eyes. Big mistake. Her heart sped up and she quickly dropped her gaze.

"The meeting broke up sooner than I thought it would. Since I knew you were here, I figured I'd take a chance."

She thought of her sister on the cruise ship, sipping champagne while Nora was living a nightmare. Irrational laughter bubbled up inside her and she tamped it down. Damn, if she'd gone to the shoe department five minutes ago he never would have found her.

Erik reached out and took the bags she was holding. "Looks like mission accomplished."

William cleared his throat. "You must be…" he was saying.

Nora felt everything slide into slow motion. She turned to stare at William. *You're a clerk,* she wanted to scream but not a word came out of her mouth. *You don't get to talk to—*

"Her boyfriend," William finished.

She couldn't breathe. Erik's eyes locked on her in question.

She forced herself to speak. "Uh, actually—"

"This is so handy," William was blabbering. "She was going to take all these things home to you. But you could try everything on right now and save time…and of course, the headache of coming back to make returns or exchanges. The dressing rooms are right over here. I've always wanted to be a writer, too."

She could hear pounding in her ears and realized it was blood trying to explode out of her head. Erik opened his mouth to say something and she quickly slipped her arm through his and began to pull him through the department. "Thanks so much for your help, William.

We've still got to get shoes, so we'll just try on some of these things later."

When they reached the central aisle, Erik stopped and faced her. "What's he talking about?"

"Oh, you know how clerks can be. It's his second day and he kept trying to help out…. I didn't want to be rude, so I told him…I was shopping for my boyfriend. *The writer.*" She laughed as light and easy as she could. "I don't always like to admit I'm a personal shopper because…" *Why not?* This was a stupid line of reasoning. What was that old saying about don't start a sentence until you know what the ending is? Or was it, don't ask a question you don't already know the answer to?

"Suzanne?"

"Oh. Right. I don't always tell because, somehow, clerks start steering me toward more expensive items. And my goal, besides to dress you exquisitely, is to save you money." More lies. And stupid ones, too.

"Thanks…I think. But money isn't really that much of an object."

No kidding. "That's good because we need to get you some shoes to go with your new clothes."

"Which I should be trying on, don't you think?"

Of course. It made perfect sense. Then she

wouldn't have to return anything tomorrow. But once they went back to the men's department so Erik could try on the clothes, she'd have to see William again. And God only knew what he might say. "I suppose you could just pop into the closest dressing room," she said, gesturing.

"In the lingerie department? Much as I might enjoy it, they'll probably call security if I go in there."

He started back toward the men's department and Nora followed, almost dragging her feet. Maybe William would have gone off duty by now. As they neared the dressing rooms, she spotted the man straightening a rack. Maybe he wouldn't notice them—

He looked up and smiled.

Fat chance.

"Can I get you a room?" he asked.

"Yes, thank you," she said.

"Right this way," he said and Erik followed him into the dressing rooms. As the two men rounded the corner, she heard William ask, "So what types of books do you write?"

To which Erik replied, "Romance."

She dropped her head into her hands and shook it slowly from side to side, mortified at how badly she was messing this up. A few minutes later, Erik stepped back out wearing tan slacks and a pewter shirt. He looked incredible. As he waited for her appraisal, he unbuttoned his cuffs and began to roll up the sleeves. She caught her breath. *Great forearms.* Slow heat slid through her. She could almost be seduced by the sight of good forearms and rolled-up sleeves. She looked up and discovered he was watching her watch him. Her cheeks flushed. Blue eyes, great forearms. She was a goner.

"If everything fits you this well, we're going to have trouble deciding what to keep," she managed to get out.

"Then I'll keep it all." He grinned and went back into the dressing room.

Before another hour passed, they'd chosen clothes for his party and bought a pair of shoes, as well. As they headed out of the store carrying several bags, Nora felt the pressure of the past two days lift. Erik had everything he needed for his mother's party and Suzanne hadn't lost the big account. Now she could go home, put her feet up and unwind, knowing that all was right with the world of personal shopping.

And she'd hold this over her sister's head for the rest of her life.

"Want to go for a drink to celebrate?"

She turned her head slowly to look at Erik. "Pardon me?" He didn't really just ask her to prolong this agony, did he?

"Want to get a drink to celebrate our success? I'm buying. Come on, it's Friday night."

No. Absolutely not. I want to quit pretending to be someone I'm not. I want to get out of these control top pantyhose and comb the gunk out of my hair. *I want to go home and take off these shoes before my toes are permanently misshapen.* Surely Suzanne wouldn't go for a drink, would she? Nora mentally sighed. Of course, Suzanne would—especially with Erik Morgan.

The problem was, Erik was too cute, way too nice and he looked too good in casual chic. Frankly, she didn't think she could maintain this facade with a drink under the belt and him sitting by her side.

So it was decided—*no way.*

"There's a great little place a few blocks up. We don't even have to drive," Erik said. "The Redwood Room at the Clift Hotel."

Suzanne was gonna owe her but good. "Sure," she said smiling. "Lead the way."

CHAPTER FIVE

FIFTEEN MINUTES LATER they were ensconced at a corner table in a cozy bar drinking imported beer and chatting amicably. Soft piano music filled the room. When their conversation lulled, Nora studied the interior, admiring the rich dark-paneled walls.

"So did you and Nora have a lot of fun switching places?"

She jerked her head back to look at Erik. "What?"

"When you were kids," he said. "Did you switch places a lot? I just saw Nora a few hours ago and if I didn't know better, I'd say you were the same person."

Nora let out a laugh, too high and too loud. "We've always confused people. Sometimes even our parents couldn't tell us apart." *Oh, well, she was going to liar's hell anyway.* "And yeah, we did switch places. Once—" she caught herself just before she said the wrong name "—Nora paid me to go out with a guy she didn't like who had asked her out."

"How did that go?"

"When he tried to kiss me, I told him that I, meaning Nora, was going to become a nun and that it just didn't make sense for us to get involved." She laughed, remembering. "And then it got all over school about Nora becoming a nun and she was furious with me because then *no one* asked her out."

He laughed with her and their shoulders brushed against one another. Nora felt a flash of physical awareness. Oh, this was not a good thing, at all.

"Did you do all those other twin things, like take each other's tests?" He took a drink of beer.

A whole series of memories raced through her mind. "Not too often. I wasn't the most dedicated student. I used to skip school, go off and have fun. I never really took it seriously until I met my—" *Husband.* Her brain skidded to a stop. She was telling him *her* story—not Suzanne's.

"Your?"

"My counselor. High school counselor who made me see how important school was." Nervous heat pricked all over her body.

"So you were the wild one and Nora was the serious one, even then, huh? She seems pretty straitlaced, like she doesn't really cut loose."

I do, too. "She has fun," Nora said defensively.

"Don't get me wrong. There's a place for those buttoned-up people in the world, too."

Buttoned-up people? First, Suzanne told her she used to be an orange and now Erik Morgan was telling her she's buttoned-up? She took a swallow of her beer. *I used to be wild once,* she wanted to shout. *Wild is still inside me.* Instead, she said, "You'd be surprised at some of the stuff Nora's done."

He raised his eyebrows. "Come on. At the hospital they call her No-Nonsense Nora."

No-Nonsense Nora? A weird pain shot through her chest and she felt her cheeks grow hot. "Really? That's what they call…her?"

"It's not a cut. Just sort of factual. She's a really nice person…just all business." He leaned toward her. "You two should trade places some time. You go into the hospital as her—no doubt you'd send people into shock."

"No doubt." *I don't even think you're cute anymore,* she mentally said to him. She played with her glass and tried to think of some way to just get the heck out of there.

"So how'd you end up as a personal shopper?"

I was dragged into it by my opposite-of-no-nonsense sister, the fun one. "I just fell into it. I've always liked working with people—"

"And shopping?" he teased.

"That, too. But it was Nora who made it possible. Without her supporting me while I got this business going, I wouldn't have been able to do it." She paused, pleased that she'd gotten in a good word for herself. "See? There are good reasons to be…responsible."

"I'm not slamming your sister. She's great at what she does. I think she's one of the best P.T.s around," he said.

"You do?" Suddenly Erik Morgan looked not just cute, but incredibly handsome. "Yeah, she really likes physical therapy. Although even No-Nonsense Nora is getting bored working at the hospital."

Surprise flitted across his face.

"What? Can't Nora get bored?" she asked.

"No, it's just she's so poker-faced no one would ever guess."

Poker-faced? Jeez, this evening was more fun every minute. She sipped her beer and decided to change the subject. "I heard the hospital's going to open a sports medicine rehab center."

"You know about that?"

She gulped. "Oh, Nora told me about it.... And I—I'm mentioning it because I think she'd like to get into—" *Careful now, don't sound too knowledgeable.* "Into other kinds of physical therapy. Like sports-related stuff."

"Seriously? I don't see her into sports."

Nora wanted to scream. "What do you see her into?" she said in a deadly calm voice.

"Knitting."

"Knitting!"

He laughed. "I'm kidding. Like I said, your sister's a nice person, but she just doesn't have your...spirit. Which is okay because she's really good at what she does and everyone knows it."

Effective, but dull. Just what every woman wanted to be. She made a show of looking at her watch. "It's getting late. I should really get going." She grabbed her purse as Erik finished off his beer.

"I'll walk you to your car," he said.

The cool night air felt good after being in the bar. Nora took a deep breath. She was relieved to be almost done with this job, almost done working with Erik Morgan. And then she realized that after tonight, she'd just be Nora again. And the comfortable feeling she had with

Erik, this easy camaraderie would be gone. A wistfulness slid through her.

"It's been great working with you," she said. "If you ever need help in the future, just give me—"

"There is one other project I wanted to talk with you about," he said.

Oh, no. Not that thing he mentioned this afternoon. She'd hoped he had forgotten about it. Even the easy camaraderie between them wasn't worth the stress she'd been living with these past few days. He'd have to wait until Suzanne was back. "I am sort of booked up right now—remember, I squeezed you in."

"I know." He leaned against her car.

Good thing she'd brought Suzanne's red BMW instead of her own aging Chrysler minivan.

"But this may be more fun than your other jobs," he said.

She hesitated. "What do you need? I can check my calendar when I get home." *To make sure it's booked solid until Suzanne gets back.*

Erik looked at her, those eyes of his glimmering with fun. "Would you like to come to my mother's party with me?"

"With you?" She suddenly felt like the class geek who'd been asked out by the star football player.

He grinned. "Yeah."

Oh, wasn't this just grand? As Nora she couldn't even get a date—that is, if she'd even been looking for one. But as a version of Suzanne, she got asked out by the catch of the century. By a guy who actually thought she, Nora, was a loser. Or something quite close to that. So, even if she came clean to him, she could never have this guy for real. *He liked Suzanne.*

"I'll level with you," he said. "My mother has a habit of trying to fix me up with single women and I suspect she's going to be in prime form at the party. I figure if I bring a date, it'll thwart her plans. What do you think?"

Yes. No! If she went, she'd have to fool his mother again. And the odds she could continue being successful at that would get lower every time she saw dear old mom. "I—I'm pretty sure I have other plans." She fought the urge to tell him exactly who she was— No-Nonsense Nora who needed to take up knitting.

Try saying that three times fast.

She unlocked the driver's door.

"Why don't you check your schedule?" he said. "I'll call you later. I think we'd have fun."

Persistent, wasn't he? She supposed that persistence is what got him to the top of his game in skiing…and medicine.

"Okay. Nice working with you." She jumped into the car and waved at him as she pushed the gas pedal to the floor, hard.

ERIK HEADED TOWARD his Subaru WRX and was surprised at the sense of disappointment he felt. Suzanne had more or less turned him down—kind of an unfamiliar happening in his life. Though, in truth he hadn't asked her for a date—just a business appointment—so he knew he shouldn't take it personally. And if she had a conflict, well, that was business.

He pulled his keys out of his pocket, clicked open the car door and slid inside, promptly dropping his keys into the darkness somewhere. He bent to fish around on the floor for them and banged his forehead into the steering wheel. "Dammit."

Rubbing his head, he sat back into his seat. A faint dusting of fog was rolling in, pale silver beneath the white glow of the streetlamps. Kind of early in the year for fog.

He wished he'd kissed Suzanne tonight.

He let his head fall back against the headrest and hoped she decided to come with him tomorrow. She so didn't match his mental image of what a personal shopper should be like, it almost blew him away. Sure, she wore those high-fashion clothes. But they didn't seem to fit her personality. She was lacking that plastic coating so many women seemed to wear. And she wasn't the glib conversationalist he'd thought a personal shopper would be, either. In fact, he found it refreshing that she pretty much blurted out exactly what was on her mind.

The oddest thing about it was, he couldn't figure out why his mother would have chosen to work with a personal shopper like Suzanne. Mom was a perfectionist—from her hair to her clothes to her house. Much as Suzanne tried to put on that air, he could tell, she just wasn't like that.

Which was another thing he liked. Because, while he valued perfection in certain things— like skiing and surgery—he saw no point in getting carried away about other things, like clothes.

He flipped on the dome light and bent once more to look for his keys, finally spying them almost beneath the gas pedal. Scooping them up, he started the engine and pulled out of his parking space.

Interesting that Suzanne had asked about the rehab center for her sister. If what she said was true about Nora's aspirations, it might be a good fit. He'd mention it to the other guys and see what they thought. Maybe Nora would be the person they needed to run the place.

Maybe he should stop at Suzanne's and talk to her about it a little more.

He shook his head. He shouldn't be thinking about chasing down a woman before he figured out what he was doing with his life. Hopefully, he'd be flying out to meet with USSA soon, so he'd know whether or not he had a decision to make.

The sooner the better, he was realizing. Because, regardless of whether Suzanne Carlisle was busy tomorrow night or not, he'd already decided this wasn't going to be the last time he saw her.

NORA STRETCHED OUT on the sofa and watched the news without seeing a thing. *No-nonsense and buttoned-up?* She wasn't that bad, was she? Part of the reason was because she had a child—a person had to be responsible with a kid, didn't they? She reached for the phone and dialed Suzanne's cell, listening while it kicked into voice mail.

"Hi, you've reached Suzanne, the Shopping Goddess. Whatever your need, you can count on me to find it. Leave a message and I'll call you back."

"Well, Goddess," Nora said, staring at the ceiling. "I just want to know if you think of me as no-nonsense and buttoned-up. The kind of person who never has any fun and should take up knitting. Call me back." She shut off the phone.

No doubt Suzanne was at another party right now, tinkle tinkle. Because somehow, over the years, Suzanne had managed to continue sparkling like silver, while Nora had tarnished to dull. Suzanne was still the fun one, while Nora was busy being the responsible one. Suzanne got asked out on dates by guys like Erik Morgan, while Nora sat home on Saturday night... *knitting*. Suzanne was the one—

The phone rang and she snatched it up. Thank goodness her sister was on the ball tonight. "Hello?"

"Nora! How did the shopping go?"

"Margo?" Her heart fell. As much as she loved Margo, she really wasn't in the mood to chat with her. What she wanted was answers from Suzanne.

"Rosie's with me, too," Margo said. "Sorry to call so late, but we're just sitting at my house and got to wondering how your shopping expedition with hunka man went."

"Fine. Mission accomplished—he's got something to wear," she said flatly.

"And?"

"Nothing."

"Oh, spill it. Something went wrong. I can hear it in your voice."

Nora debated whether to tell all, finally deciding that it might be nice to know how Margo viewed her, as well. "We went out for a drink afterward—"

"They went out for a drink!" Margo repeated gleefully to Rosie.

"Somehow we started talking about my sister… Nora. He said that Nora was buttoned-up and no-nonsense." She eyed a crack that ran the length of the ceiling and wondered how she'd never noticed it before. "Is that what I'm like?"

"No! Not all the time."

"Not all the time?"

"Hardly ever," Margo said quickly. Her voice muffled a little as she put a hand over the mouthpiece and repeated the question to Rosie.

Suddenly Rosie was on the line. "Screw him. We like you just the way you are."

"Oh, wait a minute here. So what you're saying is, I *am* buttoned-up and no-nonsense?" She felt like hyperventilating.

"That's kind of extreme and a poor choice of words. You're less buttoned-up and more starched shirt—"

"Starched shirt? That's even worse—"

"Another poor choice of words. You're not a starched—"

The call waiting beep went off in the earpiece and Nora glanced at the phone number. *Suzanne.* "Hey, Rosie? I've gotta go. Suzanne's on the other line and I'm waiting for her call. I'll call you back later." She switched over to Suzanne. "Hi!"

"What's the matter now?" her sister asked.

"You heard my message. Is that what I'm like?"

"Buttoned-up and no-nonsense?" Suzanne sounded puzzled.

"Yeah. Is that how you see me?"

"You mean specifically like that?"

My God, was her sister hedging? "Yeah. Specifically or close to it."

"Why are you asking this?"

"Why won't you answer the question?" Nora's irritation rose.

"I asked you first."

Nora pushed herself up to sitting and swung her feet to the floor. "No, you didn't. I left a voice mail first. So you have to answer first."

Suzanne made a squeaky noise. "What was the question again?"

"You're stalling. You *do* think I'm buttoned-up and no-nonsense, don't you?"

After a long silence, Nora finally said, "Suzanne? Are you there?" When her sister didn't answer, she threw herself back against the couch in frustration. Another lost connection.

She pushed the speed dial for her sister's cell phone, half expecting Suzanne not to pick up. When she did, Nora said, "Did you just hang up on purpose so you didn't have to answer me?"

"No! Now what was the question?"

"Am I buttoned-up and no-nonsense?" Nora asked.

"Not exactly."

"What exactly, then?"

"First tell me who said it," Suzanne said.

Nora pursed her lips, reluctant to name her accuser. "Fine. Erik Morgan said it. Tonight."

"Why would he say such a thing? I thought you were acting like me. Tinkle tinkle and all that. I don't need my clients to think I'm dull— not in this business."

Nora felt a slow burn start inside her. She spoke slowly. "I *was* tinkle tinkle. He wasn't saying me as you was dull. He was saying me as me was dull. Get it?"

"Oh. So you and Erik were talking about… you…I mean Nora?"

Nora straightened the magazines on the coffee table. "Yeah. We went out for drinks—"

"You went out for drinks with *Erik Morgan?*"

"No, dear sister, *you* went out for drinks with Erik Morgan. To celebrate your shopping success. The job is complete and you haven't lost your big client."

"Wow! Thanks. You may have a knack for this after all," Suzanne said.

Nora wandered into the kitchen to find something to eat. Chocolate preferably. Pounds of it. "Oh, it gets better. After he told me how Nora is so no-nonsense—and obviously, I, Suzanne, am a lot more fun—he invited me to go to his mother's party tomorrow night at the yacht club."

Suzanne screeched. "*I* have a date with Erik Morgan?"

"No. You're on a cruise ship, remember? *I* have a date with Erik Morgan." After the cupboards revealed not so much as an ounce of chocolate, she pulled a string cheese from the fridge and tore it open. "Well, actually, I don't."

"Don't tell me you turned him down."

Nora didn't reply. She was trying to figure out exactly why she had turned down a date with Erik—handsome, skier, doctor, great forearms—even if it was a *professional date.*

"Nora? Don't tell me that," Suzanne said.

"Okay, I won't." She took a bite of string cheese, not nearly as satisfying as chocolate would be, but at least it was food.

"You turned him down?" Suzanne's voice was incredulous.

"That would be correct."

Suzanne blew out her breath. "Please, please, Nora, who I know would meet the next great love of her life if only she would let it happen, please explain to me why you turned him down."

"He was saying I was no-nonsense and buttoned-up. Only he was *with* me and saying it *about* me…. Do you know what that feels like? And I know I didn't used to be like that…and I *wasn't* being like that right then—"

"Because you weren't being you! I can't believe you turned him down! Nora, I told you before. We both used to be oranges…and then you turned into an apple."

"So you're saying what he said is true?"

Suzanne hesitated. "Maybe a little."

"A little?"

"Okay, a lot," Suzanne said quietly.

"A lot? I'm a lot dull?" An ache started deep in her chest and her shoulders slumped. She'd worked so hard these past years to keep it together for her and Danny…sometimes she'd felt like she was hanging on by her fingernails.

"I'm sorry. You weren't always this way. Only since Kevin died… It's like you withdrew and never fully came back."

"I can't believe this. You have no idea how much pain I felt." *Still feel.*

"I do. You're my sister. Your pain was mine, too. If you hurt, I hurt…." Her voice broke. "All I wanted was to be able to fix it for you…and I couldn't. And when you finally started to come back from that place where all you felt was the agony of losing Kevin, you came back different."

"How could I not? How could anyone go through that and not be changed?" The ache in her chest wrapped itself around her heart, squeezing. She pressed a hand to her breastbone and tried to swallow down the knot in her throat.

"I know. But, Nora, you used to be tinkle tinkle all on your own. No one ever had to tell you how to do it." There were tears in Suzanne's voice. "And when you came back, you were functioning, doing your job, taking care of Danny… But it was like you had closed a door…protecting yourself…you weren't going to ever take a chance again. On anything or anyone. Boring and lonely was better than risking being hurt again."

Nora tried to draw a breath. She clenched her hands together in her lap and focused on the tightness of her grasp, as though the pressure of her fingers against one another would dull the pain in her heart. The room blurred behind the sudden tears in her eyes. "You don't…have a clue—"

"I didn't live it like you did. But I lived it right beside you."

"It's not the same." Her voice shook. "It's not the same. *You don't know.*"

She could hear Suzanne breathing and knew she was crying, too.

"I know I don't know. I just want to see you happy again. You don't have to go out with Erik Morgan—that's not what I'm saying."

"Then what are you saying?" *What did everyone seem to be saying these days?*

"I don't know. I just want my sister, the orange, back. I miss who you were. I love you, you know."

"Yeah, I know." Nora had to get off the phone; she couldn't deal with this conversation anymore. "I think I hear Danny awake," she lied.

"Don't be mad at me."

"I'm not. I love you, too." She shut off the phone, lay it carefully on the table and gave in to the sobs that had been building inside her—

deep, wracking sobs that seemed to lay bare her soul. She wanted to come back, too. She wanted to love and be loved. But she was so afraid. What if she got hurt? What if she hurt someone else?

No-Nonsense Nora. Even Kevin would have laughed at that one. She wiped the back of her hand across her eyes. They didn't come much better than him. She looked at the television, where *Sleepless in Seattle* was playing on cable for about the fiftieth time this year already. And the words that seemed to run through her brain on a regular basis forced their way out of her mouth. "I'm so tired of being lonely."

She stared at the phone for a minute, then picked it up and went to Suzanne's room to retrieve Erik's business card from the file where she'd put it last night. Taking a deep breath she dialed quickly and started talking as soon as he answered.

"Hi, Erik, it's…Suzanne Carlisle." She could hardly hear over the blood pounding in her ears.

"Hi." He sounded shocked to hear from her.

She plowed ahead. "I, ah, checked my schedule and actually I'm free Saturday so if you still want me to I would love to go to your mother's party," she said in one long rush. *Lunatic,* she chastised herself. *Slow down.*

"Great! I'll pick you up at seven." He laughed. "In case you're wondering what to wear…it's *casual chic*."

CHAPTER SIX

NORA PULLED ON some tan linen slacks with a white three-quarter length sleeve blouse and checked out her reflection in the mirror. Blagghh. Too tight in the butt—she looked fat. She peeled the outfit off and threw it on Suzanne's bed, which was strewn with clothing she had already discarded as she tried on one outfit after another in an effort to figure out what to wear to the party. Her stomach was nauseous from nervous excitement, she couldn't eat and she was beginning to feel weak from starvation.

And he would be here very soon.

Standing there in her underwear, she held a hand up level with her eyes and watched it tremble slightly. That confirmed it—she was a total wreck.

It had been over ten years since she'd had a date.... She sat on the edge of the bed. *Since Kevin had first asked her out.*

She thought about the past—about her husband—for a long minute, then pushed herself to her feet. She wasn't going to do this to herself, not tonight. Who knew if this was a date, anyway. She wasn't entirely certain *what* to call it. Which seemed appropriate because, regardless of what it was, she didn't know how to act, or what to say.

She pulled a blue knit top from Suzanne's wardrobe and held it up. This might work. She drew it over her head and looked at herself in the mirror and thought about Erik.

What if he didn't like her? What if he did? What were they supposed to do when the date ended?

Kiss?

Maybe she should throw up.

This was just too much to deal with. And she was way too removed from this sort of stuff. It wasn't that she thought it would be awful to kiss Erik. In fact, quite the opposite. But, oh, God, she wasn't even sure she knew how to date anymore, let alone kiss. All of this would be a lot easier if she didn't feel an attraction to the man—and if he didn't have those incredible eyes.

Well, maybe not the kissing part, but certainly the date part. It was always easy to go on a date with someone you didn't like. Well, maybe not *easy*. But at least you weren't so nervous. Then again, you could still be nervous because you didn't really want to go and were afraid the guy might try to kiss you and you knew you would have to either stop it before it started or kiss him back halfheartedly or even really kiss him back just to be nice which then made the predicament even worse—

Stop! Her brain was overheating. She sucked in a deep breath and blew it out slowly. Maybe Erik was thinking of this as strictly business and there was absolutely nothing for her to worry about.

She looked at herself in the mirror again and cringed. *No way.* Peeling off the blue top, she tossed it on the bed.

Although…she and Erik had never discussed any type of fee for tonight. So maybe he did think it was a date.

She pulled a sundress out of Suzanne's closet, slipped it on, then turned to critically appraise herself in the full-length mirror. *No.* Way too casual even for casual chic. She stripped it off and added it to the growing pile of clothes. Too bad she didn't have a ladies maid to hang all this stuff up again.

Clearly, the problem was *she had nothing to wear.* She should have gone out and bought something new this afternoon. For a moment she almost gave in to the irrational thought that she might have enough time to run out and get something new before Erik arrived. Right. She was losing her mind—all over a date.

Or a business agreement.

Whatever it was.

She sat on the edge of the bed in her underwear once again. Calm down. It was only a date. Probably just a business date. She and Erik had fun talking together, laughing together. *This was just an extension of last night's shopping trip.* It wasn't like the all-important meet-the-family date or anything.

Oh, God, yes it was! *Easy, easy, easy.* Just because his family would be there didn't mean anything. It wasn't really a meet-the-family date—it was a *business agreement.*

But what if he thought it was a date? Or what if it started out businessy and turned datey in the middle? Either way, what happened at the end of the night? Did he walk her to the door? Shake her hand? Kiss her? Maybe she could have him drop her at the corner and she could just run home…screaming.

The question did nothing to settle her stomach, which was now hungry and nauseous at the same time. She ran downstairs, grabbed some cheese and crackers in the kitchen and forced them down, swallowing hard. Then she inhaled slowly and shoved her racing thoughts away. Forget what was going to happen at the end of the night. Erik would be here any minute. If she didn't figure out something to wear soon, he was going to find her in her underwear.

Mortified, she raced for the stairs. Good thing she sent Danny and the sitter to the park a half hour ago; she didn't need Erik calling her Suzanne and her son pointing out he had the name wrong.

ERIK PULLED UP in front of her house and killed the engine. A little boy and a young teenage girl sat on the front steps eating Popsicles, the frozen treats melting in the seventy-five degree heat and pooling on the ground at their feet. For a moment he wondered why the neighbor kids were hanging out on Suzanne's porch and then he remembered being a kid and hanging out on whatever porch was available.

He shoved open his car door and started up the walk. "Hi," he said.

The little boy grinned at him, lips, teeth and chin stained blue. "Are you here for my mom?"

Erik stopped. *Mom?* "Do you live here?" He

looked directly at the girl. If this was Suzanne's daughter, she would have been pretty young when she gave birth.

Or maybe Nora. These could be Nora's kids.

"I'm the babysitter," the girl said. "Ashley. And yeah, he lives here. This is Danny. His mom is getting ready. I'll tell her you're here." She jumped up and dashed into the house.

Wow. Suzanne had a kid. And she hadn't mentioned it. He hadn't really thought to ask, either....

Danny stood up and stuck out his hand. "Nice to meet you."

Erik shook Danny's hand, feeling the sticky Popsicle juice migrate from Danny's fingers to his own.

"Do you have a wife?" Danny asked.

Ashley pushed through the screen door just in time to rejoin the conversation. "If he had a wife, he wouldn't be taking your mom out, Danny." She held the door open. "She said to tell you she's running a little late and you can just go in the living room if you want."

"Or you can stay out here with us." Danny looked up at him with big brown eyes.

"I think I'll stay out here with you."

Ashley let go of the screen door and it banged shut.

"Do you have a bike?" Danny asked.

"Yeah, I do."

"I do, too. Want to see it? It's a two-wheeler."

Ashley snorted. "With training wheels."

"My mom's gonna take 'em off." He started down the driveway toward the garage. "Come on."

Erik followed him down the drive, with Ashley right behind. "So, Danny, you like riding?"

The little boy nodded and disappeared through the open garage door, returning a minute later proudly pushing his bike, a shiny new red number.

Erik ran a hand over the top tube and rang the little bell attached to the handlebars. "I used to have a red bike, too, when I was about nine. Had a lot of fun with that bike." Lots of fun. The first winter he had it, he and a friend took the wheels off and attached the front and back forks to two halves of a broken ski. Since it was his idea, he got to be the first one to take it down the sledding hill—after they'd iced a section of the hill but good with buckets of water. His wipeout had been spectacular. So had the broken arm.

"So you're ready to take off the training wheels, huh?" he asked.

Danny nodded. "My mom said she would do

it a million years ago. Zach doesn't have training wheels anymore. And I don't want them, either."

"Who's Zach?"

"My friend. Next door." He knelt next to the bike and tried to twist off the nut that held the training wheels in place. "Can you take this off for me?"

Erik frowned. "I don't know, buddy. Your mom probably wants to do that."

"She says she's going to, but she's always too busy," Ashley said.

"I need to ride with Zach," Danny said.

"You know you can't just jump on and ride when those training wheels are off. You've got to learn to get your balance first," Erik pointed out.

The kid ignored him, just tried to twist the nut off again.

Erik turned to Ashley. "You're sure she was planning to pull them off?"

"Uh, yeah. She's said it, like, every day for the last two weeks. I babysit here a lot."

"You think she'd care if I took them off?"

Ashley shrugged. "One less thing for her to do."

Erik thought about it for a minute. Hell, Suzanne would probably appreciate him helping her out like this. "Okay." He went into the garage and grabbed a wrench from the pegboard on the wall. As he knelt by the bike, Danny began to hop from foot to foot in adrenaline-fueled anticipation.

Within a couple of minutes, he had the training wheels off. He wiped his hands against one another to remove the dust, then took hold of the handlebars and gestured at his new friend. "Okay, kid, hop on. Let's go for a spin."

Danny ran into the garage and came out wearing a helmet, kneepads, elbow pads and wrist guards.

"You wear all that stuff riding your bike?" Erik held in a laugh.

"Mom says I have to."

Seemed a bit over-the-top. For about four seconds he wondered whether Suzanne really intended to take the training wheels off or not. Then Danny climbed onto the bike and he put the whole thought out of his mind.

"Take those wrist guards off," Erik said. "Those are for Rollerblading. You won't be able to hold on right. Here." He pulled the guards off Danny's wrists and tossed them to the ground.

"Now, let's ride." Erik high-fived the kid, then started to gently run down the driveway while holding on to the bike seat.

"Pedal, Danny. Harder. Steer! Steer the bike!" They headed down the sidewalk and the front wheel veered from left to right and back again as Danny worked to find his balance. Erik jogged a little faster.

"Don't let go!" Danny cried.

"I'm not. You just steer. Pedal. Keep pedaling. *Pedal, Danny!*" He ran faster and let go of the seat for a second as he ran alongside the bike. "You're doing it, Danny!"

The bike wobbled and Erik grabbed hold of the seat again. Danny braked as they reached the end of the block. Erik's breathing was coming a little hard, it crossed his mind that casual chic probably wasn't the best choice for this activity. "Okay, let's go see if your mom is ready."

Danny turned the bike around and they flew down the sidewalk toward his home. Erik spotted Suzanne on the porch, one hand on her hip, the other shading her eyes as she watched them. Standing there in a pink sleeveless dress and sandals, a soft breeze blowing the fabric around her legs, she looked like she belonged in a painting of a glorious summer afternoon. His breath caught for a moment and all he could do was look at her. He could freeze-frame this shot forever.

"Hey, Mom!" Danny yelled.

"Keep pedaling, Danny, pedal." Erik picked up the pace so the bike was moving along at a brisk clip. Then he let go and watched proudly as Danny rode untethered along the sidewalk for a ways before veering onto the grass.

"Steer, Danny, steer!" Erik took off running in pursuit.

"Danny!" Suzanne screamed.

The kid's feet were off the pedals now, out straight to either side for balance, the bike barreling right for the hedge between two yards. Danny hit the bushes and tipped sideways, landing sprawled across his bike.

Suzanne raced down the stairs and got to Danny just as Erik did. She picked her son up and started running her hands over his arms and legs. "What hurts? Does anything hurt? Are you okay?"

Danny pushed his mom's hands away and grinned at Erik. "Did you see me, Mom? I rode by myself."

"Yes, I saw you." Her voice grew stern. "What were you doing? Look at that scratch on your leg. You could have been killed."

Danny pulled out of her grasp. "Mom, you're a worrywart and a spoilsport." He grabbed Erik's hand. "Can we go again?"

"Who took the training wheels off?" Suzanne asked softly. There was a definite frozen quality to her voice and Erik felt suddenly like he was about to be sent to the principal's office.

"Mom, did you know he's not married?"

Suzanne rolled her eyes. "Yes. I did. What does that have to do with taking training wheels off?"

"Well, Ronald was married."

A faint blush crept up Suzanne's cheeks and he wondered if Ronald was an old boyfriend. She looked at Erik. "In case you're wondering, he's talking about Ronald McDonald."

"I wasn't wondering," he lied.

"So?" Danny asked his mom. "What do you think?"

"We'll talk about that later," she said. "Now how did the training wheels get off your bike?"

Erik raised an eyebrow at Ashley. He should know better than to believe teenagers. "I took them off," he said. "I...thought you were planning to do it and just didn't have the time."

"Daniel—" Suzanne frowned at her son.

"You said you'd take them off."

"When you were ready. And clearly you aren't ready."

"Yes, I am," he said defiantly.

"Where are your wrist guards?"

Danny scowled. "I can't hold on right with those."

Based on Suzanne's response so far, Erik knew Danny was heading into really big trouble now.

"So you just didn't wear them?"

The kid shrugged.

Unbelievable. Danny was taking the fall for him. "That would be my fault, too," he said. "I told him not to wear them. But he's right, he can't hold on properly with them on—they're designed for Rollerblading...not biking."

Suzanne glared at him and somehow, the evening of fun he had pictured them having seemed very far away. "Sorry," he said.

"Let's go wash up that cut." She marched Danny back inside.

"I guess I'll put the training wheels back on." Erik started down the driveway.

Ashley sauntered along beside him. "His mom's kind of overprotective."

"It might have been nice if you'd mentioned that before."

"Yeah, well, Danny's right. She is a worry-wart and a spoilsport."

NORA SAT STIFFLY in the passenger seat of Erik's car and tried to calm her jackhammer heart. She couldn't believe Erik had taken her son's training wheels off without asking permission. And she couldn't believe Danny and Ashley had come home early from the park. No wonder her heart was pounding a million beats a minute. Besides her child almost getting hurt, she had just dodged one of the biggest bullets of her life—that being, her own child unmasking her.

At least these new events had temporarily buried her concerns about whether Erik was going to kiss her at the end of the night.

"I'm sorry," he said.

The sincerity in his voice melted her anger and she began to relax.

"It just didn't seem so out of line, especially when both of them said you'd been promising to take off the training wheels for weeks."

"I had. But I didn't really mean it. You don't have children so you don't realize what can happen to them." She knew she sounded overly cautious and, for the first time ever, felt a little embarrassed about it.

"Considering that, since the age of five, I threw myself down mountains on two thin pieces of wood, and survived—"

"It's different when it's your own child."

Erik just looked at her and she had a hard time telling if he was getting her point of view or not.

"I guess," he said. "You know, I didn't even know you had a son."

Her brain kicked into overdrive. *She was Suzanne—not Nora.* Suzanne had no children. Good God, she'd just given it all away. Her heart started to pound all over again. She knew she shouldn't have agreed to come out with him. "Oh," she said weakly. She frantically scrambled to come up with the next lie to add to the pyre that would soon destroy her life. "I guess I didn't have any reason to mention it before. It's not the thing I typically talk to clients about because you know, I'm typically talking—" *stop talking* "—about shopping."

Erik nodded, but he had a strange expression on his face. She tried to figure out if he'd just worked everything out.

"So…are you divorced?" he asked.

Divorced. Hmm. *Should she be divorced?* What was the answer here? He couldn't possibly know her story—Nora's story. She hardly knew the man. Unless someone at the hospital had blabbed it to him. But, no, that was unlikely. So, should she be divorced? Or widowed? Or— *Stop thinking.*

She drew a breath. Okay, she'd just go with the truth—her truth, not Suzanne's. A fine bead of sweat prickled across her shoulders. "My husband was killed shortly before Danny was born."

"Oh, God, I'm sorry."

She had to be more careful. She'd actually succeeded in getting the shopping done and the account saved. Then, in the space of a few minutes, she'd almost blown the whole thing on a date—a date she was going on just to prove she hadn't become dull. "My friends say it's made me too cautious with Danny…and maybe it has."

"Makes it more understandable, anyway." He gave her a sideways glance. "So, I just have to ask. Did you go on a date with Ronald McDonald?"

Nora laughed, a big rolling laugh that shook loose all the tension that had built up inside her.

"Not that I don't think he wouldn't be a great catch," Erik continued.

She laughed again, warmed by the teasing in Erik's voice. He really was a nice guy. "No, I did not go out with Ronald. But Danny thought he'd be the perfect man for me."

"You wouldn't have to make dinner anymore."

"That was his point," she said.

Erik laughed then and pulled the Subaru up to the yacht club, with its impressive white colonial revival facade and Corinthian columns. A valet, dressed in a black tux, opened Nora's door and helped her out of the car.

"Okay, let's forget about training wheels for the rest of the night," he said. "I'll show you a better time than Ronald ever could. Come on, the grand ballroom's upstairs." He reached out to take her hand and, at his touch, a thrill raced through her. Wait until she told Suzanne all this—she would die.

As they stepped into the high-ceilinged grand ballroom, Nora caught her breath, completely captivated. The room was finished in redwood, and had gleaming hardwood floors and a stunning stone fireplace. A large crowd of people had already arrived for the party and their voices and laughter mingled into a happy sound.

They weren't in the room more than a minute before one of the waiters tapped Erik on the shoulder and pointed him toward his mother. Erik took Nora's hand again and led her through the crowd to where Camille was holding court. She spotted them right away and stood, using a cane for support.

"Oh, Suzanne—" She smiled at her son.

"Sounds like a song," he muttered.

"Erik looks wonderful." She clasped one of Nora's hands with her own. "I'm so glad you could come." Her gaze roamed over the crowd. "Mary Jean is here…so is her daughter. I'm sure they'd both like to meet Suzanne. Once they see what a nice job she's done with you, Erik, they may want her services, as well."

Nora mentally cringed. *Oh, great, more people to lie to.*

"Be sure to tell Mary Jean that I've got a hot date," Erik said.

Camille's lips quirked a little. "I suppose I'll have to. Your sister is here somewhere, too. I told her and Bill you were bringing Suzanne so be sure to do the introductions. Oh! And don't forget to register for the door prizes. Right over by the bar."

"Isn't it kind of poor form for family members to enter?" he asked.

"Nonsense. Go on, you two, and have some champagne. Enjoy yourselves." She waved them off and turned to talk to someone else who was waiting.

Erik looked around. "I have no idea where my sister is. I guess we could get the door prize thing out of the way." As soon as they were out of earshot of Camille, he said, "My mother. She's the epitome of 'you can take the girl out of the small town but you can't take the small town out of the girl.'" He shook his head. "Door prizes."

A waiter passed by holding a tray filled with flutes of champagne, each with a strawberry in the bottom. Erik snagged two glasses and handed one to Nora. Well, wasn't this the cat's meow? No longer was Suzanne the only one having a grand time. Nora took a swallow and relished the bubbles wiggling their way down her throat. This was exactly what she needed. A little champagne to calm her nerves and she'd be just fine tonight, no matter how much lying she'd have to do.

As they were filling out the entry forms, Erik pointed to a woman standing near the large windows overlooking the bay. "There's my sister, Jenny. Come on. I'll introduce you."

Nora dropped her entry into the fancy decorated box on the table. Oh, no. What if his sister asked for shopping advice?

Jenny saw Erik coming across the room and a grin lit up her face. "I thought you'd never get here!" She launched herself into his arms and he spun her around.

"You should talk. When did you finally get in?"

"Oh, don't even remind me," she said as they pulled apart. "I knew we should have flown in yesterday. The flight got delayed and I thought we were going to miss our connection and then miss the party." She smiled at Nora. "You must be Suzanne."

Nora nodded and extended a hand.

"My mom told me all about you," Jenny said. "Maybe you can give me some fashion tips."

Nora felt her smile begin to freeze. Could she call this stuff or what? She took another sip of champagne and nodded.

"Nope, she's not working tonight," Erik said. "You want tips, call her next week and make an appointment."

She could have kissed him. And then she realized what he'd just said. *She's not working tonight.* Did that mean this was a real date?

With Erik Morgan?

Suddenly she couldn't even look at him— what if she turned red? Unable to think of a thing to say, she turned her attention to the bay, sparkling beneath the setting sun, the water dusted gold and pink. Out in front of the yacht club, piers stretched out like fingers, with boats of every shape and size docked along them.

"This is really gorgeous. Does your mother have a boat?" she asked.

"Yeah. Well, her husband does," Erik said. "He's a big sailor. Got a Swan fifty-six that he races. Built for speed but with a cruising interior. Best of both worlds he always says."

"Speaking of him, I want to find out if he's racing tomorrow," Jenny said. "I haven't been sailing in a long time. See you in a bit." She danced off.

"Do you ever race with him?" Nora asked.

"Sometimes. I always spent my free time skiing. Never really learned to sail so well—it's pretty different... Sailing you have a whole crew, skiing you do alone."

"Are they so different really? Flying down snow instead of flying across water?"

He narrowed his eyes, thinking. "I suppose you're right. At least until the wind dies. Then you can go nuts from the sound of the sails flapping because there's no wind in them and the boat is just rocking on the water."

"Since I've never been sailing I'm having a little trouble sympathizing," Nora said wryly.

"Be nice to me and I'll get you out sometime."

Be nice to me. No problem. The only issue she could see was, he thought Nora was a drip and Suzanne was a barrel of fun. So, maybe Suzanne would get to go sailing sometime, but, she, Nora, would never get the chance. She took another swallow of champagne. "Okay."

By the time she'd finished her second glass of champagne, she wished she hadn't been too nervous to eat lunch because the bubbles were going straight to her head. And by the time she finished her third glass, she vowed not to have another. But, by then, they were seated for dinner, and, wouldn't you know it, she was at the head table with the entire family.

She watched as waiters attended to each table, pouring wine for dinner, and knew that if she had even one sip it would be the end of her. Already when she turned her head, her brain came along later. She could only imagine what it would be like if her brain just didn't come along at all.

A few minutes passed, then dinner arrived, every table served at the same time. She looked at her plate. Filet mignon, crab, with swirls of sauce over everything and all sorts of green and yellow vegetables piled on top with some long crunchy things sticking out like big needles. Looked kind of like an art exhibit thing that Selena would do.

She took a bite; it tasted incredible. As she ate, she tried to pay attention to what people were saying as they came up to the microphone to speak. Most were toasting Erik's mother, some told funny or touching stories. Finally, when the main course was finished and the waiters were passing out dessert, Camille took the microphone, thanked her publisher and everyone else in the room and announced that the door prizes would now be distributed.

Someone brought the entry box forward and Camille began to pull names, one by one, as she gave away signed copies of her latest book, fancy pads of writing paper, elegant pens and—

What? Who? Everyone was clapping and smiling. Nora gave her head a little shake to clear the champagne bubbles from her ears.

"Suzanne, you won! Get up there!" Jenny motioned at her excitedly.

Her mouth dropped open and she quickly shut it. "Won what?" she managed to say without slurring.

"You're in the next book," Erik said. "It's your fifteen minutes of fame."

People were clapping and looking at her and she flushed—who knew if it was from alcohol or embarrassment. Heat rolled over her. *Help me,* she said in her head and quickly added *St. Jude* to the end of the sentence. Then she drew a deep breath, pushed her chair back and stood.

So far, so good. Thank goodness she'd worn flat sandals and not Suzanne's stilettos. She concentrated on making sure she didn't sway as she made her way to where Camille Lamont waited to give her a hug.

"I am delighted that Suzanne has won this prize," Camille said into the mike. "She's my personal shopper and fantastic at what she does.

I can't wait to work her character into the story." She took Nora by the arm and pulled her toward the podium. "Suzanne, how about giving us an idea…something just off the top of your head you think I should put into the book."

Nora looked out over the audience. An idea? How about not drinking too much champagne on an empty stomach? "Maybe she could have a twin sister," she said giddily as she accepted the award certificate. "Maybe she could change places with her sister and find out what people really think about her." *What the hell was she doing?* "Or, you know—" she gestured weakly with one hand "—maybe not." She stepped back from the microphone and slunk back to her chair.

Leaning over to Erik, she excused herself to go to the ladies' room. Once there, she splashed a little cold water on her face, careful not to smear her makeup, and dabbed it off with a paper towel. She felt a little more alert now. Clearly, a Diet Coke was in order, or some coffee. She stepped out into the corridor and started back to the grand ballroom feeling a little more coherent than she had earlier. Thank goodness she'd finally eaten.

Someone grabbed her by the arm and pulled

her toward a dark corner. As she turned her head, her brain only slightly slower in its response, a male voice said, "Hello, Nora."

CHAPTER SEVEN

SHE FORCED HER EYES to focus and found herself face-to-face with Suzanne's ex-fiancé— all dark good looks and very little gray matter. Her heart rate slowed and she sobered even more. "Keegan! Shh. What are you doing here?" She knew the answer before he even spoke. "You're setting up the band."

He worked a toothpick between his teeth. "What's going on? Why are you pretending to be Suzanne?"

She shushed him again. "It's a long story. I'm just helping her out, so keep your mouth shut."

"Huh." He eyed her thoughtfully for too long. "What's it worth to you? And Suzanne?"

"What?"

"You heard me."

Nora laughed. "Keegan, you'd make a lousy Mafioso."

"How come Suzanne won't return my calls?"

Very little gray matter. "Maybe because you dumped her."

"Yeah, well, I need to talk to her. That cruise we were going to take on our honeymoon? I paid for it."

Uh-oh. "I don't know anything about all that stuff." She tried to move past him but he blocked her way.

"You tell Suzanne to either return my calls so I can get refunded for the cruise—"

"You want the money back?" She felt the room begin to spin. She was going to really kill her sister this time.

"Damn right. And she's got all the paperwork."

He wanted his money back. And Suzanne and a friend were, at this moment, enjoying that cruise…or actually a different cruise…just earlier than the one she had planned to take on her honeymoon.

Nora put a hand against the wall for support. "Well, Keegan, see, I don't think she has the money because, you know, she's still trying to get this business going." She paused to try to pull her thoughts together. "Which is why I'm helping her out tonight."

"She just has to give me the paperwork—she doesn't need to come up with any money. Then I can get a refund."

Nora thought of champagne and parties and light, easy, happy laughter, tinkle tinkle. "She's been so busy lately…."

"I'll tell you what." Keegan's voice took on an edge. "You tell your sister to give me my tickets or I'll tell Mrs. Big Client Lamont that her personal shopper is not what she says she is."

Nora dropped her fake smile.

Keegan leered. "And, I'll also tell her that you two have a history of scamming people."

"What? That's ridiculous!"

He shrugged. "And maybe," he added. "I'll tell the hospital what you're doing in your spare time."

"The hospital isn't going to care if I'm a personal shopper in my spare time." Except, if she ever did apply for a job with the new sports medicine rehab center…then getting caught lying to Erik Morgan might just mean the end of that dream. The thought disquieted her.

"We'll have to see, won't we?" Keegan looked down the hallway and she followed his gaze. Erik was coming toward them.

"I was wondering where you went," he said.

"Erik, this is an old friend—"

"I was engaged to her sister—"

"Nora," Nora said, locking eyes with Keegan.

He paused. "Nora," he said around the toothpick.

"He's with the band," Nora said evenly. "A roadie."

Erik shook hands with Keegan. "Good to meet you." He touched Nora on the arm. "Hey, want to go outside? I can only take so much of this."

That made two of them. "I'd love to. Good seeing you, Keegan, I'll tell…my sister to give you a call."

"Do that." He turned and sauntered back toward the party.

Unbelievable. Why was it whenever she agreed to something with her sister it turned into a fiasco? She needed to talk to Suzanne—*now*.

She opened her purse and pulled out her cell phone. "I— Can you excuse me just one more minute?" she said to Erik. "A call came in on my cell and I just want to make sure everything is okay at home." She hurried downstairs and stepped outside, frantically dialing Suzanne's cell phone number as she wandered down one of the long wooden docks. A breeze ruffled her hair and she could hear the rigging on the boats softly clattering as they rocked gently in their slips. Under other circumstances she would consider this an incredibly romantic night. But not now….

"All right, smarty party girl," she said when Suzanne finally answered. "We are now in deep, deep, deep, deep trouble. Deep with a capital *T*."

"Have you been drinking?"

"No, why?"

Suzanne laughed. "You can't spell. You never could hold your liquor."

"Oh, fine, I had a couple glasses of champagne. That, my dear sister, is the least of our worries. Does the name *Keegan* ring any bells?" She stopped at the end of the pier and looked out into the darkness.

"Gee, I don't know. You mean like Keegan, the rat who decided he didn't want to marry me? Like Keegan, the jerk who decided he needed to go out with some babe twelve years younger than him? Like Keegan—"

"That would be him."

"What about him?" Suzanne said in a bored voice.

"He's here at the party, doing setup for the band. And he wants to know why you won't return his calls."

"*What party?* And excuse me? He wants to know why *I* won't return his calls? Tell him what's good for the goose is good for the gander. Kindness is as kindness does and all that crap."

Nora controlled the urge to yell at her sister. "Suzanne. Has he left you any messages about getting the paperwork back for the cruise tickets *he* bought?"

"Yeah. So what?"

"Well, he wants the paperwork so he can get a refund."

"Too bad, so sad. You tell him that I, and Emmy, a dear friend who stood by me when my fiancé didn't, are taking a little mental rehab cruise through the Alaskan Passage. Tinkle. Tinkle."

"It ain't gonna be that easy," Nora said. "Because Keegan recognized me. *He knew I wasn't you.* And he said if you don't give him back the tickets, he's going to tell everyone the truth about us. So you're—"

"Screwed. About to lose the Camille Lamont account." Suzanne's voice pitched up. "Nora, you can't let it happen!"

"*I can't let it happen?* You've already set the stage for it to happen. This isn't just about you. If Keegan talks, I could lose the chance to get the job of my dreams, too."

"He wouldn't dare."

"He seemed awfully set when he talked to me. Suzanne, this is the kind of mess I got into ten, fifteen years ago when I was a kid. Not now. I'm responsible now. I've built a life…and I'm trying to build you one, too." Realizing she was getting a bit loud, she lowered her voice. "So may I suggest you give old Keegie a call and, at least, put him off a bit. And may I also suggest that you get the heck off that boat and get home, for a multitude of reasons, but particularly because you now have a pressing need to find the money to pay Keegan for the tickets you just used."

She saw Erik coming down the dock toward her. "Here comes Erik. I've gotta go before he figures this all out." She closed her phone and dropped it into her purse.

"Everything okay?" he asked, coming close to her.

She nodded. *If he only knew.* "You know kids. Danny just wanted to ask about riding his bike tomorrow. Without training wheels."

"I know we were putting the training wheels issue aside tonight, but, the kid is ready. You should let him."

She frowned. "He might get hurt."

"He might also get self-confidence."

She contemplated his words. *"He might get hurt."*

"And he probably won't. Like I said before, I started skiing when I was his age."

"That's the problem. When you're young you don't realize how quickly it all can end. You don't have any idea the pain that comes with risk." For a moment, those words sounded odd coming out of her—at least the her she used to be.

He took a step back. "I don't know…. What is life without risk? Are you really living if everything is smooth all the time?"

"You like bumpy?"

He grimaced and shoved a hand through his hair. "Sometimes life bumps are good—like moguls on a ski hill. You learn to control your skis, to concentrate, maneuver through tough terrain and come out standing. In the end, you have this exhilaration at having conquered and, depending on how hard the hill was, at surviving."

This conversation was cutting too close to home. She looked up at the moon so she could avoid looking at him. "You think pain is worth it just so you can celebrate surviving?"

"I wouldn't exactly put it that way. But, when you survive you always come out stronger. That strength is what lets you challenge life again. And challenges are what make us feel alive."

She thought of Kevin. "Sometimes it's not that easy."

"You mean a death."

She nodded.

"How did he die?"

She tamped down the ache that always seemed to well up when she talked about Kevin dying. "Car accident. Irresponsible teenage kid driving a stolen car, ran a red light one night…"

"Oh, God, I'm sorry."

"Yeah. He kind of saved my life. And then he lost his. He was a cop. I used to skip out of high school and he'd pick me up and haul me back there."

The breeze messed her hair into her face and she brushed the loose strands back. "In the squad car, he'd give me lectures about the importance of education. Something must have sunk in, because after high school ended, I got my GED and then went to college. After graduation, I tracked him down to thank him."

"He gave you something to hold on to."

"Yeah." She thought back to those years and felt the pain of missing him again. "He was only six years older than me…we started dating, got married. He wanted to get on the other side of the law and become a lawyer. I wanted to go on to become a physical therapist—"

"Like Nora?"

She froze. Damn all that champagne. She was going to blow this thing one way or another. "Ah, yeah, like Nora. But then, I got pregnant. He never made it to law school… never met his son." Her voice dropped to a whisper and she looked out over the bay, dark in the moonlight. "He always sacrificed for me. And then he died too soon…before I could give back to him."

Erik didn't say anything for a long time and she finally turned toward him. He was looking at her, just looking, his gaze so intense it almost scared her.

"I think you're probably underestimating the value of what you did give him," he said. "Most people just want happiness, acceptance—" He broke off for a moment. "It isn't about jobs, and money, and trips and owning things. I know, easy for me to say when I have all that. But it's not…" He glanced away and Nora knew suddenly that Erik Morgan was not content, had a longing, a hole in his soul he was searching to fill.

"My dad," he said, "died when I was eleven. He used to recite this poem to my sister and me at bedtime… about a child running to his father when he got home after work and showing him all the bruises and cuts he'd gotten that day. And, as the father makes them better, he laments the fact that the greatest hurts his child will someday have will be those of the heart. Sometimes I can still hear him as he sat on the edge of the bed in the dark." He paused. "And then he got sick. And died within six months."

"So you know."

He nodded. "Not exactly what you feel, but, yeah, I've done that mogul run."

"Sometimes, the reminders come out of the blue and hit me…and I have to back away from everything," she said softly.

"And then what happens?"

"I come back out. I have to. I have a child, a job…" *I want to have a life again.*

He looked at her curiously, just watched her as though assessing something. Finally he nodded. "About Danny and the training wheels…"

She laughed, and the touch of sadness she was feeling seeped away. Her eyes met his and she saw understanding there…and she thought to herself that, for being a wild hotshot skier, this man had a gentle soul. Her heart stirred. She wished he would put his arms around her and hold her close.

And then her cell phone rang and she wanted to crawl under the dock. She checked the caller ID. Jeez… *Now what?* "Hold that thought," she said to Erik. "The babysitter is calling again."

She hurried down the dock and turned on the phone. "What now?" she said in lieu of hello.

"What party?" Suzanne asked. "You never answered me before—where are you?"

"That's what you're calling for? I'm busy."

"Don't tell me you actually went to Camille's party."

"Okay, then I won't," Nora said, enjoying herself.

Suzanne squealed. "You went? I thought you told him *no!*"

"Yes, well, I decided to put a little risk back in my life. Because this charade of ours wasn't quite enough."

"I can't believe it. *So you're busy, huh?* Making out with Erik in a corner somewhere?"

"Right. That's not going to happen." Nora checked to make sure Erik was still way down at the end of the dock.

"Erik Morgan can kiss me anytime he wants," Suzanne said.

"Well, when you get back, he may have to. Because then you'll be you and I'll be me and *you'll* be going out with him."

"Oh, God, Nora, this is getting way too complicated."

"I'm glad you're finally reaching that conclusion."

Erik turned and waved at her.

"I have to go," she said. "Erik's gonna get suspicious if I'm on the phone all the time. I keep telling him the babysitter's calling."

"Don't hang up on me! We need to figure this Keegan thing out."

"I already have—it involves you getting off that ship and coming home. I'll call you later." Nora clicked off the phone, dropped it in her purse and hurried back toward Erik. "I'm really sorry. Danny isn't feeling that well."

"Do you want to get going?"

She shook her head. "I think he's just tired. Overexcited from riding his bike, I bet…"

"I've been standing here thinking about him, too. How about teaching him to ski?"

She froze. "Isn't that sort of a big leap from training wheels? I could never send him off on a mountain with a stranger—"

"You mean a ski instructor?" He bent toward her, and the nearness of him and the smell of his aftershave almost made her catch her breath. "What if it's not a stranger? How about I take the two of you skiing? Some hills are open until Memorial Day. Hell, most years you can ski at Mammoth Mountain until July."

A shiver of fear ran through her and she shook her head. "He's so young—"

"Yeah, exactly. It's a great age to learn. When I lost my dad, skiing gave me something of my own to hang on to."

Nora thought about Danny's obsession with finding a dad. Could something like skiing help him past that? As an outlet? Did five-year-olds really need outlets? Wasn't life just one big fun outlet anyway when you were five? "You also got really hurt." She looked pointedly at Erik's knees.

"Skiing gave me far more than it took away... So what do you say?"

She couldn't bring herself to reply.

"Tell you what," he said. "You think it over and I'll ask you again in a few days. Come on, I'll show you my stepfather's boat, *Mojo*."

"That's its name?"

"Yeah." He took her hand in his and she loved the warmth of it, the way it made her feel secure as he led her down another dock. Mojo. Erik had it, that was for sure.

They halted next to a big sailboat with a striking white hull and a large cockpit where several people were sipping drinks and chatting. Nora was impressed; she only wished she knew more about boats so she could tell what she was looking at.

Erik stepped onto the teak deck and held out

a hand to help her aboard, then introduced her to his stepfather, Jack Lamont.

The man had an open, friendly face and she liked him immediately. "Good to meet you, Suzanne. I understand you're responsible for Erik's new fashion sense," Jack said. He laughed jovially and Erik laughed with him.

"Jack's not into clothes, either," Erik said, stepping down the companionway that led below deck. "I wouldn't doubt if my mom has you shopping for him soon."

She followed him below and was awed by the sense of luxury that was evident in the stunning varnished wood interior, the *L*-shaped settee and teak chairs around a large table. Soft lighting gave the space a romantic glow. "They race this?" she asked.

"Yeah. But it's a really comfortable boat to cruise in, too." They stepped into the galley, which was beautifully designed with a sink and stove. She rubbed her hand on the counter. "Is this Corian?" This boat must have cost a fortune.

He laughed. "Only the best." He pulled a couple of clear plastic glasses from a stack on the counter. "Want a drink?"

"I think a Diet Coke is what I need right now."

"Coming right up." He scooped ice into the glasses.

Nora shook her head. "Somewhere between seeing Keegan and taking all those phone calls I sure lost my champagne high."

"I can see why." He popped open a Diet Coke and poured it into the cups. "I don't know your sister well, but that guy really didn't seem like her type at all."

She felt a niggling irritation. Here they were discussing No-Nonsense Nora again. "Oh, really?" she said as nonchalantly as she could. "What *is* her type?"

"You know, a more staid kind of guy. An accountant or an engineer...not a roadie."

Staid? She wanted to tell him that *she* was the one who used to cut school. *She* was the one who used to sneak out of the house at night to meet her boyfriend. *She* was the one who used to get the party started, so to speak.

Then it hit her that all her thoughts contained the words *used to.* Suzanne was right—she had changed. "So, if Nora's type is an accountant, then what's my type?"

He turned, a glass in each hand, and looked at her. Looked at her so long she had to break eye contact just so she could breathe.

But when she glanced back, she was caught instantly in his eyes again. Heat slid through her veins. He took a step toward her, then another

and backed her right up against the companionway wall until she couldn't move away from
him, until their bodies were touching and their
eyes were still locked. And then, arms out to the
side, still holding a glass in each hand, he dipped
his head and covered her mouth with his own.

He kissed her.

Her heart clutched with such intensity that
she trembled. She hadn't been kissed in five
years. His lips moved over hers, his tongue
teasing, playing with her mouth. Her body
tightened and she brought her hands up against
his chest, could feel the beating of his heart
under her palm, and wanted to bury herself in
the warmth of him, the smell of him. She took
hold of his shirt with her hands and pulled him
closer, gave herself up to the kiss as he pressed
her back into the companionway wall. Her
body went into a slow melt, every nerve
relaxing as she leaned into him, happily
drowning in the heady sensations of his kiss.

When they finally pulled apart, she stared up
at him, stunned by his actions—and her
response. Suddenly, irrational fear filled her.
What was she doing?

At the sound of voices at the top of the companionway, Erik took two steps back and held
out a glass. "Diet Coke?"

She shook her head. This was definitely not something she should be doing. Her heart actually hurt right now. Besides, Suzanne would have a nightmare to take care of when she came back. *Not that she didn't deserve it.* "I'm sorry. Now that I think of it, I probably should get going. I'm worried about Danny and it's getting late."

He gave her a puzzled look, then set the glasses in the sink. "No problem."

Ten minutes later they were in his car, headed home, making small talk the entire trip. Her cell phone rang twice more and Nora ignored it. She hoped it was Suzanne calling to say she'd found a way off the cruise, but no way could she answer the phone right now and risk having Erik overhear their conversation. If only she hadn't been so stupid to think going to this party would make her fun again. So much had gone wrong—from drinking too much on an empty stomach, to seeing Keegan…to kissing Erik.

As soon as they pulled up to her house, she popped her door open. Erik did the same.

"You don't have to walk me up," she said. "It's been great working with you. If you ever need Shopping Goddess services again, be sure to give me a call." She jumped from the car and raced up the walk before he could reply. *That certainly eliminated her worries about what would happen at the end of the date.*

Once inside the house she put a hand to her forehead. What was wrong with her? The minute she met someone with potential, someone she wanted to get close to, someone who appeared to want to get close to her, she ran. She and Erik had a connection—she could feel it. She'd felt something special between them all night, especially when they kissed. And that had made her want to run all the more.

Rationally, she knew she shouldn't get involved with Erik—not when she was pretending to be someone she wasn't. So, regardless of what the heck was up with her heart, she'd been smart to discourage him. She'd done the best thing for Suzanne's business, the best thing for her own future.

So why didn't she feel so great about it?

She watched the sitter get safely home cross the street, then punched in speed dial for Suzanne. A deep male voice answered the phone. For a moment she was taken aback, speechless. "Ah...I'm calling for Suzanne Carlisle...."

"Suzanne is somewhat...*indisposed* at the moment," he said lazily.

Her sister's laughter fluttered in the background.

"You tell Suzanne that she has five seconds to get herself *un-indisposed* or Keegan and Nora are going to have a chat." She had no patience for romantic dalliances at the moment.

Five seconds later, Suzanne was on the line. "It was just a joke, Nora. Settle down."

"It's not funny. You've been calling me all night and now you're *indisposed?*" Nora paced from the living room into the dining room and back.

"You weren't returning my calls, so I found something else to do."

"Don't get indignant with me. I didn't get us into this disaster that seems to be quadrupling by the day," Nora said. "So why did you call? Please say you're coming home." She started up the stairs, so wound up she didn't want to sit down.

"No. But I thought of another solution. I'm going to call Keegan from here. He won't have any idea I'm on the cruise ship…and I'll stall him until the cruise is done."

Nora's optimism evaporated. "What about the garden club speech on Tuesday? I thought you were going to come back for that."

"I checked. We're on open water now…and we'll be on it then… There's no way off the ship unless it's an emergency." She paused. "So…the thing is…if you don't do it for me, I'll miss this opportunity, and think what that will mean."

You'll live with me for the rest of my life. Irritation flared within Nora.

"How come I feel completely trapped?" she said.

Suzanne didn't answer.

Nora felt her anger fade to resignation. She'd managed to do the initial client assessment with little to no help from Suzanne; she could do this, too. She blew out her breath. "Whatever. Fine. You'd just better prepare me this time so I have plenty of things to say."

"I will, I will! Thank you, Nora. I owe you big-time."

"Yeah, yeah. Just don't blame me if Camille Lamont figures it all out and you lose the account anyway."

"She won't. Half the time she's so caught up in the plot of her latest book, she's, like, walking around with her head in the clouds."

Nora peeked into Danny's room to check on her son; he was sound asleep, sprawled across the bed, uncovered. "I thought writers were supposed to be really observant. Like they notice things about people, understand their feelings, read their emotions…"

"They do? I never saw her doing that. Do you think she already knows you're not me?" Suzanne asked, her voice panicked.

"I doubt it." Nora pulled the Spider-Man quilt up to cover Danny. "So, now, back to Keegan," she whispered so as not to wake him.

"Don't worry. I'll take care of Keegan. By the time this is done, he'll be putty in my hands."

CHAPTER EIGHT ·

ERIK PUT HIS CAR into gear and pulled away from the curb. What had happened tonight? Based on Suzanne's sudden need to leave the party and her businesslike goodbye, he had obviously done something wrong. He hadn't planned to kiss her and once he'd started, hadn't planned to make it so...pleasurable. But she'd kissed him back. Had pulled him closer. So what had gone wrong?

Maybe he'd moved too fast. He shook his head; he'd brought Suzanne to the party to ensure his mother didn't try to foist single women on him tonight. And instead, he'd foisted himself on Suzanne.

She had come along as his hired help for the night and, somehow, he'd started treating her like a date. He wasn't entirely sure how he'd let it happen. Except, whenever he was with her, he found himself wanting to touch her, kiss her.

He'd thought she wanted the same thing. And

yet, after the kiss, she'd backed away at warp speed. He knew he shouldn't care, should just let her go— especially with a potential coaching job in his future that would involve being gone ten months of the year. But he also knew that the kiss had said far more about the connection between them than did her quick retreat.

Something just didn't add up. He turned his car back toward the yacht club. He wasn't ready to go home yet. There was more to this woman than met the eye and his mother was the only person he could think of who might be able to give him some insight into her personal shopper.

Twenty minutes later, he was back at the party, had grabbed a beer and was sitting at a table near the dance floor with his mother and sister. The band was loud enough that it was a little hard to hear. And though the crowd had thinned a bit, a lot of people were still there.

"You took her home already?" Jenny frowned.

"The babysitter called—her son wasn't feeling well."

"Her son?" his mother asked.

"Yeah. Danny."

His mother's brow furrowed. "Her son?" she repeated.

"Yeah," Erik said louder.

"I didn't know she—"

"Are you going to see her again?" Jenny leaned forward onto her elbows and grinned at him.

He laughed. "We had fun. She's nice."

"Oh! He avoids the question! You'll be seeing her again—I can tell." Jenny clapped her hands.

"Maybe. She's sort of hard to read."

His mother nodded slowly and looked about to say something before stopping herself. Finally she spoke. "Sometimes Suzanne can be a little…" she searched for a word "…reserved. She's probably just nervous about involving someone new in her—son's—life."

Maybe that's what it was. Maybe she was worried about Danny getting attached to him if it didn't work out. "So she's like that with you?" he asked.

His mother hesitated a moment. "Yes. Yes, she is. Quieter, more reserved."

"I think part of it might be because her husband died five years ago."

His mother's eyes widened. "Suzanne's husband? What?"

He raised his voice again. "Why don't you tell the band to turn it down? Her husband died. Didn't she tell you that?"

For a moment Camille didn't answer. "She told me—"

"Maybe that's why she's so reserved," Jenny offered.

"I asked her to speak at the garden club meeting," his mother said randomly.

"Oh, really?" Jenny winked at Erik. "When is that going to be?"

Leave it to his sister to make sure he hit paydirt.

"Seven o'clock Tuesday night." His mother absently stirred her cocktail with her straw. "She's supposed to get back to me, but I haven't heard anything yet."

"Maybe you'd better follow up," Jenny said. "Tell her how *important* it is that she be there." She grinned at him.

This wasn't a bad idea. He could drop in at the event and hang in the back. Suzanne didn't even have to know he was there. But it would give him a chance to just watch her, see if her appeal still held, find out if that mysterious allure he found so enchanting was just a figment of his imagination—or an innate part of her being.

He smiled at his sister. "I think she's right, Mom."

And his mother smiled at him. "Oh, don't I know it."

EARLY THE NEXT AFTERNOON, Nora sat on a sunny
bench in Golden Gate Park and watched Danny
on the playground while she waited for Margo
and Peter to arrive. The air smelled of spring and
flowers coming into bloom and she drew in a
slow breath. For weeks, the boys had been
bugging them to come to the park and ride the
carousel, and they'd finally settled on this Sunday.

She heard a whoop from behind her and
spotted Peter racing across the grass toward
them, his blond hair shining in the sun. She
stood and went out to meet Margo, who was
strolling more sedately behind him.

"Didn't Ellie come?" Nora asked, looking
around for Margo's daughter.

"She went to a friend's house," Margo said.
"It's just me and Peter today. So, I'm dying to
hear. How'd the date go?" Margo asked.

Nora shrugged. "I don't know." She watched
the boys, already running down the path toward
the carousel.

"That doesn't sound good. What happened?"

As they followed the boys, Nora recounted
the evening's events, from drinking too much
champagne to her encounter with Keegan, to
the kiss and her sudden decision to go home.
For a moment, she debated whether to say
more, finally blurting out, "I think something's

wrong with me. Maybe I need professional help. There I was, really enjoying being with this guy and then, suddenly, I was thinking *I can't do this* and I just wanted to get home."

"Fear," Margo said.

"Tell me something I don't know."

"You've come to the right place. I'm going to have to start charging for all the advice I give out," Margo said.

"I'll buy you an ice cream. So really, what do think is wrong with me? Great guy. Seems like he might like me. I run. Am I just out of practice?"

"Hurry up!" Danny yelled from ahead and she waved at him.

"You like him a lot?" Margo asked.

"Yeah, I do."

"That's what it is, then. The more you like him, the harder it'll be for you to get involved."

"Margo, honey," Nora said. "You're losing your touch. That doesn't make any sense."

"Yes, it does. Think about it. The more you like him, the greater the risk that you could get hurt if it goes bad, so it makes getting involved scarier." She took hold of Nora's arm and made her stop, as if the mere act of walking caused too much distraction. "If he were some guy you didn't like, you wouldn't care if he rejected you, so no real risk of pain there. But caring about Erik means you have to open yourself up to the risk of a broken heart if he decides down the line he doesn't like you."

Nora blinked. "You're saying this is about me actually being afraid of pain that may never even happen?"

Margo nodded. "You're just trying to protect your heart."

"Mom!" both boys yelled in unison. "Keep moving!"

They starting walking again, this time a little faster.

"Letting yourself care about someone else opens up the potential—no matter how remote—that he could leave you, walk out—"

"Die," Nora said quietly.

"Right. And that's where your fear's coming in. What if you care about this guy, and you have to live through the pain you felt with Kevin all over again?"

Nora thought through what Margo was saying. "So if I don't let my heart go out there—if I pull back—I can't get hurt."

They caught up with the boys at the concession stand and Margo reached a hand out to tousle Peter's blond hair. "So, one ride apiece. Does that sound about right, boys?" she asked, teasing.

"Mom!" Peter shouted as Danny groaned loudly.

Nora dug a twenty-dollar bill out of her pocket. "I think I'm going to buy a long period of peace. Let's see, fifty cents a ride… Margo, you want that ice-cream bar now?"

"Drumstick."

Nora handed the money to the concession-stand worker. "How about six tickets for starters? And two drumsticks."

She handed the tickets to the boys and they dashed onto the carousel, weaving their way among the colorful prancing horses, arguing over which was the most perfect stallion, then finally clambering onto their mounts. She and Margo took up a spot along the fence in the shade. They stood in silence for a minute, watching as the carousel began to pick up speed.

"You might be right about this," Nora said. "I don't think I could bear having my heart broken again, no matter how wonderful Erik seems to be. I'm just not sure I can do it again. There's a big part of me that says it's easier not to get involved than to take that risk."

"Then you spend the rest of your life alone. And you've already said you're tired of being lonely."

Nora waved at the boys as the carousel turned past. "Yeah. But what if I get hurt?"

"And what do the nights feel like?"

"I miss Kevin. I want someone."

"I know," Margo said softly. She put an arm around Nora's shoulders and gave her a squeeze. "That's why you have to think about taking the risk with Erik. You can't run forever."

"Some people never fall in love again," Nora said.

"And that's a good thing? I don't think so. It's human nature to want someone to love, to want someone to share with, to want someone to just *have*. Don't bury that part of you. Not when you've actually met someone you have a connection with."

Deep inside Nora knew Margo was right. But when she got scared, like she did last night with Erik, it just seemed easier to be alone. Until she was alone again. And then she hated it.

"Yeah…" Nora said. "But even if I wasn't scared, there's the whole problem of Erik thinking I'm Suzanne. I'm lying to him."

Margo nodded. "If you decide to get involved, you'll have to tell him the truth."

"I can't even conside it until after the garden club speech."

"I thought Suzanne was coming back for that."

"Can't get off the ship," Nora said.

Margo gave her a disbelieving look. "So she wants you to do it?"

"Basically."

"Hey, Mom! Look at this—no feet!" As the carousel rounded past them, Danny stuck his legs out from each side of his horse.

Both women waved.

"Are you going to?" Margo asked.

"If I want Suzanne to keep her client—and I do—I don't think I have a choice. I just have to call Camille and let her know that I'll be there."

"You want me to go with you?" Margo asked.

"What? For moral support?"

"Yeah. I could be your assistant. Hand out business cards." Margo made a little bow.

"You'd do that?"

"That's what friends are for."

Nora opened her arms and gave Margo a hug. "Thanks. I'd love to have a face I trust in the audience."

"It's done, then. Seven o'clock Tuesday night."

NORA PUSHED THROUGH the doors into the meeting room for the garden club and, for about the fiftieth time in a week, wondered how she had gotten herself into this nightmare. This must be payback from all the times she'd dragged Suzanne into messes when they were kids. She hadn't heard from Keegan since Camille's party, so Suzanne's plan of leaving a message on his answering machine must have worked. How long it would continue to work she had no idea—hopefully the rest of eternity.

Suzanne had helped her prepare for the speech—well, as best she could when they kept losing the cell phone connection. Finally she told Nora to get over to the library and page through a bunch of high fashion magazines—*Women's Wear Daily, Vogue, Elle*. "Check out the Collections issues," she said. "That'll give you a good idea of the season's upcoming fashions."

So, last night, after doing multiple Internet searches on personal shoppers, she and Margo had gone to the library. Now Nora could safely say she'd just finished looking at some of the ugliest clothes she'd ever seen. Some styles combined multiple plaids with totally unmatched prints. It was like *The Emperor's New Clothes*. No one wanted to admit that this stuff was hideous.

Well, she would. She'd shout it from the rooftops.

Just not tonight.

Tonight, she wanted to get this thing behind her and, if she was lucky, get out of here in time to catch the tail end of Danny's soccer game. It boggled her mind that she was skipping her son's game to give a speech about fashion. Forget about skipping the soccer game—it boggled her mind that she was giving a speech about fashion. A feeling akin to panic hit her in the chest and she took a breath to calm herself. *She could do this.*

And when she was done, she would never do anything like it again.

She stood in the back with Margo and looked slowly around at the hundred or so women in the room. "There's a lot more people here than I thought there'd be," she whispered.

"Ten or ten thousand," Margo said reassuringly, "doesn't make a difference." She shifted the stack of business cards from one hand to the other, revealing her own nervousness, despite her strong words.

"Easy for you to say. You're not the fashion expert." They'd purposely arrived with only fifteen minutes to spare so as to minimize inter-action time, and especially limit time with Camille Lamont, the one person who could blow this out of the water if she ever got truly observant. Nora spotted Camille across the room and went over to say hello.

As she drew near, Nora suppressed a shudder. The woman was wearing one of those three-plaid outfits she'd just seen in *Vogue*. It was like a train wreck. "Your clothes are exquisite," she said.

"I should hope you think so." Camille patted her on the arm. "You helped me pick it out."

Nora laughed, tinkle tinkle. *Get me the hell out of here.* "Are we almost ready to start?"

"Yes, I was beginning to get a bit nervous. It's not like you to cut the time so close." Camille introduced her to the current club president, who promptly swept her away to the front of the room.

"As we discussed on the phone," the woman said, "you'll talk for twenty minutes, take questions and then we'll socialize for the rest of the meeting... You can just mingle among the group at that time and concentrate on answering individual questions."

Mingle? Individual questions? Her shoulders tightened as her stress level increased. She'd rather concentrate on handing out Suzanne's business cards and encouraging people to call in a week or so.

A few more minutes passed, then Camille

went to the microphone. "This month, we're taking a little detour from making beautiful gardens to making the rest of our lives beautiful. To that end, I asked Suzanne Carlisle to join us. Suzanne is a personal shopper— in fact, she's my personal shopper—and she really knows colors, styles, fashions and how to put things together…."

Nora regarded her own outfit, taken directly from Suzanne's closet. She did look great, even if this push-up bra of Suzanne's felt like it was pushing her right up and out of her white V-necked blouse…and her feet were so badly squashed in Suzanne's shoes her toes were falling asleep. She tried to wiggle her toes to get the blood circulating again.

"I give you Suzanne Carlisle."

Gradually her brain registered that her sister's name had been spoken and everyone was clapping. She smiled as though she had been paying complete attention and stepped to the podium, almost dropping the notes she'd put together late last night.

"Thank you for having me," she said. She spotted Margo hovering at the back of the room near the door and her self-confidence rose. "Tonight I'm going to talk about 'You are what you wear.' Everything you put on, from the top of your head to the tips of your toes is making a fashion statement about you. Clothes talk. So the question is, what are yours saying?"

The women's faces showed their interest. Nora glanced at Margo and was pleased to see she was rubbing her nose, a signal they had set up in advance to let Nora know everything was going well. As long as Margo didn't scratch her head, which meant abandon ship, everything would be all right. Nora began to relax. She slid easily into the rest of her prepared speech and finished up at just about the twenty-minute point. "Are there any questions?" She held her breath, hoping she'd covered anything anyone would ever want to know. Her toes throbbed in her too-small shoes.

For a moment, there was no response, then slowly, toward the back, a tentative hand came up. "What is the most interesting thing you've had to buy for someone?"

Uh-oh. She tried to think of some of the stories Suzanne had told her. Why hadn't she paid better attention when her sister was regaling her with her client tales? "Oh, gosh— I guess maybe the time I had to... Oh, there are so many different situations," she blabbered as she frantically tried to think of *any* story Suzanne would have told her. Something had to come to mind…anything. "I once had to…buy anniversary gifts for a husband and wife to give one another and neither knew the other was using my help. That was pretty interesting." Ohmigod, an out-and-out fabrication—and a stupid one at that. She had better remember to tell Suzanne this story just in case anyone ever asked about it.

The ladies tittered and Nora gave herself a little pat on the back. She just might make it through this thing in one piece after all. "Any other questions?"

A middle-aged woman stood. "What statement is my outfit making about me?"

Nora blinked. *Maybe that you blindly follow fashion without ever bothering to see if it suits you.* "Um, well, it very much shows…that you have an eye for sophistication and a zest for embracing whatever comes your way." *What was she saying?* "It's a…style that says you know who you are and aren't afraid to show it."

The ladies applauded. Another woman waved her hand and stood. "What statement do I make?"

Margo was gently scratching her head. Nora tried not to panic; there was no way she could make up something about every woman's outfit in the room. She looked at the questioner and thought *you wouldn't catch me dead in those clothes.* "Your style is definitely one to…live in." Her brain stopped and she tried to jump-start it. *Something else. Say something else.* "You know, I think you have a knack for finding clothes with a real…casual chicness."

CASUAL CHICNESS? Erik crossed his arms over his chest and leaned against the doorjamb. That phrase sure was popping up a lot lately. He was tempted to raise his hand and ask her to define the term just for fun, but changed his mind. He'd talk to her once she was off center stage.

She'd invaded his thoughts a lot since Saturday, in fact, too much. And that wasn't a good thing because he had work to do, a clinic to plan, a coaching job to chase down… And he kept getting distracted by thoughts of kissing her and touching her and stripping her clothes off—

Not a good train of thought. He dragged his attention back to the podium and admired Suzanne's ability to come up with something flattering to say no matter how ridiculously these women were dressed.

Another hand waved. "I've heard corsets are coming back. What do you think of that?"

"So much for women's liberation," he muttered.

At his words, the cute blond woman a few feet away from him glanced up and began to scratch her head like she had lice. He took a step away from her, and another, then went out into the hall to wait for the program to end.

NORA CHOKED OFF a laugh. *Corsets? What liberated woman would even consider wearing a corset?* "To each their own. I personally won't be wearing one, but there are those who will follow the fashion."

She smiled at the audience. These questions had to stop—*now*. "I think we could break here. I have business cards if anyone would like one. I'll leave a stack up here on the front table— and my assistant has some, as well."

Margo waved a hand in the air, then began to pass out cards.

The women gave Nora a round of applause and she stepped down from the podium, stopping briefly to talk to Camille and the garden club president. "I'm going to run to the ladies' room," she said. "Be right back."

As she passed Margo, she whispered, "Let's go."

Once out of the meeting room she headed straight for the front door, not even looking to see if Margo was following her or not. She wasn't answering any more questions. *She was out of here.* With over a hundred women milling around in there, no one would notice her absence.

Besides, she had to get out of these shoes before her toes required physical therapy. She peeked at her watch. If she hurried, she would be able to catch the last half of Danny's game.

"Hey, wait up!"

Nora turned just as Margo jogged up next to her. "Sorry."

As they walked, Nora pulled her shoes off and wiggled her toes back into their normal shape. Who cared if her pantyhose was torn to shreds by the time she got to the car? No one wore pantyhose anymore—the only reason she had them on was because her legs were so white. "My feet are killing me," she said.

"Erik Morgan's here," Margo said.

Nora's heart skipped a beat. "What? Where?"

"Didn't you see him standing in the doorway near me?"

"No. He wasn't there the whole time, I would have noticed. He's not a garden club member, is he?"

Margo snorted. "Right. He came to see you. Go back inside."

"Please." Nora opened the front passenger door of Suzanne's car. "If the guy wanted to see me, he would call. He wouldn't go to a garden club meeting."

"After all the mixed messages you're sending? I bet he doesn't know what to think. That's why he's here tonight."

Nora hesitated. "I promised Danny I'd be at his game."

"You also said you weren't going to keep running away."

"I said I'd think about it." She gave Margo a hug. "Thanks for coming. Being able to see you in the audience made it so much easier." She climbed into the passenger's seat and shut the door, feeling a twinge of guilt as Margo walked away shaking her head.

Should she go back inside? The thought of seeing Erik again gave her butterflies—good ones. But what would she say? She shook her head. Just stick to the plan for tonight—get out of these clothes and get to Danny's game. Thank goodness she was parked between an SUV and a minivan—it gave her privacy to change into something more comfortable.

The pantyhose were going first; the bra was a close second. How did Suzanne stand these push-up underwires? She'd only worn this one because of her low-cut top. And it wasn't worth the discomfort. Suzanne would probably be one of those women who got a corset now that they were in style. She leaned over the seat to grab her capris and casual shirt from the back, then began to peel off her clothes, all the while debating with herself whether she should stick around and *accidentally* run into Erik.

ERIK FOLLOWED SUZANNE out into the parking lot. She sure hadn't stuck around long to answer questions. The woman with the itchy head had chased her down and the two crossed the lot together, Suzanne flipping off her shoes and walking most of the way to the car in her stocking feet. Yeah, he knew there was more to this woman than met the eye.

He waited a moment for the blonde to leave, then started toward Suzanne's car. Itchy woman passed him going the other way. "Lovely night for romance, isn't it?" she said, grinning.

He ignored her. Off balance, as well as infested it seemed. As he neared Suzanne's car, he saw her feet appear on the dashboard, then disappear again. What the hell? Was she okay? He went over to the car and tapped on the window just as she pulled her bra out of the sleeve of her shirt.

She jerked her head around to look at him through the closed window and her mouth made a shocked little circle. He winced.

Changing clothes.

He knew this. Women changed clothes in cars all the time. They could change clothes without taking other clothes off. They were born with some sort of skill that way. He gave a wave and stepped back from the car. "Great way to make an impression," he muttered to himself. "Surprise her when she's taking off her underwear."

A few minutes later, Suzanne was out of the car, casually dressed, slightly breathless, her dark hair mussed around her face—probably from pulling shirts over her head. *And from taking off her bra.* He thought about her breasts under that T-shirt without a bra and willed his eyes not to look. His mind swerved back to where it had been earlier, stripping her clothes off, and it was all he could do not to pull her into his arms and kiss her.

"You a new member of the garden club?"

He smiled sheepishly. "Sorry about the… interruption."

"Don't worry about it," she said. "Did you need something?"

She seemed a little rushed. That, combined

with the Herculean effort he was making to keep his eyes from straying to her breasts and his mind from undressing her, scrambled his brain. "Ah, ah, yeah. I was just wondering if you'd eaten yet? Do you want to get something? To eat, I mean?"

"I haven't, but—" She made a vague gesture with one hand. "I can't. I'm trying to get to Danny's soccer game before it ends."

He shoved his hands in the back pockets of his khakis. *Say something.* But he couldn't think of anything to say. He really wasn't into rejection and sensed she was about to hand him an even bigger one than she'd given him on Saturday.

And then she said, "Um, maybe another night," and raised her hazel eyes to his. And smiled.

So maybe it wasn't a blow-off after all. He grinned back at her. "Yeah. Okay." As she turned toward the car, his brain finally kicked into gear. "Hey," he said. "How about you and Danny going skiing with me this weekend?"

She looked over her shoulder at him, her expression totally unreadable, and he knew she was thinking about Danny getting hurt. As she opened her mouth, he fully expected her to say no.

"Danny would like it," he said before she got a word out.

She smiled. "I know. Where would we go?"

His heart warmed at the effort he knew she was making to give her son some freedom. "We could run up to Squaw Valley. It's only four hours away…spend the weekend."

She caught her lip between her teeth and he thought about what it had been like to kiss those lips.

"I can't really afford—"

"My treat," he said. "Let me take the two of you."

She took so long to answer, he was stunned when she suddenly grinned and said, "Okay."

He blinked. "Okay." *Okay*. "Great. I'll get all the details and give you a call."

"I'd better get to the game before it ends." She hopped in her car and drove off.

He walked across the parking lot kicking at the loose stones on the blacktop like a carefee kid.

CHAPTER NINE

LATE THURSDAY MORNING, Erik grabbed a cup of coffee in the hospital cafeteria and headed to his favorite corner table to think over the phone conversation he'd just finished with USSA. Things were moving forward nicely; he was flying out next week to talk with them in more detail.

He'd rather have gone out this week, would like to put some closure on the whole thing one way or another, but he had surgeries and other appointments scheduled that couldn't easily be changed on such short notice.

As he crossed the cafeteria, he realized someone was already at *his* table doing paperwork. The woman moved her head and for a moment he was taken aback. *Suzanne*. His heart sped up. But, as quickly as that thought entered his mind, it was replaced by the realization that this was Nora.

He stopped. Here was the sister of the

woman who seemed to be taking over his thoughts. Couldn't hurt to say hello. He strolled over to where Nora was sitting and bent down to ask, "Need some help with a patient's treatment?"

STARTLED, Nora jerked her head up. Erik Morgan stood next to her holding a cup of steaming coffee.

"Mind if I join you?" he asked.

Her thoughts froze and her mouth moved but no words came out. Unbelievable. She'd just spent the better half of an hour mentally debating whether she should really go skiing with the man this weekend.

Margo would say her mental debate was nothing more than her getting ready to run away again. And yet, if she didn't run, it meant she had to continue lying about who she was. Which brought her to the fundamental question—did she want to go out with Erik again?

And now, here he was. Adorable as ever.

"Sure," she finally croaked out.

She couldn't keep going on like this. Before she knew it, Suzanne would be home and the problems would be compounded. If she'd never agreed to switch places, none of this would have happened. Then again, if she'd never agreed to switch places, she would never have gone out with Erik.

Because he thought Nora was boring.

Well, okay, maybe not boring. But certainly not worthy of his attentions. And God only knew what he would do if she told him Suzanne was really Nora and it was all just fun, tinkle tinkle.

He slid into the opposite chair. "Thanks for letting your sister know I couldn't make it shopping last week."

Was this a sign? Did it mean she should tell him the truth? Did it mean she should definitely go skiing with him, start a relationship? Maybe it was a sign that she should leap to her feet, scream, "Fire!" and race out of the building.

"Sure," she managed to say. Ohmigosh, all she could say was *sure?* No wonder Erik thought Nora was dull. "She's used to shopping without the client along, so it didn't faze her." That sounded better.

She looked across at him, met his eyes, started to sink into their blue depths and thought, yeah, I would like to see him again. An inkling of panic ripped through her and she pushed the fear away as hard and fast as she could.

"We're going skiing this weekend," he said.

"She mentioned that. I think she's really looking forward to it."

"She is? That's great." He sipped his coffee. "She was kind of apprehensive about it when I first invited her."

"Sometimes she gets protective because, well, she lost her husband, so she…"

"Worries about losing her son, too. I know. But the hills we'd be on with Danny would be pretty flat."

Silence fell between them, stretched out too long until it felt awkward and she searched for something to say. "We used to ski a lot when we were younger. Haven't gone in a long time, though…"

He leaned toward her and she caught a whiff of his aftershave and was sucked back into the memory of kissing him on the boat Saturday night. She wrenched her thoughts back to the present.

"You should come with us, too," he was saying. "I rented a two-bedroom condo, so there's plenty of room."

She started shaking her head. "Oh. I don't know—" She took a drink of her cold coffee and almost choked. "Actually I already have plans for this weekend." *To go skiing with you.* "But thanks for asking."

"If you change your mind, just tell your sister." He set his elbows on the table and narrowed his eyes. "I'm going to have to see you and Suzanne side by side so I can try to tell the difference between you. Right now, you've really got me stumped."

She laughed. *Great. Why don't you stop over tonight?*

"Hey, before I forget, Suzanne asked me about the sports medicine rehab center the hospital's opening. Said you might be interested in a job."

She sat back in her chair, stunned, a shy smile slipping onto her face. She thought this conversation had gotten lost the other night in all the discussion about Nora being dull. She couldn't believe he even remembered, let alone was following up on it. "Yeah, actually, I would be."

"The director position just got posted Monday. Whoever gets hired, we want them on board right away to help with purchasing and design decisions. You should apply." He smiled and she melted.

"For the directorship?"

"You'd be good at it. A couple of us were already discussing possible candidates and your name came up more than once."

"It did?" Her voice pitched so high it almost

squeaked. Oh, how professional…and self-confident. She took another drink of her ice-cold coffee just to have something to do.

"I don't know how soon interviews will be, but it never hurts to get a jump on it." He grinned at her, then pushed back his chair and stood. "I've got to go—work beckons."

As he walked away, Nora stared at his back—his broad, strong back—and his thoughtfulness touched her. Ever since their date on Saturday, she'd found herself thinking about him a lot. He popped into her mind when she least expected it, could see him smiling at her, hear his laughter, *feel his kiss.*

And then she would remember Kevin. And what they had together. And how easy it had been after knowing him all those years. She knew his face, his touch, how to touch him, what he loved, his hopes, his dreams…his soul. *As he knew her.*

She wanted that easy understanding with someone again, that comfort that came with time spent together. That place she'd already found with Kevin.

Tears filled her eyes. She knew she would never find any of that again unless she went out there and tried, unless she forced herself past the fear of getting hurt, past the fear of feeling loss again.

The thing was, this attraction to Erik, she hadn't even realized it was happening. And now she cared for him more than she knew was safe. She was hiding the truth from him—and her heart was out there. He didn't know who she really was and there was no telling how he would react when he found out he'd been lied to.

She felt the flutter of fear; she might have already set herself up for major heartbreak.

NORA HAD HARDLY PULLED into the driveway after work before the sitter was out the door, quickly explaining about a special band sign-up meeting she had to get to. Nora went into the house and spotted Danny on the living room floor building a colorful Lego tower.

"How's my favorite boy?" She kicked off her shoes in the front hall and sat next to him, reaching over to pull him close and kiss his head.

"Good."

"Anything exciting happen at school today?"

"A guy came to our class." He sorted through the Legos, searching until he found a rectangular blue piece.

"A guy. What kind of guy?"

"A fireman. We talked about stop, drop and roll."

"In case of a fire, huh? That's good." She nodded.

"I'm gonna be a fireman when I grow up." He concentrated on putting more Legos on his foot-tall stack.

Amazing how every kid wanted to be a fireman at some point in their lives. "Oh, well, that'll be exciting."

After watching him a while longer, Nora stood. "Okay, well, I think I'll go put together some dinner for us."

"He was really nice."

Oh, no.

"He said he doesn't have a wife. But he wants one someday."

"He does, huh?"

Danny looked up at her, his face hopeful. "Maybe you could go to the fire station and say *hi.* I told him I would tell you that."

She sat down cross-legged beside him again. "Honey, I would give the world for you to have a dad." *I would give the world to love a man who would be your dad.* "But things like this can't be forced. You just can't go out and find someone to be your dad. One of these days, I'm going to meet someone…." Anger welled up inside her, then quickly dissipated into sadness as tears sprang to her eyes. "Someday I'll meet someone and we'll feel this connection and before you know it, we'll be in love, and getting married and you'll have a dad." She lifted him into her lap and kissed the top of his head.

"Just like that," Danny said.

"Yeah. Just like that."

"Okay."

She drew a long, slow breath. "Ashley's coming over tonight to watch you for a while. You know I'm going to my coffee group."

"Okay." He grinned at her and kept building his Lego tower. "Can we have ice cream later?"

"You bet. I got some cones, too—they're in the cupboard." She pushed herself to her feet and went into the kitchen and stared into the refrigerator without seeing anything.

SHE PULLED OPEN the door to Margo's Bistro and stepped inside, eager to see her Thursday night coffee group. After the week she'd had, she really needed the support of friends. She loved the atmosphere Margo had created in the bistro; she always felt like she was enveloped in warmth when she was here. Glancing at the chalkboard as she walked past, she noticed the listing for Soup of the Day was conspicuously absent of any soup name.

Margo spotted her and came toward the door, coffee mug in hand. "You're early."

"There's no soup listed on the chalkboard."

"We sold out of everything. Something wrong?"

The woman was way too intuitive. "Maybe."

"Want your usual?" Margo asked.

She nodded and Margo turned to the college kid behind the counter. "Edward, can you get a chai latte?"

As soon as the drink was made, Margo linked her arm through Nora's and headed toward the back of the bistro. "Come on, let's go into the annex. We've got a little time before the rest of the gang shows up."

Nora dropped down on a comfy rattan chair and sipped her chai as Margo pulled a pack of matches from her pocket and lit several candles in the room. "Tell me what's going on," Margo said. She sat opposite Nora on the matching sofa. "Erik Morgan?"

"No. Yes." She tried to focus her thoughts. "Sort of. He's just one piece of the puzzle I now call my life. I'm going away skiing with him this weekend—and he thinks I'm my sister. Keegan wants his money back from Suzanne— and she's off on a cruise and won't come back. Danny wants a dad—and I think any man would do. Erik told me—Nora—to apply for the job as director of the new sports medicine rehab center. And—" Her voice dropped. "He does something to me—" she touched her chest above her heart "—here. And, it's scaring me."

"So...what's the problem?"

Despite herself, Nora laughed. "Yeah, I don't know what I'm so worried about."

Margo sat for a minute. She took a long drink of her coffee.

"What?" Nora asked. "I can almost see your mind working in there."

"I'm just thinking about what we talked about on Sunday. About fear...and your heart."

"I've thought about it, too."

"I know you want Suzanne to get it together and move out. And I know you want this new job. And I know Keegan could blow it all if Suzanne doesn't pay back his money." Margo drank some more coffee. "But that's all secondary."

"Secondary? It's turned my life into chaos. If something doesn't give pretty soon, I'm going to have to start taking antacids. Or Valium. Or hemlock. And if that doesn't work, I'm going to need a long vacation—which I can't afford because I'm supporting my sister who can't afford to move out."

Margo nodded knowingly. "Secondary. The

biggest issue I see in your life is that you're falling for Erik."

"Don't you think that other stuff is more import—"

"No. That's just life. Yours may be a bit more complicated than most right now, but...you know, life comes, it goes. These problems, too, shall pass." She took another sip of coffee. "But, Nora, this thing with Erik—" her voice took on a passionate edge "—*it's what living is about.*" She glanced away for a moment. "When my marriage broke up, I was devastated. And when I met Robert, well, everything was all wrong for me to get involved with him. He was obsessed with finding a job, the bistro was struggling, then Peter was diagnosed with diabetes..." She looked at Nora. "That was all *just life.*"

"In other words, deal with it."

"I might not put it quite so bluntly, but, yeah. I'm trying to figure out a way to say this that makes sense. Life is all the junk that happens. But living is...stepping deeper into life, taking risks, allowing yourself to feel, to love, to care beyond the bandages you've wrapped around your heart." She leaned forward, both hands around her coffee mug. "Because, really, how much can you feel on any part of you when you're all wrapped in bandages?"

"But it holds back the pain."

"And it blocks the pleasure, too. You know how when you hurt yourself, the muscles tighten up around the injury to protect it?"

Nora nodded.

"I think that's what happens with broken hearts, too. The muscles tighten up to protect the heart from more pain and the wound never heals. The only way out is to let those muscles relax. Take the bandages off…and open yourself up again."

"But what about Kevin?" Nora whispered. "I really loved him. How many times in one life does someone get that kind of love?"

Margo's eyes filled with understanding. "You're looking at it all wrong. You'll never duplicate the love you had with Kevin. *Because no two people are the same.*" She shook her head. "The love you feel for one can't possibly be the same as the love you feel for another. And that's okay. It doesn't mean one is any better or worse than the other. *They're just different.*" She drew a breath and exhaled. "No one ever said you have to stop loving Kevin. Why would you? He was your husband, the father of your child."

Tears bit at Nora's eyes and she wiped a hand across them. "But if I don't stop loving him, then how—"

"Oh, Nora. I said this once before, you don't need to just move on, you need to let go—of your anger, of your guilt, of your regrets...of Kevin. I'm not saying you have to stop loving him. You just need to accept that it's okay to let go, that he won't be angry or hurt that you fell in love with someone else. You need to accept that, though life with him was wonderful, it was in the past." She teared up then grinned sheepishly. "See, I'm gonna cry now. I'm no expert, but I do know this—letting go doesn't mean you didn't love him, won't always love him. But it's the only way you can give yourself a future that involves loving someone else."

"But what if I risk again and it doesn't work, or the next guy dies, or—"

"There are no guarantees with anything, except this. Life is better well-lived. You can float along, never venturing out much beyond your security zone and you'll never have to worry about being hurt—not much anyway. But you also won't ever feel the great highs that make life so absolutely grand."

"Nothing ventured, nothing gained," Nora said wryly.

"Yeah, I guess I could have skipped all that other stuff and just said those four words." Margo leaned forward again. "From my own experience, all I can say is this… If you are lucky enough to find someone who makes you laugh and brings you joy, and for whom you do the same… Someone with whom you have things in common, with whom you feel contentment when you're together…" She choked up. "God, now I really am crying. Then you should grab it. Because it's a gift. A chance to—"

"Hey, ladies!" Selena swung into the room, danced over to where they were and dropped down onto the sofa next to Margo. She looked from one to the other. "Let's see. Red eyes, sad expressions. You guys are telling jokes in here, right?"

They both laughed.

"We're talking about Kevin," Nora said. "And Erik." She didn't want to go over the whole thing again, needed some time to digest everything Margo had said.

"You know I'm not big on getting into serious relationships." Selena drummed her fingers on the armrest. "But what's right for me isn't necessarily right for you. Oh, and by the way, I already had a ton of coffee today—can you tell? Anyway, I'll give you my piece of unsolicited advice because…well, because I happen to be here right now…and I'm wired."

She gave a delighted chuckle. "Life is short. God isn't up there with a stopwatch saying 'Nora has more grieving to do.' And Kevin isn't flying through heaven saying 'She'd better not be making it with another guy.' They both have plenty of other things keeping them busy."

She pushed her fingers through her curly hair. "I'll tell you this. If you could somehow ask Kevin whether he wanted you to stay alone the rest of your life because of him, I will guarantee—without ever having known the man—that he would say *no*. I promise you, if he was half the man you've said he was, he would want you to fall in love again. *He would want you to be happy*. And he wouldn't want you down here comparing every other guy to him and saying they come up short."

She sat back and took a drink from her espresso cup. "And that's all I have to say on that topic—for at least the next ten seconds."

Margo raised her eyebrows at Nora and they both started to chuckle.

"I just have one comment," Nora said between laughs. "Please tell me that's decaf."

AFTER MAKING SURE the sitter got safely home, Nora took the stairs slowly, weary despite the caffeine she'd had tonight. Her conversation with Margo kept replaying in her mind. She didn't know if she really had it in her to try again—at least not with Erik. What if it didn't work and all she got was more pain?

And what if she didn't try and spent the rest of her life in regret?

She stepped into her room and let her gaze roam. This was the bedroom she once shared with the man she loved. She ran a hand over the blue-and-tan comforter she had picked up on sale years ago and remembered how happy she had been to put it across their bed. Moving slowly, she changed into a comfy pair of gray knit pajamas, then dragged a box down from the top shelf in her closet and set it on the bed. She hadn't gone through this stuff in a long time—too many memories.

She lifted the top off the box and sat there for a minute before reaching inside to pull out an old, worn navy blue polo shirt. It had been Kevin's favorite; he'd refused to get rid of it no matter how beat up it had gotten. He used to joke about how everyone else bought shirts that were enzyme-washed and faded so they looked old, but he had the real thing. She held it to her face, tried to find the smell of him in it, but, after five years, it was gone.

"Oh, Kev, everything would be so much

easier if you hadn't died." Tears filled her eyes. "It'd be you and me sitting on the front stoop watching our children ride their bikes. You and me who would have known each other for all those years already. I wouldn't be out in the world meeting some new guy and kissing him and messing it all up."

She set the shirt on the bed and took out his robe, heavy white terrycloth. She never knew exactly why she'd kept it—he only wore it when her parents came to visit. And then he'd rip it off when they were alone in their room and he would kiss her passionately and threaten to make boisterous love to her with her parents down the hall. They'd laugh like teenagers who were getting away with something. And then they'd make love quietly, their every breath soft and tender.

She'd kept a pair of his jeans just because. Because she loved his legs, big and muscular, and his tight butt and how well he fit those jeans. She used to wrap her arms around him and shove her hands in his back pockets and pull him close. The pain hit and she squeezed her eyes shut, sucked in a breath through clenched teeth and waited for it to ease, as she knew it would.

Then she opened her eyes and took his watch

from the box, a sport watch, the kind with a timer in it and a stopwatch. The battery had long since gone dead. It hadn't been expensive, but it had been his and he'd liked it and she just hadn't been able to give it away.

And there was all that other stuff she saved. The last issue of *Sports Illustrated* that had come when his subscription ran out, the dog-eared paperback dictionary that he kept on his nightstand so he could look up words he didn't know whenever he came across one reading in bed at night, the ticket stubs to the last movie they'd seen together.

She pushed around the little things, then refolded the jeans and the robe and the shirt and shoved them back inside and put the lid back on. Then she went to her jewelry box and took out his wedding ring and held it in the palm of her hand, just felt the weight of it. She slipped her own gold band onto her finger. It felt cool next to her skin…and odd. So many years had gone by since she'd worn this ring. So many years and yet, it didn't really feel like that much time had passed at all.

She sat on the edge of the bed, filled with a sense of melancholy and longing and regret. For things she wished she'd said to Kevin and not said, for things she wished she'd done or not done, for things she wished she could take back. She looked at her hand a long time before finally taking the ring off and putting it away.

What was past, was past. All her wishes in the world wouldn't bring it back. Theirs had been a good marriage. And somewhere deep within her, she knew that Kevin, if he could be here now, would probably have gotten angry and said, *what matters is that we were happy.* She could almost hear what he would say next—*go find that again.*

The ache returned, filled her heart, and she lay her head on the box and let the tears flow. She thought to herself that Margo was probably right. It was time to let go.

"Hey, Kev," she said quietly. "I kind of figured something out tonight. It's not just about getting Suzanne moved out... And it's not just about Danny getting a new dad... And it's not just about me being more challenged in my job." She wiped her nose with the back of her hand. "I *can't live* without loving someone, Kevin. I thought I could, but I can't."

She stopped crying and sat up. "I've gotta say goodbye, Kev, because I can't fathom living the rest of my life like this. I'll always love you.... But I've got to take a shot at loving someone else."

She waited a few minutes, then picked up the box and put it back up on the shelf in her closet. The phone rang and she reached over to the nightstand to pick it up. Her sister greeted her from the other end. "What's been happening? You haven't called me in two days," she said accusingly.

Nora sighed. "I don't know."

"Are you okay?"

"Just missing Kevin."

"Oh, honey—"

"No, it's not so bad. I've come to realize something. I'll always love him. I'll never forget him. But I can love again." Her voice cracked. "It won't be the same—it'll be a different person, a different time. But I don't want it to be the same. That was Kevin. This will be someone else. There's no way it can be the same, but that doesn't mean it can't be just as wonderful."

"Nora—"

She could hear the smile in Suzanne's voice. "Yeah, I know. It's taken me a long time to get here."

"Nora—"

"Mind you, I'm only going to stick my toe in the water and see how it feels."

"Nora!"

"What?"

"I think Erik Morgan might be one lucky guy."

CHAPTER TEN

"I'M TELLING ERIK the truth this weekend. Come hell or high water, he's got to know who I really am," Nora said into the phone to Suzanne. She zipped her black suitcase shut and hoisted it to the floor beside her bed. "My stomach's already in knots and we haven't even begun the trip."

"Let me know when it's a done deal, because I'm going to have to tell Camille," Suzanne said. "And I'm not savoring doing this via cell phone from Alaska."

Nora snorted. "I'm not exactly savoring telling Erik, either."

"Do you have a plan?"

"No. I'm just going to wait for what seems like an opportune moment."

Suzanne laughed. "How about when he calls you Suzanne and Danny tells him he's got your name wrong?"

Nora sat abruptly on the edge of her bed.

"I know. I've worried about that happening ever since Erik came to pick me up for his mother's party."

"If Danny does let the cat out of the bag, it could be a nice segue to baring your soul."

"Yeah, except I don't think it's the best idea to have this unveiling discussion in front of my son. Danny doesn't know I'm pretending to be you. In his eyes I'll just be a liar. Not exactly the best role model."

"I'll keep my fingers crossed for you," Suzanne said.

"Thanks. If Danny outs me before I tell Erik, then I'll just have to deal with it. That's the price of dishonesty, I guess." Nora carried her suitcase downstairs and set it on the living room floor next to Danny's smaller one. The thought of telling Erik the truth was making her crazy inside. Her stomach was almost quaking and she could feel a headache coming on. "Any word from Keegan?" she asked. "I'm starting to feel like something's going to explode when we least expect it."

"No, no. He's fine. He called my cell again, and I called him back. I told him I'm out of town for a client and won't be back for a week—"

"Great, more lies. And what happens in a

week when he wants the cruise paperwork or his money, and all you have are souvenirs from Alaska to give him?" Nora peeked out the window to see if Erik had arrived yet.

"Stop worrying. I know how to handle Keegan. You just go on your ski trip and make sure that, when you're done, you haven't lost the man of your dreams."

EARLY THE NEXT MORNING, all decked out in ski gear, Nora drew in a breath of fresh air and looked up at Squaw Mountain, snow-covered and dotted with skiers. Temperatures were in the mid 50s, the sky a clear, clean blue.

"We really couldn't have picked a better time to teach Danny how to ski," Erik said.

"Yeah," Nora lied. Last night she'd vowed to herself that she wouldn't let on how apprehensive she was about Danny starting to ski so young. She was dumping Nora the apple and bringing back Nora the orange.

Erik handed her a set of ski poles. "Since you haven't skied in fifteen years you might as well follow along as I teach Danny, 'cause skis have changed—and so has technique."

"I'm a beginner again?"

"Close." Erik patted Danny on top of the head. "You ready, bud?"

Danny nodded, his expression open and full of contagious excitement.

"He's a good kid," Erik said to Nora. "You've done well."

His compliment touched her heart.

Erik stomped his skis up and down on the ground and grinned, his own enthusiasm obvious. "Now, you two, here's how you stand on skis. I want you to make French fries with them."

"Hey, Mom, just like Ronald's wife."

Erik caught her eye. "I'm starting to think there was more to this thing with Ronald McDonald than you're letting on."

She laughed. "Oh, yeah. A lot more. I was using him for apple pies and hot fudge sundaes."

He grinned and turned back to Danny. "Okay, line your skis up even with each other—flat on the ground. Like this," he said, demonstrating. "Two crispy French fries in a row. Then flex—that means bend—at your ankles, your knees and your waist."

Danny followed his directions, bending so low his face was almost touching the snow. Nora could see a small smile on Erik's lips. "Not quite that much, kid—just a little," he said, his voice never wavering from its patient tone.

For not having children, he certainly had the ability to relate to them.

Erik checked Danny's stance and hers, then nodded. "Now, hands in front. Like you're holding a tray of—oh, let's see—hamburgers, and look ahead with your eyes."

They imitated his arm position.

Erik pointed a pole at Danny. "The kid's a natural."

"Don't even think about teaching him to race—I don't want him to break his neck." She mentally groaned. That sounded like an over-reaction even to her.

"Ski racing's not until this afternoon's lesson. Right now, we're just going to glide down this little hill. Follow me."

"Wait a minute," Nora said. "Shouldn't he be on a leash or something? I've seen people with those—they seem like a good idea. You ski behind him and hold on to the leash so if he falls, you can stop him from rolling down the hill."

"Leashes pull kids too upright—make 'em off balance. I want him comfortable on his skis, not tipping backward."

"But what if he falls?" Nora asked.

"I'm not gonna fall," Danny said.

"Even if he does, it isn't far to the ground."

"And the snow's soft, Mom."

Erik didn't wait for any more discussion. "Okay, class, follow me." He pushed off and slid down the small incline they'd been standing on.

Becoming an orange again would be a lot easier if Erik would take it more slowly. She tried to hold herself back from saying anything more and failed. "Shouldn't Danny try gliding along flat ground for a while first?"

"Sweetheart, if this part of the hill were any more level, it would be called a flatland. Come on, you two."

She flushed, feeling a little silly.

Danny followed without hesitation, so Nora did, too.

Erik nodded approval. "Won't be long and you'll be ready for the big time."

Nora looked up at the mountain's most difficult runs. *Over her dead body.*

Erik caught her glance and laughed. "Not all the way up there. We're going to the beginner runs."

After they repeated the exercise a few more times, Erik stopped in front of Danny and said, "You ready to go up the mountain a little?"

Danny's head bobbed enthusiastically and Nora could tell that Erik had passed over the line from man to hero.

"This is plenty steep down here for a five-year-old." She cringed at how completely she was failing to hide her concern.

"Mom, this is boring."

"Ditto," Erik said.

"It's my job to make sure you don't break your neck." She hated what she sounded like.

"You're a worrywart and a spoilsport."

"Quit saying that," she said. Those words had become a sort of mantra for him lately—and a regular reminder of how cautious she'd become.

Danny wriggled his body. "I wanna ski."

Erik placed a hand flat on Danny's head. "Your mom just wants to make sure you don't get hurt, Danny. That's what moms do. My mom even still worries about me." He flashed an understanding smile at Nora and warmth washed through her. "We're gonna take everything slow, so she knows it's not dangerous, okay?"

Danny threw his head back in melodramatic exasperation. "I bet your mom doesn't worry about you falling like mine does."

"She's more worried that I'm *not* falling," Erik said.

"Huh?"

"Has to do with love. You'll understand when you're older." He turned to Nora. "As for skiing, we're not gonna do anything even remotely dangerous for him. I want Danny to *like* skiing at the end of the day—not walk away and never do it again. So, let's go try a beginner run."

Fifteen minutes later they had ridden the chairlift and gotten off without any mishaps.

"That wasn't so bad, was it?" he asked.

"If you like heart palpitations," she said, reliving Danny scootching himself to the edge of the chair and jumping off when they reached the disembarking point.

"If you haven't noticed by now, I live for heart palpitations," he said. "That's what makes life exciting."

They glided to the top of a small beginner hill. "What I'm going to do now is make a snow snake down this hill and you two follow me," he said.

Nora held up a hand, stop-sign style. She felt more than a little foolish. "I just have to ask this. What if he loses control and goes too fast?"

"I think I'm with Danny. You're a worrywart and a spoilsport," Erik teased.

Her eyes widened.

"But I still like you," he said. "Let's just take it down this hill and see how he does. It'll be okay. He'll be fine. You'll be fine. *Let go a little.*"

She hesitated, knowing he was being inordinately patient with her. She also knew he was right; kids learned to ski at age five all the time. Danny was growing up—he needed room to take chances. And she needed to let go a little if she was ever going to get past everything she'd been through. She drew a breath. "Okay. Ready when you are."

Erik winked. "Follow the leader." He set off down the hill.

HOURS LATER, Nora tucked Danny into bed in the mountainside condominium Erik had rented for the weekend. She pulled the fluffy down comforter to his shoulders and sat on the edge of the bed. "So you liked skiing, huh?"

He yawned. "It was the best," he said sleepily. "I want to be a ski racer when I grow up."

Oh, brother. She gave him an inch and he wanted a mile. "What happened to being a fireman?"

Danny scrunched up his face. "I guess I could be a ski racer in the winter and a fireman in the summer."

"Sounds about perfect."

His eyes drifted shut and his breathing grew slow and even. She bent to kiss his forehead.

"Mom…"

"Yes?"

"Maybe Erik wants to be a dad." He opened his eyes a little.

She ran a hand through his silky soft hair. "Maybe he does. But, sweetie, that isn't something I'm going to talk to him about. Not unless he brings it up first."

"But, Mom, if he maybe does—"

"What did we talk about just a couple of days ago?"

"I know…*someday.* But how do you know when *someday* is? Maybe if you fell in love with him, *someday* would come."

Her heart wrenched. She'd loved someone once. And here she was talking to that man's son about loving someone else. Fear tried to make an inroad into her mind and she pushed it away. Her choice had been made…she was moving forward.

"Good night, honey. I love you." She kissed him on the cheek.

The door opened. "Hey, buddy," Erik said from the doorway. "You did good today."

Nora turned and her heart nearly stopped. He was leaning in the doorway in jeans, the sleeves of his casual shirt rolled up, a bottle of beer in one hand. He looked incredibly handsome.

She stepped out of the bedroom and closed

the door behind her, sneaking a glance at those forearms. If he only knew the effect they had on her.

"There's more beer in the fridge unless you'd rather have wine?"

"A beer is fine. I'll get it." Anything to get his arms out of the line of her sight. Nora grabbed a Corona from the refrigerator and joined him on the couch.

"Sorry I was so overcautious this afternoon," she said.

"It's okay. You got much better as the day went on. Besides, it's not like you don't have good reason to be that way…." He paused. "Do you miss him a lot?"

"Enough. Sometimes the most unlikely thing will trigger a memory. Buying an anniversary card for a friend a few weeks ago made me melancholy. I wonder if it'll ever completely go away."

"I don't think it does. But why would you want to completely forget someone you loved?" He took another swallow of beer. "I still get reminders of my dad. Still miss him. Yeah, the raw edges smooth over, but love doesn't just stop…."

"Because that person is gone," she finished.

"Yeah. It's more like an acceptance that

they're gone, that things will remind you of them and that's okay."

She wrapped both hands around her beer bottle. "A lot of people don't get that. They want you to just get over it."

"That's because our society doesn't do grief well. We'd rather pretend the sad stuff isn't happening."

Nora relaxed into the couch, touched by his insight, his understanding. A sense of contentment filled her. Maybe Danny was right. Maybe this was a man to love.

He took a drink of beer and wiped his mouth with the back of his hand. The movement—his forearm flexing, his hand in motion across his mouth—made her heart begin to pound. She thought of sliding her hands up those forearms, across those shoulders, around that neck. Of kissing him again, long and deep.

She inhaled slowly, then lifted her beer to her mouth and took a swallow. She shouldn't be thinking these thoughts. Not now, anyway. What she really should be thinking about was telling him she was Nora. Right. Just open her mouth and say *I've got something to tell you.*

She looked at him and he smiled at her, and, somehow, that discussion at this moment felt like an intrusion. She took another look at his forearms again.

There would be time enough for the truth later.

ERIK RUBBED THE BACK of his neck and turned his head to stretch the muscles. "I don't know why I'm sore—it's not like I did a lot of hard skiing today."

"Maybe it's from looking backward watching Danny and me. He had so much fun. Good thing he's exhausted because otherwise I think he'd stay up all night talking about it."

"He's really a good kid. Fearless," Erik said. Just the kind of kid he'd always figured he'd have. One he could take on adventures. Yeah, he liked her kid.

"Fearless is a good thing?" she teased.

"He'll know what it's like to live." He rubbed the back of his neck again. "Maybe I need to take some Advil."

Suzanne looked at him sideways. "I could probably get that stiffness out of your neck in a few minutes."

He mulled over what it would be like to have her hands on him, working his muscles—*all of them*. He shoved the image away. "Nora teach you everything she knows?"

She blinked and opened her mouth to speak, hesitating a moment before saying, "Yeah. She did. Makes me work on her neck and shoulders sometimes when she's had a long day. Go sit in the chair so I can get behind you."

He moved over into the upholstered chair and braced himself for her touch, expecting her fingers to be cold. But nothing prepared him for the jolt of heat that slid through his body when she actually laid her hands on his neck.

She began to knead the muscles, putting pressure at the tight spots, forcing him to relax. The tension in his shoulders eased as another tension began to build inside him and take its place. He closed his eyes and pictured her hands on his chest, his hips, his legs, pictured her holding him, stroking him. He thought of kissing her, of stripping her shirt up over her head and cradling her breasts in his hands, of tracing her curves with his tongue as he unzipped her jeans.

His body tightened. This was the dumbest mind game he had ever played. He tried to think of something else. "So Danny's ready to go tomorrow, huh?" The calmness of his voice belied the tension inside him.

"Hmm," Suzanne said absently. Her fingers worked at his neck and moved down to his shoulders and his brain was stolen again, back to sliding off her jeans and trailing kisses down her belly until he stroked into her with his tongue and made her writhe with need, made her want him as badly as he wanted her. His heart was already pounding, his breath almost coming short, the pressure inside him growing as her hands kept working his neck and shoulders. He wanted her lips where her hands were now, wanted her hands where his thoughts were now and her mouth to follow—

He tried to freeze his thoughts, to think of snow and skiing—something *cold*. He really should know better. Somehow the combination of fresh air and exercise always made him…randy. He glanced back at Suzanne, to see if she had any inclination in the same direction, but she merely smiled serenely down at him.

"Getting better?" she asked.

He gulped. "Not yet," he lied. *Not until I have you beneath me.*

He sat there, every nerve in his body aware of the woman behind him, wanting her, fighting it until finally, action took precedence over thought and he reached back to take her arm.

"What?" she asked.

"Stop." He drew her around so she was

facing him, looking at him with those big hazel eyes. "Or don't stop. One or the other."

She smiled again, as if she knew his every thought, and that was all the invitation he needed. He pulled her down onto his lap and kissed her hard, took her mouth in exactly the way he wanted to devour the rest of her.

NORA TREMBLED at the suddenness of his movement, met his eyes for an intense moment before his lips were on hers again and she opened her mouth to him, tasting him in awe as if this were their first kiss. He cradled her head in his hands and sensation skidded through her like fire and her whole body tightened from the heat of it. She slid her hands over his shoulders and pulled him closer, and he kissed her deeper, his hot mouth drawing her with him into a dark sensual place. Something began to build in her, a need long suppressed that she didn't think she'd be able to push back again—and didn't want to. And then his mouth was on her neck, trailing kisses, his tongue teasing that tender spot at the base of her throat, touching her with fire. She whimpered.

"Sweetheart," he whispered. "Stop me now or I'm not stopping."

She met his eyes again, saw her own need

mirrored there, and shook her head, her decision made. "I don't want you to stop."

He didn't kiss her then, just looked at her and looked at her as he slid his hands under her sweater, trailing heat with his touch, across the soft skin of her lower back and around to her stomach. He caressed her breasts through the silky fabric of her bra, slipping the clasp with one hand. She sucked in a breath, letting her eyes close as she leaned into his strong, warm hands and brushed her mouth over his. He kissed her back like she was everything he'd ever wanted and couldn't get enough of all rolled into one. And it made her want him more.

Then he grasped the hem of her sweater and pulled it up over her head, sliding her bra off at the same time.

"You're making me crazy," he said. He bent to kiss the curve of her breast, his tongue tracing circles until finally he took her in his mouth and sucked hard, sending heat shooting through her.

"Crazy's not the word for it," she said on a gasp.

He kissed her throat, her cheeks, her forehead, her hair, and she knew, without a doubt, that she wanted this man.

She paused a moment at the thought and

knew Erik felt her hesitation because he pulled back to look at her. "You really okay with this?" His lids were heavy on his blue eyes, drunk with passion.

"Yeah, I am." The sense of freedom was incredible, to face her fear and step over it. She grasped the front of Erik's shirt and pulled him toward her, slowly popping open each button and kissing his chest all the way down to his stomach. She heard his breath catch and smiled, knowing it was her having this effect on him. Then she pushed the shirt from his shoulders and he shrugged it off the rest of the way as she ran her hands over the hair on his chest, over those glorious strong forearms and up his biceps. She touched a wide scar on his shoulder.

"What's this?" she whispered.

"Rotator cuff surgery."

"When did it happen?"

"Who the hell cares?" he said and kissed her again hard and long, making her too dizzy to want to ask anything more. Mouth still on hers, he pushed forward in the chair and stood, setting her on her feet. Without breaking the kiss, he walked her into the bedroom and locked the door behind them.

She shivered against the heat of his body and he kissed the curve of her neck, her jaw, her eyes, her mouth. "You're incredible," he said and she laughed because it had been so long since she'd gotten a compliment like that. He unzipped her jeans and slid his hands into the back of her pants to cup her bottom and pull her tight against him.

She thought she might die at the nearness of him. She could feel his heart beating against hers, could feel the strength of his need for her and the tremble of her own need building. He pushed her jeans down, sliding his hands along her legs. She stepped out of them as he pulled his own off.

And then he laid her down on the bed and she stretched against him, reveled in the heat of his skin, the feel of his hard body against hers. He kissed her deeply, thoroughly, and slid a hand between her legs, pressed against her, stroked her, tormented her as the blood pounded in her veins and the pressure built until she broke, arching toward him as the world exploded into waves, one rolling over the next and the next, taking her breath with it.

As she floated there in a pleasured haze, he grabbed a condom from the nightstand and put it on. She reached for him and he rolled her beneath him, pressing into her, loving her then until the weight of him on her, inside her, his mouth possessing hers, drove her up and over the brink again.

Later, he held her in the darkness, their breathing calm, and she drifted, content with the feel of his skin against hers, the soft touch of his breath on her neck. In her heart she felt the stirring of emotion and she refused to acknowledge it. *Too soon,* she warned herself. *Don't care too soon.*

He ran a hand down the curve of her back and across her rear end, pulling her tight to him. "I think we should do that all night."

She snuggled back into him, could feel the heat begin to build between them. "I might be persuaded."

His hand stroked up her thigh, across her belly to cup her breast, while his mouth came down on hers, hot and insistent. She felt that dizzying thrill as the world tilted deliciously and she let herself slide away with it, gave herself up to the moment, shoving aside the inkling of disquiet that she had, once again, postponed telling Erik the truth.

"I've got something to tell you," he said when they woke in the middle of the night, his arms around her from behind, his hips cupping her bottom.

"I've got something to tell you, too," she whispered. *My name is Nora.* "You go first."

"Okay. I'm thinking about taking another job." He nibbled at her ear and she felt a rush of warmth inside her.

"You mean with the new sports medicine rehab center," she said.

"No. I used to ski on the Olympic team—"

"Really?"

"Yeah, a long time ago." He ran his fingers over her hip.

She gave him a playful nudge. "Of course I know you were on the Olympic team. Who doesn't know it?"

"Probably lots of people. It's been over fifteen years—"

"You were on the Wheaties box."

"Okay, so maybe people do know. It still was a long time ago. Anyway, I'm talking to the U.S. Ski Association about coaching the men's A team. It's something I've always wanted to do—just never pursued it at that level. I've been coaching nationally ranked juniors part-time for a few years."

"You'd leave orthopedic surgery?" She struggled to make sense of what he was saying.

"That's the big decision."

She looked at him over her shoulder. "Might be a pay cut," she teased.

"Just a bit. Like three-quarters of a pay cut."

He paused. "My years on the team, though, were some of the best of my life. I miss it. Being part of a team like that."

Nora squirmed out of his arms to roll on her back and look at him. Despite everything he'd accomplished in his life, Erik Morgan was still searching. She'd thought as much that night on the dock when they were talking. She knew it as a fact now. She pressed a hand against his chest above his heart. "Aren't your partners like your team, now?"

He exhaled. "In a sense. But at the end of the day, we go our separate ways. They go home to their families… and I just go home. With the team it'll be different."

"How?"

"Ten months of the year we'll be traveling together—training and competing all over the world. You get close…like a family."

She lay there in the darkness feeling the heat of him next to her and wondered whether there would be any room in his life for her once he had this new job. Erik was lonely. *Just like her.* But he thought the answer was to run away.

And she'd finally realized just this week that running away never worked.

She wanted to wrap her arms around him and tell him that. Wanted to make him see that he didn't need to coach skiing to belong to a team—he just needed to stop running. But that was something he had to learn for himself. "So when do you find out?" she asked.

"I fly out to Utah Tuesday to interview and talk through the details. Nothing's for sure. The job isn't mine yet—I'm just talking to them."

She nodded, her heart bereft. Even with her limited knowledge of the ski world, she knew that Erik, with his incredible background, would get the coaching job. This was a done deal, regardless whether he'd interviewed yet or not. "That's pretty exciting," she said with forced enthusiasm. "So does this mean the Olympics?"

"I'd take them to the next Games."

"You'll be pretty busy for a few years then." A dull ache started beneath her breastbone.

"Yeah. I'll be gone a lot." He ran his thumb over her jaw and a shiver slid through her. "Even though it's not for sure yet, I wanted to be up front about this."

She nodded.

"I haven't even told my partners yet. But I wanted you to know…even if I get the job, I still want to see you." He brushed a kiss on her lips and she kissed him back.

When? The third Tuesday of the second week in July? Why was it that when she finally decided to let go of the past, the man she decided she wanted was leaving her? For a moment she had the sense that she'd done this once already, had lived through this before. She drew a slow breath to still her racing heart. No, this wasn't the same as Kevin dying, it wasn't. This was completely different.

"So what did you want to tell me?" he asked. He played with her hair, ran his hand over her shoulder, pressed his lips to the soft skin of her throat.

She hesitated. Was there a point anymore in telling him who she was? He was going to be gone very soon—for a very long time. And even though, at this moment, he thought he wanted to see her again, she knew how it worked—*out of sight, out of heart.* Soon she would be a nice memory, an interlude between one life and the next. The ache spread across her chest. Once Erik was deep in his ski world again, Suzanne Carlisle would likely never cross his mind again.

In light of that, was it really necessary for him to know she wasn't Suzanne?

No.

Even though she might be interviewing for the job at the new rehab clinic and he would likely be one of the interviewers?

No. He'd probably be gone before the interviews even got scheduled. There was no guarantee she was going to get one anyway.

Her heart shattered. She'd let herself get attached—too much, too soon. No wonder she hadn't dated these past five years—it came with pain.

"So?" he asked.

"Oh, it's nothing as exciting as your news. I just wanted to say how glad I am that you brought Danny and me skiing."

CHAPTER ELEVEN

BY FOUR O'CLOCK Tuesday afternoon, Nora was ready to call it quits. For the week. Ever since they'd gotten home from skiing, time had dragged. No matter how much she tried to ignore her thoughts, she couldn't get the weekend out of her mind, couldn't stop thinking about how Erik had flown out to Utah to talk to USSA, couldn't forget how much her heart was hurting.

She'd called Suzanne late Sunday night to tell her the news and her sister had been stunned speechless, which was a rare thing indeed. Nora smiled as she remembered Suzanne's righteous indignation. Her sister was nothing if not loyal.

When she'd finally been able to form words again, Suzanne had burst out with, "After the weekend you two had together—after you had sex with him—he has the gall to tell you he's taking a job that will keep him busy ten months a year?"

"It's not a sure thing yet," Nora had replied.

"Oh, please. Former champion wants to coach and they'll turn him down?"

Once Suzanne calmed a little, they'd gone on to talk about how Nora decided not to tell him the truth. They both agreed it was the right decision because, with this turn of events, putting the truth out there would just bring another unnecessary complication into both their lives.

Nora put her elbows on her desk, stuck her chin in her hand and forced herself to concentrate on work again. She contemplated opening the patient charts in front of her and procrastinated some more. The phone rang and she snatched it up eagerly—anything was better than finishing her paperwork.

The caller identified herself as being from the hospital's human resources department. Then she said, "You put in an application to work at the new sports medicine rehab center."

Nora's heart gave an excited flip. She hadn't expected anything to happen with the application for weeks.

"I've got good news," the woman was saying. "I'm calling to set up an interview with you."

"Already?" This was way too soon.

"The doctors want to get the director on

board right away to help with planning decisions. The rest of the positions won't be filled
for a few months."

"Oh, that's great." Nora's stomach felt like a
lead weight had dropped into it.

"Are you available to meet Friday?"

Four days? Panic darted through her. Erik
would still be here in four days. Surely he'd be
part of the interviewing process; he and his
partners were integrally involved in the
planning for this clinic. Then again, this being
the first interview, maybe she'd only be meeting
with a human resources person—sort of a preliminary screening to narrow the field.

She quietly blew out the breath she hadn't
even known she was holding. Of course, that's
why they were calling so soon—only the top
couple of candidates would make it through to
an interview with the docs themselves. Those
guys were far too busy to spend time interviewing lots of candidates. She relaxed a little.
"That's fine. Whatever the time, I'll make sure
my schedule is clear."

"How about early afternoon. Say one-
thirty?"

"Perfect." She wrote it in her calendar and
drew swirls around it.

"You'll be meeting with several people at

once," the woman said. "The hospital administrator and the orthopedic surgeons who will be involved with the center."

Shit. So much for preliminary screening interviews. "Ah, which surgeons would that be?" she asked, already knowing the answer.

"Dr. Chapman…Dr. O'Connell…"

And Dr. Morgan, she said to herself as the woman said his name aloud. *The man she'd just slept with a day ago.* The one she was still lying to.

Nora let her head fall forward into her hand.

"Do you have any questions?"

Yes, can you get Dr. Morgan off the committee? "Not at the moment. But if I think of something, I'll give you a call."

As soon as she hung up, Nora dropped her head to her desk. "I knew I should never have agreed to switch places. I knew it. I knew it. I knew all this lying would come back to haunt me," she muttered. "The piper always wants to be paid."

She mentally ran through all the issues. Erik thought she was Suzanne. Erik had made love with her. Erik could determine whether she got her dream job or not.

How did she get herself into this mess? A simple decision to help her sister had snowballed into an out-of-control nightmare. She tried to assess the situation rationally. How angry, really, could Erik get if she told him she had taken Suzanne's place?

Pretty angry. Because the switch hadn't been just a one-time deal. And, not only was Nora lying, but Suzanne was, too. To him. His mother. His sister. And just about everyone else who came along.

She should have gotten out of this before. It might have been okay if she'd just done the "shopping for Erik" thing. But it had gotten so much bigger. She rubbed a hand over her eyes. So now what did she do? Come clean? Or just keep it up?

Erik scrunched down into the hard plastic seat in the Salt Lake City airport waiting area and tried to read the local paper. Boredom had set in an hour ago when his flight was delayed due to mechanical problems. He had just spent the better part of the last two days in meetings with USSA officials about coaching.

The job was his—if he wanted it. And he'd done his best to assure them he was almost certain this was exactly what he wanted—even if, deep inside, he wasn't so sure anymore.

He thought about last weekend with Suzanne

and reached for his cell phone, wanting to just give her a call, hear her voice, talk through this new job with her. She'd probably be able to give him a whole different perspective. Then he stopped himself. It wasn't as if she had any sort of interest in his future—they'd only just met. This was his decision to make…alone.

Before today, he hadn't thought he'd need to move to Utah, had kind of been thinking he could keep San Francisco as his home base so he could still keep his hand in orthopedic surgery even while he was coaching. But during the past days' meetings, USSA officials had strongly encouraged he move. Though it wasn't a requirement, more and more ski team coaches were making Park City, Utah their home.

It was probably unrealistic of him to think he'd be able to fit medicine in with the schedule he'd have as a coach anyway. Problem was, if he moved, would he ever see Suzanne again?

May and June the team would be practicing in California, at Mammoth, because it always had snow late in the season. The resort was only a seven-hour drive from San Francisco— maybe he could get Suzanne to come out once in a while.

Part of August they'd be up at Mt. Hood in Oregon. The rest of that month and all of September they'd be in New Zealand or Chile. Late September and October would be Europe—Austria, Italy. Then back to the U.S. for the World Cup in November, and the rest of the circuit to follow, running through March. After that, they'd have a little time off, attend ten days of meetings in Utah in April and then start it all over again.

He was really looking forward to the competition, the emotion, working with the skiers to help them improve, the feel of winning again, even the dejection of losing. But somehow, the schedule didn't sound as appealing as it had two weeks ago. He shifted into a more comfortable position.

Then there was that waiting in airports thing. There would be a lot of that in the coming years.

He shoved the negative thoughts away and focused on the positives—on working with talented athletes, building a good relationship with them, creating chemistry on the team.

He checked his watch. He'd be getting in really late tonight. Which was fine. He was in no hurry to talk to his partners about the offer—and what it would mean for their partnership if he took the job. What he needed was a little more time to really think this through and make sure he made the right decision.

NORA PULLED THE CLOTHES from the washer and shoved them in the dryer. She'd survived more in the last two weeks than she'd ever thought possible— impersonating a personal shopper, giving a speech to the garden club, making love with Erik… She should be happy she'd pulled it all off.

And she would be. Except she was too depressed about Erik taking the coaching job and leaving. And her having to interview with him as Nora.

A sock fell to the floor and she bent to pick it up, noticing then the trickle of water running from beneath the washer across the floor to the drain. Oh, damn. What now?

She unplugged the machine, got on her hands and knees and tried to peer under it.

Danny rounded the corner and got down on his knees next to her. "Whatcha doing, Mom?"

"The washer's leaking," she said. "I'm trying to see where the water's coming from."

"Oh." He sat back on his heels. "Too bad we don't have a dad."

She lifted her head. "Danny! Men aren't the only ones who can fix washers. Women can fix washers, too. *I* can fix this washing machine."

"You can?" He sounded impressed.

She looked at the machine and the water

running from beneath it. *Yeah, right.* "You bet. Let's go get the fix-it book."

Hand-in-hand they went upstairs. Nora pulled an oversized volume, *How to Fix Anything,* off the shelf and flipped to the pages on washing machines. Hmm, it looked sort of complicated. She read down the list of potential problems and probable solutions. Might as well just take it in steps. First, take the back off the machine and see if you can figure out where the water is coming from. She could do that.

"Come on, Danny. Let's go fix it," she said with more confidence than she felt. She rummaged through the kitchen junk drawer until she found a screwdriver, then marched back downstairs with the fix-it manual in one hand, the screwdriver in the other and Danny right behind her. "The first thing we have to do is take the back off," she said.

"How do we get back there?"

"Actually, the first thing we have to do is move it out." She grabbed two corners of the machine and began to rock it from left to right, pulling forward at the same time to move the washer away from the wall. Then she climbed over the top and dropped down behind it.

"Cool! Can I come back there, too?"

"No. It's dirty and linty back here," she said,

but Danny was already squeezing his little body between the washer and dryer.

He sat on the floor beside her. "This is like a fort."

"Yeah." Nora began to unscrew the back of the washer, shoving each screw into the pocket of her jeans as she removed it.

"Hey, Mom, check out this spider!" Danny practically shouted.

Nora lurched away from him.

"It's eating a bug! Look, Mom!"

She eyed the nature show he was studying and suppressed a shudder. "We'll have to vacuum him up later."

"Miss Joy at daycare says spiders are our friends."

"Let them be someone else's friends," Nora muttered. She pulled the back off the washer and realized she couldn't see much of anything by the light of the single bulb hanging from the ceiling. She drew an irritated breath.

"Danny, honey, run upstairs and get me the yellow flashlight in the kitchen drawer, will you please?"

"I wanna stay in my fort."

"When I'm done with it you can use it to

watch your new friend, Mr. Spider." *Before I vacuum him up, that is.*

"Okay!" Danny raced upstairs.

She waited behind the washer, eyes on the spider. "You stay over there or it's squish time—got it?"

From upstairs came Danny's yell, "Mom, I can't find it."

"In the junk drawer!" she called back. "It's yellow."

After another few minutes passed with no sign of Danny, a wave of impatience enveloped her. Nothing was ever simple anymore. Everything was just one big complication. She was tired of it all—the washer, her sister, Erik, her dead husband, her job, even her son. She let out an angry huff.

Danny squeezed back behind the washer with her and held out a pack of matches.

"Where's the flashlight?" She was ready to scream.

"I couldn't find it."

"It's right in the junk drawer." It took everything she had not to shout at him.

He held out the matches again.

"It's right in that drawer," Nora repeated, as if insisting it was there would make it magically appear in Danny's hand.

He bent to look at his spider, still holding the matches out toward her.

"Matches won't work, honey." She sighed. "I'll get the flashlight."

She took the matches from him, climbed over the washer and marched upstairs. For crying out loud, why was it that no one ever could find what you sent them to find? She knew darn well that she would get upstairs and not only would the yellow flashlight be in the drawer, it would probably be right in front.

She yanked open the drawer and dug around, spotting the flashlight almost immediately. Par for the course. Kevin could never find anything, either. Maybe it was a male thing.

She glanced at the clock; it was already past Danny's bedtime and here they were taking apart a washing machine. Great mother she was. Shaking her head she went back downstairs and climbed behind the washer again.

"It was right there in the drawer," she muttered to her son, who was bent over his spider and poking at it with a Popsicle stick. "Some spiders bite," she warned him.

"We're playing a game."

Whatever. She wasn't in the mood. She flipped on the flashlight and shot the beam into the cavern of the washer. As far as she could tell, water wasn't coming out of anywhere. She looked at the trickle on the floor and tried to follow it back to the machine. She felt the hoses at the top of the washer, thinking they might not be tight enough. Everything was dry.

Frustration sent a feeling of despair through her. If she had to call the repairman he would probably cost a hundred bucks an hour and it wasn't like she was rolling in extra cash. She peered inside the washer again. *No leaking water.* So where was it coming from?

She slumped against the wall. What more? Behind her eyes, tears pricked and she let them come. She was so tired of facing decisions—facing life—alone. *Damn you, Kevin,* she thought as the tears flowed. *Why did you have to die?* Even if he knew nothing about fixing washers, at least they would have had each other to lock arms with, to lean on, to support one another when the world got overwhelming.

She swung a hand out and smacked the side of the machine. Probably too old and too expensive to fix. So now she'd have to buy a new one. *And damn you, too, Erik Morgan,* she thought. *Why did you ever ask me to go to your mother's party?* The tears flowed steadily now and she let her head fall back against the concrete block wall, spider friends be damned. What a case she was, sitting on the floor in the basement behind the washer, sobbing, while her son played with a spider—probably a black widow—next to her.

Danny was right. Where was a man when she needed one? This was a man's job; men fixed washing machines. It was in their genes or something. God, she was tired of doing it alone.

The irony of it was breathtaking. When she'd finally decided to let go, to move forward with a guy, he promptly told her— after having sex, of course—that he was going to be extremely busy for the next four years. But just so she didn't think too poorly of him, he tossed in one of those throwaway lies guys say to make themselves feel better: *I still want to see you.* What was with guys that they had this stupid need to say something about getting together in the future when they didn't have any intention of following through?

She'd never expected Erik to be like that. She thought of last weekend, of making love with him—and of the possibility of never making love with him again. And she crumbled.

Danny spotted her tears and sat back on his haunches. "Why are you crying, Mama? Should we call a man to fix it?"

Nora drew a hand across her eyes. "No, honey, we don't need a man," she said. "I'm crying because I'm so happy. I fixed it myself."

LATE THURSDAY AFTERNOON, Erik shoved open the front door of his mother's home and stepped quietly across the large foyer.

"Hey, Mom, how's the knee?" he called out as he neared her office. He could hear the light tapping of her fingers on the keyboard of her computer. "How's the knee?" he repeated from the doorway.

His mother turned. "Were you talking to me?"

"Is there anyone else in the house whose knees I would be concerned about?" He walked over to her desk.

"Now, Erik—"

"You doing your exercises?"

"Every day." She exited the document on her screen and spun her chair to face him. "And how's my personal shopper doing these days?"

"How should I know?"

His mother laughed. "Erik, I've known you for every one of your thirty-nine years. I know you've been seeing her and I couldn't be happier about it. Why don't you bring her to dinner Sunday night?"

Erik gaped at her. What was it about mothers? Did they have an entire network of spies? And what age did their children have to reach before they were safe from their mother's meddling?

"Oh, all right," she said. "Jack saw you kissing her on the boat. And I write romance, you know. So—"

"Naturally, you created a romantic story to go along with Jack's report."

"Naturally." His mother gave him her "I'm the mother and always right" smile.

"What if I said you were wrong?" Although after the past weekend, he found he had no desire to deny his involvement with Suzanne.

"It's certainly within your right to say that. Go ahead. I'll sit back and decide whether I believe you."

Erik bent to open the small refrigerator in his mother's office and pull out a can of Coke. He held it up. "You want one?"

She shook her head.

He popped the top and took a drink. "Okay, so you're right. I've been seeing her."

"Is it serious?"

He thought of their lovemaking just a few

days ago and desire skimmed through him so strong he physically felt it. Under other circumstances, he might think things were getting serious. But not now, not with a possible job change and move looming ahead.

"No. We have fun together, laugh. But no, it's not serious." He shook his head as if to underscore his words.

"Laughter's important in the long haul."

"Mom," he said patiently. "We have fun. But this isn't the long haul." He dropped down into the plaid overstuffed chair in the corner. "The long haul is why I stopped over today."

"Oh?"

"You know how I told you I wanted to coach the A team? I just got back from Utah, talking to USSA about it."

"You mean you were really serious about that?"

He couldn't believe how taken aback she looked. "Mom, how can you be surprised? I told you I was talking to them."

"I thought it was just another wild idea of yours—like becoming a freestyle skier."

"I actually did that," he said.

"It was still a wild idea." She waved a hand at him. "I'll take one of those sodas now. Seven-Up. Put a little vodka in it."

He rolled his eyes. "Mom—"

"But you have a career. And what about the new rehab center? You've been pushing for that for years."

He grabbed a Seven-Up from the refrigerator and handed it to her. Yeah, that was the rub. To have this coaching opportunity come up at the same time as the clinic—and especially now that the hospital was offering them complete control—made the whole decision all the harder. "It's not the same. Skiing was always my first love."

"Isn't it enough that you coach juniors? And the schedule, Erik. You were gone three-quarters of every year. What kind of a schedule would you have now?"

"The same."

She popped open the Seven-Up as she shook her head. "And what about Suzanne?" Her voice went up a notch. "How can you carry on a relationship when you're gone all the time?"

He'd been trying not to think about Suzanne as he worked his way through this. He didn't think his decision should be influenced by feelings for a woman. "Mom, I wouldn't be able to carry on a relationship with her anyway—I'm probably moving to Utah."

Her eyes widened and her mouth dropped

open. It wasn't often he shocked his mother. Kind of gave him a perverse sense of satisfaction....

"Erik! Out of the blue you come up with this coaching idea and now, suddenly, you're moving to Utah and leaving your girlfriend?"

"It's not out of the blue. And she's not my girlfriend," he said irritably. He hadn't talked to Suzanne since the weekend, had left her a message this morning on her cell phone and, as yet, she hadn't called him back. So, at this moment, he wasn't exactly sure what she was.

"Moving...when you've just met a young woman whose company you enjoy?"

"Life is all about timing," he said. "Unfortunately, she and I seem to have *bad timing*." He pushed aside the vague emptiness that he'd been feeling whenever he thought about never seeing Suzanne again.

"Don't be so cavalier. Finding someone you connect with is not an easy thing in this world." She paused— no doubt for effect. "Especially when you get to be your age."

"Now that you mention it, I do feel decrepit."

"Erik," his mother said in her ultrapatient voice, "it's a rare thing when you find someone you're comfortable with. You would give that up for one last shot at glory—"

"This isn't about *my* getting another shot at glory. It's about helping other athletes get their shots at glory. It's about being part of a team."

His mother shook her head. "There are many different kinds of teams in this world."

Oh, hell, here it came, the lecture. He wondered whether she'd still be lecturing him when he was sixty. He glanced at his watch and started to stand up, ready to make an excuse that he had to be somewhere.

"Don't you dare think of leaving yet," his mother said, her voice stern. "You may be grown up, but I'm still your mother."

He dropped back into the chair and looked at her, waiting.

She gave him a nod. "When you make this decision, you need to fully understand what you're giving up. Not just your job and the income…but a chance for real happiness."

"I hardly know Suzanne." He actually felt like he knew her pretty well, but he wasn't going to admit it here. "This could fizzle out in six months for all I know and then I'd have given up the chance to coach." He pushed himself out of the chair and wandered across the room to look at the row of framed book covers on the wall—all of them romance novels written by his mother. "Life doesn't play out like a romance novel, Mom. At the risk of sounding cliché, life is what you make it."

He could hear her sigh.

"So is love, Erik. *So is love.* If you never let it have the chance to germinate, if you never water it, if you run from it whenever it begins to sprout in your life, then you will never know what it is to be *whole.*"

"You're a romantic." He picked up one of her novels from the side table and flipped through the pages, then pretended to read aloud, "Darling, you mean everything to me—"

"Oh, stop it. I've never written drivel like that," she said with a laugh.

He closed the book and set it down.

"I may be a romantic," she said quietly, "but I also lived through your father's death and thinking I would never love again. I know that love heals, that it creates teams where none existed before. Love can be grand and powerful and fulfilling and humbling. *If you let it in.*" Her expression grew soft. "Love is what you make it, Erik. I would hate for you to grow old, still searching, never having let yourself feel all that, never having realized that all you ever really needed was love."

"Is that a speech from one of your books?"

"You're determined to do this, aren't you?"

He nodded. "I like Suzanne, Mom, but I wouldn't consider giving up an opportunity like this for her. I hardly know her." He shoved his hands in his pockets. "I just came by to let you know about my decision—not discuss my entire future."

His mother pushed herself out of her chair and gave him a hug. "I guess you're old enough to know your own mind. So, I'll just leave you with this. One of the things I've learned writing all these romance novels is that love and commitment are a tug of war between intimacy and identity."

"Mom, I really don't want to know, but what does that mean?"

"It's kind of simple," she said. "In order to achieve intimacy with someone else, you have to give up a part of your identity. It's a hard balance—some people never get it." She slid her arm through his and began to walk with him toward her office door. "Your identity is wrapped up in who you are. Injured skier whose incredible future was cut short by a knee injury, dedicated coach who gives up his personal time to work with junior skiers, brilliant doctor, perpetually single, hard-to-get... If you ever want to have a truly intimate relationship, then you will have to sacrifice something of that identity. The question is, my dear son, do you ever want a truly intimate relationship? And if so, what are you willing to give up for it?"

She let go of his arm. "Lecture ended. I'll plan on the two of you for dinner Sunday unless you let me know otherwise."

CHAPTER TWELVE

"COME ON, DANNY, we're going to be late." Nora grabbed her son by the hand and hurried across the asphalt parking lot toward the grade school. She put a hand up to shade her eyes as the blinding rays of the setting sun shot over the top of the building.

Danny hung back, dragging his feet.

"What's wrong?" She tried to be patient, but it was the night before her interview and her stomach was already nervous. Besides that, Erik had left two phone messages for her that she hadn't returned.

She just couldn't bring herself to talk to him with all that had passed between them last weekend and then the interview ahead. Her stress level was through the roof. She'd never told him the truth because she thought he'd be out of the picture. And now she had to interview with him, knowing she was still lying to him, knowing that every time he saw her as Nora made it a little more likely he might realize the truth.

"What's wrong?" she repeated, kneeling beside her son.

He shrugged.

"Sweetie, it's Family Fun night. Come on, we're going to have *fun*. All your friends are probably in there already."

He shrugged again.

"Cookies, punch, games...*come on*."

"Who's gonna be my free throw partner?"

Nora's heart stopped. *Not this dad thing again.* "I will. You and me—we're partners." She gave him a hug.

"You're a girl."

"Girls play basketball, too, you know." *Stay calm...patient.*

"Couldn't Erik come with us?" He kicked at the asphalt.

Why did it seem like everywhere she turned lately it was Erik, Erik, Erik. She held in the urge to scream. "No, Erik couldn't come with us. He's just a friend. And Danny— Look at me." She waited until her son raised his head. "Erik is going to be really busy soon, gone away for a long time...traveling."

Danny's expression clouded. "He said we

would go skiing again. He needs to watch me ride my bike."

She shook her head. "He may do all that before he leaves. But, Danny, he *can't* be your new dad."

"Why not?"

Because he thinks I'm Suzanne and I'm never going to tell him otherwise. Because he won't have time in his life to fall in love. "He just can't."

"It seemed like you felt a conniption."

"Conniption?"

His earnest expression brought a pain to her heart. "You said someday you would meet someone and feel a conniption."

She started to laugh. "Connection. I would feel a connection."

"Didn't you feel it?"

She sobered. "Yeah, I felt it. But sometimes it isn't enough. Sometimes people have reasons for staying apart—like moving." And like protecting themselves from getting hurt and like searching for something to make them feel as if they're part of a team and not realizing they've already found it.

"Couldn't you just ask him to stay?"

"I don't know him that well, sweetie." She brushed a hand over his head. "Besides, it's his decision to make."

"But— Couldn't you just tell him about your conniption? And see what he says?"

"Oh, Danny—"

"Pleease, Mom."

Tell Erik how she felt about him? No. That would also mean she'd have to tell him she'd been deceiving him. And her interview was tomorrow. Suddenly she wished she was five years old again and life was simple. "I'll think about it," she lied.

"I bet he felt a conniption, too."

She nodded. "He'd probably have an even bigger conniption once he heard what I have to say."

"Really?" Danny's eyes lit up.

"Oh, I have no doubt." For a moment, she wished she didn't have to miss her coffee group tonight, because she sure needed her friends. She grabbed Danny by the hand and started for the school building. She didn't want to think about Erik anymore—all it brought her was pain. "Come on. If we don't hurry we'll miss all of Fun Night out here in the parking lot."

MID-AFTERNOON THE NEXT DAY, Nora stepped out of the hospital conference room where she'd just had her interview, and held herself back from dancing down the hall. She'd just faced

Erik, his partners and the hospital administrator and it had gone really well. She'd been herself, just Nora. And as far as she was concerned, she would never be Suzanne again. Her sister was due back in two days and the charade was over.

Life would be back to normal in no time.

She'd thought seeing Erik would be painful, but it hadn't been as bad as she expected. He related to her differently as Nora, more businesslike, so he felt like a different person to her. She had almost been able to compartmentalize their relationship—shove it into a little box in her mind and close the lid.

Almost. But not entirely.

When she least expected it, and her guard was down, she would remember the time they'd spent together and pain would arc through her like an electrical shock before she pushed the memory away.

She brought her thoughts back to the present. Now that the meeting was past, she could feel her tension seeping away, the nervous energy that had been part of her the past couple of days evaporating. She stopped at a drinking fountain near the bank of elevators and drank thirstily. All that talking had left her parched.

Not that she was complaining. She grinned and punched the elevator button.

The interview had begun with the usual, expected questions—where did you go to school, do you have any specialized training, here's the kind of injuries we're expecting to see and do you have any experience handling similar cases?

They'd really liked the fact that she had experience working with athletes. She'd seen the approval on their faces when she described her internships and the job she'd held in college, working with injured athletes at the university's athletic training facility.

That was when the meeting seemed to kick into high gear. Their questions had quickly evolved into a planning discussion about equipment, organization, logistics, patients and virtually everything else anyone would want to nail down before opening a clinic.

By the end of the interview, they'd almost guaranteed her the job. Erik had given her a look as if to say *it's yours* and she'd shaken hands all around and headed out of the meeting walking on air.

The elevator doors opened with a ding and she stepped inside the empty car. As soon as the doors closed, she did a little dance all the way to the next floor, her reflection in the shiny metal walls dancing with her.

The only downside had been continuing to lie to Erik. Her conscience weighed on her. Guilt. It was nice to see all those years of Catholic school were having an impact on her life. She thought about telling him the truth now and decided it was too late to clear the air. He would be gone within the month, off with his *team* on their grand adventure. And she would be here with the pain of being left behind—a pain that could only be worse if she told him what she and Suzanne had done. No way was she going to do that to herself.

Two hours later she was sitting at her desk, daydreaming about getting the job, when her phone rang and she absently picked it up, expecting it to be a typical call from one of her patients.

Instead, it was the hospital administrator.

She wrenched herself back to reality and tried to sound coherent. "Oh, yes, hi," she said.

"I know this is quick, but we talked everything through right after you left and the group is unanimous. We want you to run the center," he said.

A grin burst across her face and she laughed, tinkle tinkle. *Ohmigod, she was a Nora/Suzanne cross now.* "Oh, thank you. That's great—I'm really excited about it." She thrust a triumphant fist in the air.

"I can't give you any details yet as far as the

start date," he said. "But the docs want to make sure you're involved in the whole process—from equipment purchases to space design. So, next week, we'll get together and work out a different schedule for you so you have the time to get going on this."

As soon as they hung up, Nora called Suzanne's cell. "Hey—I got the job!" she practically shouted when her sister answered.

Suzanne screeched. "I knew it! I was praying to St. Jude for you all morning—well, okay, twice."

Nora leaned back in her chair, still smiling. "That guy really delivers—I'm gonna owe him big-time."

"Just don't forget to thank him in public or he won't come through again."

"What?" Nora doodled on a notepad, writing her name and then Sports Medicine Rehab Center Director several times beneath it.

"You have to publicly thank him," Suzanne said as though Nora were a small child. "Haven't you ever seen those little want ads in the newspaper that say something like, Thanks to St. Jude for prayers answered?"

"No. Why would I see those?"

"Don't you read the want ads?" Suzanne sounded incredulous.

"Do you?"

"Well, sure, there's always something interesting. You never know what you'll see—stuff like, Mary Lou, come home or I'm throwing all your possessions on the front lawn. For sale—wedding dress, never worn, fourth owner. And then there are all those Thanks to St. Jude ads."

Nora put her hand to her forehead. "I had no idea. I probably need to take out a full page."

Static crackled through their call. "I think we may lose this connection," Suzanne said. "So congratulations again—we'll celebrate when I get back." She laughed. "I'll get the champagne. Hey, good thing you never told Erik the truth."

"Yeah. Good thing." Nora hung up the phone. She stared at her notepad. Yeah. Good thing.

"YOU'RE THINKING about quitting?" Tim asked, gape-mouthed. "We just hired the director for the clinic."

The three partners were sitting at the small conference table in the corner of Erik's office. Erik wrapped his hands around his ceramic coffee mug and waited for Andy's reaction.

"The hell you're quitting!" Andy didn't even try to disguise his irritation. "What is this? A mid-life crisis?"

"Give me a break." Erik leaned back in his chair. "I've wanted to coach for years."

"Right. That's why you're coaching juniors," Andy said.

"This is the *A* team—"

"You've also wanted to open a sports medicine rehab center for years. You fought for this thing—and now you're going to give it up?" Tim said quietly.

Erik shook his head. He had hoped his partners would understand, but it was becoming clear they didn't get it at all. "I didn't ask for both things to happen at the same time."

"But they did. Don't go back to adolescent decision-making—choosing what sounds the most exciting at the moment," Andy said.

"I'm not," Erik snapped. "I've given this a lot of thought."

"Not enough apparently or you wouldn't have come to this conclusion. It's a big mistake." Andy sounded disgusted.

Erik tamped down his anger. Between his mother and his partners, he felt besieged. He'd expected Tim and Andy to be upset; he just hadn't expected them to fight back with such ferocity. "You were never on the team so you don't understand."

Andy shook his head. "Nope, I understand all

too well. What you're doing is that impulsive, fly-down-a-mountainside-get-an-immediate-rush thing. *And you know it.* Except this mountainside is your life. And you're about to throw it away."

"I'm with Andy," Tim said. "Five years ago, the three of us formed a partnership—we're a team. You don't get to quit now just because someone else wants you."

"This isn't kickball," Andy said. "And we're not the scrubs." He stood. "You're already on the *A* team, Erik. And you're a blind fool if you can't see that." He headed out the door, then wheeled around in the hall and stepped back into the room to shoot off another volley. "And what about that woman—Suzanne? You're just going to blow off the first woman you've met in years that you actually like?" He shook his head and went into his own office.

Tim stood. "Give it some more thought before you make up your mind, Erik. We'll accept whatever you want to do. We'll even get by without you—we just don't want to. Just make sure it's really what you want."

An hour later, Erik still sat at his desk, staring through his open doorway to the ski painting hanging straight ahead in the hall—and not really seeing it. He was mentally hashing over everything he'd been thinking about lately—coaching, moving, the pros, the cons, what his partners had said, what his mother had said... Suzanne.

Tim had already left for the day, had stuck his head in and told Erik to call him this weekend if he wanted to talk about it. Andy, though, was still in his office. Probably brooding. Probably debating whether to come in and broach the subject again. Andy hated to lose—especially when he was convinced he was right. He and Erik had become friends during their residency and had gone into business together afterward, their goals the same. Andy had great business sense and tremendous drive—he knew how to make things happen and he was almost never wrong.

But was he right about Erik? Was this just an impulsive get-an-immediate-rush kind of decision?

He didn't think so. He was truly excited about working with the skiers—coaching, traveling, spending the upcoming years all over the world... He was really looking forward to the sense of belonging that came with being part of the team, a feeling he hadn't had since—

—*he was with Suzanne.*

He shook his head. No. This wasn't about Suzanne. He wanted to coach the *A* team. He wanted this as much as he'd wanted anything—including getting the rehab center going.

He flashed back to his trip to Park City, when he'd met with USSA officials. It had been great on all fronts...until he'd gotten stuck in the Salt Lake City airport, waiting for his delayed flight.

There would probably be plenty of delayed flights to come. For all the benefits, there were downsides, too. Being away from home nine months of the year, a massive pay cut, days that began at 5:30 in the morning and didn't end until he fell into bed, setting training courses and inspecting courses when the sun came up, videotaping from the hill and analyzing technique at night, tight quarters, driving, hauling, checking ski waxes, airport food...

What the hell was he thinking?

Nothing. He wanted this job. He liked doing that kind of shit. But considering that most of the time he'd be somewhere else in the world, it sure didn't seem crucial that he move to Utah. His home base could be anywhere...like here.

Besides, if he kept his home in San Francisco he could still see Suzanne. Once in a while, anyway. Especially when they were practicing at Mammoth in May and June.

And then his mother's words rolled into his thoughts. *The question is, do you ever want a truly intimate relationship? And if so, what part of your identity are you willing to give up for it?*

Nothing, apparently.

The reality stunned him. He was willing to give up everything—his career, the new clinic, a relationship with an incredible woman—just to coach, to be part of the ski team again. And yet, if he was honest with himself, what he wanted most, right now, was to call Suzanne and ask what she thought about it.

And if he did, and she asked him not to go, what would he do?

The answer came upon him before he'd even fully formed the question, the strength of it so overwhelming, he knew without a doubt it was true. He would stay.

He thought of his mother's question again. What was he willing to give up of his identity to have an intimate relationship with Suzanne?

Whatever she wanted.

He pushed back his chair and stood, knowing then that he was going to turn down the coaching job—and that he wanted to. His heart felt lighter than it had in a week. Stepping out of his office, he stuck his head through Andy's open doorway. "I'm not saying you're right, but you do make some good points." He grinned. "Want to go walk though our new clinic? I've got a couple of ideas."

Andy threw back his head and laughed. "I knew you'd figure out the right answer eventually."

NORA WANDERED THROUGH the gutted space that would soon be remodeled into the new sports medicine rehab center. Her happiness over getting the job had quickly been tempered by uneasiness. She thought of what it had been like to look into Erik's eyes during the interview and know she had made love with him less than a week ago. She thought of the very real probability that she might never be with him again. *And her heart broke with the knowledge that he didn't even know it was her.*

Once her workday had ended, she'd come to the clinic space, needing to feel the energy here, to try to figure out what it was she really wanted, *to come to grips with what was right and what was just easy.*

There were so many complications. Erik did deserve to know the truth. But if she told him, she might lose the job she'd just been offered. Not to mention Camille Lamont would find out and Suzanne would probably lose the account.

And yet, did that make it right?

PAMELA FORD 269

She didn't even have to ask the question to know the answer. She thought of Erik again, how he'd been honest enough to tell her he was looking at a new job that would take all his time. He'd told her the truth…and she'd kept on lying.

She wasn't like this—she was honest, trustworthy. She remembered a quote she'd once heard that had struck a chord with her: *Veracity is the heart of morality.* She pressed her lips together. From that standpoint alone, even if she never saw him again, she wanted him to know she had the integrity to tell him the truth.

And there was more. Selfishly, she wanted him to know that the person he had connected with was Nora, not Suzanne. She wanted him to know that the woman he'd made love to was Nora. She wanted him to know that Danny was Nora's son. And she wanted the chance, however slim, to see what there might be between them.

She walked to the window and stared out at the parking lot. Margo's words about the difference between life and living made so much sense to her now. No matter how great this job would be—and it would be wonderful—it was just another part of life. Living came when we allowed ourselves to care about others enough that we actually let them into our lives—and hearts. She knew then, without the shadow of a doubt, that the night she'd made love with Erik she'd stepped back into living.

St. Jude might have gotten her this far. The rest of the way she had to go herself. She couldn't carry on with this pretense any longer. Erik deserved to know the truth.

She wanted him to know the truth.

Her eyes filled with tears. And the sooner she told him, the better.

ERIK SPOTTED NORA across the empty office space, staring out a window. "Hey, look," he said in a lighthearted voice. "Our new director can't stay away, either."

She started, and turned to smile at them.

"Welcome aboard," he said as they came up next to her. "Sorry if we just scared you."

"Oh, thanks. Yeah, I was a million miles away."

He saw the tears in her eyes. "You okay?"

She nodded. "I—" She glanced at Andy and stopped. A tear slipped over her lower lashes and she quickly dashed it away.

Unsure what to say, he hesitated a moment. "Is this about the job?"

She shook her head. She looked so much like

her sister, he almost felt as if it was Suzanne who was hurting. Seeing Nora made him all the more confident in his decision. He wanted Suzanne in his life.

Problem was, he just didn't know what she wanted—she wasn't returning his calls.

"It's nothing really...." Nora said.

"We're here to help," Andy said. "Former Boy Scouts, both of us."

She shifted her gaze between them as though debating whether to reveal a great secret. "I have to tell you something...." Then she drew a breath and paused. "I am—" Her eyes darted toward Andy again. "I am—" She stopped as though searching for the right words. And then she sighed. "Upset about my washing machine. It's not working right."

"Your washer?" Erik looked at Andy.

"Water is leaking out of it."

"Have you called a repairman?" Andy asked in the nicest possible voice.

"No." She almost seemed to wince. "They can be so expensive." Her tears were gone.

A series of thoughts started to merge into an idea in Erik's mind—that Suzanne wasn't returning his calls, that the sisters needed a repairman, that said repairman would be in direct contact with Suzanne...

"I know how silly this sounds," Nora was saying. "I took the back off it yesterday thinking I'd be able to see where the water was coming from…but I couldn't find it. I have a book on repairing appliances—"

Andy shook his head. "I think you're going to need a repairman—"

"I could take a look at it," Erik said quickly.

"What do you know about fixing washers?" Andy asked.

Not much, but he knew how to use Google. "Oh, you'd be surprised."

"I bet," Andy muttered.

Nora looked stunned. "Oh, no. Not necessary. Really."

"You don't want to be stuck paying some exorbitant repair bill," Erik said.

Andy was staring at him, slack-jawed. So was Nora.

"Will you and Suzanne be around tomorrow?" Erik asked.

Odd…she seemed almost horrified. "Um, you mean Saturday?"

"That would be tomorrow," Andy said.

"I—ah—I— Well, it's Memorial Day weekend."

"Do you have plans?" Erik pressed.

She shook her head.

"Tell you what. I'll swing by in the morning and see if I can figure out what's wrong," he said. *And have a face-to-face with your sister.* He couldn't wait to tell her he wasn't going to coach the A team after all.

"No, really. You don't have to," Nora said.

"No problem. I'm happy to do it." He let his insistence show in his voice.

"Oh, let him," Andy said. "When he gets on a path, it can be a bear to change his mind. And after today, I don't have the strength to help you out here, Nora."

said so. I'll show you in the closet." The sound of voices faded as the two, still whisper-

ing, went inside. Jake moved uneasily and he knocked over a...

CHAPTER THIRTEEN

LATE THE NEXT MORNING, Nora was tidying up the kitchen when she heard the front door open and a familiar voice yell, "I'm home!"

She jerked her head up and a chill ran through her. Suzanne was back? *Now?* Erik would be here any minute.

She dropped her dishcloth into the sink and hurried toward the living room in disbelief. "What are you doing here? I thought your flight didn't get in until tonight."

"Nora!" Suzanne set her suitcases on the floor and threw her arms around her sister. "A fine hello to you, too! Yes, I know it's hard to believe, but I did take everything you said seriously— And I tried to call but I couldn't get a cell connection."

"Listen, Suzanne, this isn't a good time to chitchat. Get your suitcases and—"

Suzanne plopped down into the blue corduroy chair and put her feet up on the ottoman. "I'm exhausted. Once the cruise ended, I changed my flight. Took the red-eye so I could get home as soon as possible." She let her head fall back against the chair cushion. "I was practically up all night."

"No, I mean it. Grab your bags and get this stuff upstairs," Nora said.

"Cool it, sister. I just need a few minutes. Keegan's coming over today and I—"

"What? Keegan's coming over? Why would you do that? We don't have a few minutes!" She picked up one of Suzanne's suitcases. Waves of heat rolled over her. "Come on, we need to get your stuff off the first floor. Why is Keegan coming over? Suzanne?"

Her sister didn't move. "What's the rush? Why are you so nuts this morning?"

"The washer's leaking."

Suzanne looked at her like she was insane. "You think the water's going to rise from the basement up to here?"

Despite her panic, Nora laughed. She started to lug the suitcase up the stairs. "What do you have in here? Ice chunks?" Just as she reached Suzanne's room, the doorbell rang. *Oh, God, he was here.* "Don't answer it," she shouted from upstairs. "Don't answer—" she raced down the stairs and shoved Suzanne's other suitcase behind a chair at the same moment Suzanne opened the front door "—it!" She skidded to a stop right behind her sister.

Erik smiled broadly at Suzanne and said, "Hi, Suzanne."

She turned toward Nora, her brows scrunched together in the center as if to ask a question. Nora gave what she hoped was an imperceptible nod.

Suzanne turned stiffly back toward Erik. "Nora. I'm—Nora." She let out a light laugh—a tinkle tinkle failure as far as Nora was concerned.

"Right. I'm Suzanne." Nora leaned around her sister to give a little wave. "Come on in."

"Sorry about that," Erik said. "You two really look a lot alike."

They both laughed—chortled, choked, whatever. Just not light and easy that was for sure.

For a moment, all three stood in the living room just looking at one another. Nora tried to figure out how to tell Suzanne why Erik was here. But she couldn't come right out and say it because if Suzanne was Nora, then she should know why he was here because she was the one who told him about the washer yesterday. Or at least that's what he thought.

Her brain hurt.

She knew she should just tell him the truth.

She planned to tell him today. But not now and not like this—not with them standing here in the midst of chaos lying right to his face.

She restrained the urge to press her fingers into the pain that was throbbing in her temple. Finally, she gave up on subtlety and said, "I'm so glad Nora told you about the washer yesterday because we've been at wit's end not being able to figure out what's wrong with it. Thanks for coming over." *Sounded a little fake, but oh, well.*

Suzanne's head bobbed up and down. "Right."

Nora wanted to wring her sister's neck. *Right?* That's all she could add to the conversation, when she had to have figured out by now that she was responsible for him coming over? Well…sort of responsible anyway.

"What exactly is it doing again?" Erik asked Suzanne.

Suzanne looked at Nora and Nora tried to send her a telepathic message. *I told you it was leaking,* she shouted in her head. Suzanne smiled as though the message had gotten through and Nora felt a rush of relief.

"Oh, you know, the clothes don't get so clean—"

Nora shook her head slightly.

Suzanne cleared her throat. "What I mean is, the clothes don't get so clean because—"

"Water's leaking out of it," Nora said flatly.

"Oh, yeah, right," Suzanne said. "So there's probably not enough water in the machine to get the clothes clean. Or properly rinsed…or something."

Nora closed her eyes and willed her sister to disappear. She counted to three and reopened her eyes. *Well, that didn't work.*

The whole thing was just so unbelievable. All the time she'd spent insisting Suzanne come home early… and then, once she did, disaster broke out. Truly a case of *be careful what you wish for.* She gestured toward the kitchen. "Would you like something to drink? A Coke? Water?"

"Water's great. Thanks," he said.

"I'll have a Coke. I'm really beat," Suzanne said.

Nora glared at her, then went into the kitchen where she closed her eyes, leaned her head against the refrigerator door and begged St. Jude to help her survive this latest fiasco. She was now beginning to understand Erik's point about celebrating the mere act of survival— even at the smallest level.

Pulling a Coke and a couple of bottles of water from the fridge, she returned to the living room, and handed them out. Suzanne headed for the stairs, Coke in hand. "Nice meeting—seeing—you again, Erik," she said.

"Follow me. The washer's in the basement." Nora couldn't wait to get him hidden away downstairs.

Before they had taken more than a couple of steps in that direction, the front door flew open and smashed against the opposite wall. Danny raced into the living room, yelling, "Hey, Mom!"

"What?" Both women answered in unison. Nora cringed and hoped Erik didn't notice.

"Can I go over to Zach's house?"

Please. Oh, yes, please go. Stay there all day if you'd like. "Sure, honey, go ahead."

She could see Suzanne eyeing her from the stairway, her expression asking, *If I'm Nora, how come you're acting like Danny is your son?*

She gave her head a little shake, hoping Suzanne was smart enough to translate it to mean, *just roll with it and don't ask any questions.*

Danny looked up at Erik. "I can ride my two-wheeler by myself now. Want to see?"

"Okay with you?" Erik asked Nora.

"Absolutely."

As soon as he was out the door, Suzanne ran back down the stairs. "Why didn't you tell me he was coming over?"

"Why is Keegan coming over?" Nora asked.

They stared at each other a moment. Finally Nora said, "I was going to tell you about Erik, but I was so stressed about you being here all I could think of was hauling your luggage upstairs and getting you out of sight."

"Is this a date? Why's he fixing the washer?"

Nora threw her hands in the air in frustration. "No, it's not a date. He's fixing the washer because he volunteered to fix it."

"An orthopedic surgeon is fixing our washer?"

"He insisted," Nora said, frazzled. "Just remember, you're going to have to be me for a while until I tell him who I really am. Which, by the way, is happening today, one way or another." She peeked through the mini-blind in the front window to make sure Danny was still showing off his bike-riding skills for Erik.

"Today?"

"Yeah. So get ready to call his mother."

"I can hardly think straight—I've been up all night," Suzanne said frantically. "Don't tell him right this minute. I need some time to figure out how to break it to Camille so I don't automatically lose the account. So that everything we've done up to now isn't for naught."

Much as Nora hated to admit it, Suzanne had

a point. "Fine, you've got until he's done with the washer."

"That could be five minutes!"

"So think fast. Until then, you're me."

"My, my, my. This is like old times." Suzanne grinned wickedly. "Thing is, I can't. You made me promise I would never be you again."

"Suzanne."

"Okay, okay. I'm a little confused, though. Whose kid is Danny—Suzanne's or Nora's?"

"Suzanne's. I forgot I was you and ended up giving him my background instead of yours." She gave Suzanne a nudge. "Come on—get upstairs so Erik doesn't come back in and overhear everything."

Suzanne hurried up the stairs and into her room, Nora right behind her. "So we keep our own backgrounds—all we have is each other's names," Suzanne said.

"Right. Oh, except jobs." Nora winced at how confused this had gotten. "I'm Suzanne. I have Suzanne's job. But I have Nora's background and Nora's kid."

"Got it," Suzanne said.

"Oh. Except for Keegan. Keegan used to be engaged to Nora now."

Suzanne groaned. "You mixed everything up? What happens when Keegan gets here?"

"Why's he coming here anyway? The last I remember, you said 'don't worry about Keegan, by the time this is done, he'll be putty in my hands.' So, where's the putty?" Nora thought her nerves might burn out from the stress.

"Don't worry, I'm handling it. He's been leaving messages on my cell almost every day.... Got kind of demanding—"

"The jerk. Imagine wanting his money back."

"Yeah, well, now he wants the engagement ring back, too," Suzanne said.

"I thought you gave it back to him already."

"The ring represented a promise—one that he broke. So since he never asked for it, I wasn't going to offer it up," Suzanne said with a sniff.

Nora pulled the window curtain aside and looked out to check on Erik. "He's coming back in. *Stay up here.* And hurry up and figure out how to tell Camille so I can get this over with." She shook her head and went back downstairs, her stomach churning with nervous energy.

As long as Danny stayed at the neighbors and Suzanne stayed out of sight, everything would be fine. She took Erik to the basement and showed him the washer. Then she chugged down her bottle of water, made an excuse about needing another and raced all the way up to the second floor, bursting breathlessly into

Suzanne's room. "If Keegan wants the ring back, it must be worth something," she said.

Suzanne was stretched out on her back on the bed. She opened her eyes. "He won it in a poker game. Somehow, I don't think it's going to be worth much."

"He won it in a poker game?"

"Yeah. I didn't find that out until just before we broke up. And he only let it slide because he was drunk."

Nora snorted. "So much for the romance of choosing a ring for your beloved."

"Right. So, considering the effort he put into it—not to mention the money he *didn't* put into it—I don't know why he's so hot to get it back."

"Which brings me to my previous conclusion. If he wants it back that bad, it's got to be worth something—"

"Or whoever lost it in that game is desperate to get it back and is ready to ante up big money for it."

"Either way, it's worth something." Nora sat on the bed.

"Exactly," Suzanne said, sitting up. "Which is why I came back on the red-eye. Because he said he absolutely needs it before tonight. So I cut a deal with him. I give him the ring and he forgets all about the cruise tickets."

"And he went for it?"

"In a heartbeat. You want to hear the cherry on the sundae? Emmy and I were talking about this very thing on the cruise. She tried to resell some ugly jewelry that she inherited from her great aunt. And the most anyone would offer was ten cents on the dollar."

"Ten percent?"

"Yeah, even for diamonds. She checked all over and it was the same. So he can have the ring, but good luck getting cash for it," Suzanne said, lying down again.

"Sounds like a fitting ending for a blackmailer," Nora said wryly. "Have you figured out what you're going to say to Camille?"

"I need a little more time."

"Why? To lie on the bed some more?"

"I'm mulling my options."

Nora sighed. "Fine. I'd better get back to the basement before Erik comes looking for me."

"I think he really likes you." Suzanne gave Nora a nudge.

"No, if there's anyone he likes, it's you. And therein lies a great deal of our problem."

A half hour later, Erik had determined that the water was leaking from a loose hose. "I checked those," Nora said, embarrassed. "They didn't feel loose and there wasn't any water around them."

"Probably because it had dried on the hose by the time you noticed the water on the floor." Erik wiped a hand on his jeans.

He glanced at her for a moment as he tightened the hose. "I left you a couple of messages."

"Yeah, sorry… I've been really busy. Work… Danny…client shopping…" She tried to sound sincere even though she was lying again. Now might be the perfect opportunity to tell him the truth—if only she hadn't promised Suzanne she'd hold off a while longer. "How'd your trip to Utah go?" she asked.

"Got the job."

Her heart dropped. "Must be a lucky week for job offers," she said too brightly.

He stopped what he was doing and faced her. "I turned it down."

She caught her breath and raised her eyes to his, those incredible blue eyes. "You turned down your dream job?"

"Mom! Hey, Mom!" Danny came bounding down the stairs, rounding the corner to the laundry area at full force, with his friend, Zach, close on his heels.

Nora felt the return of panic and she prayed Erik didn't call her Suzanne in front of her son. Now that she was so close to the end, she wanted to be able to control when and how she told Erik the truth.

"Mom! I want to show Zach—" Danny pulled up short at the sight of Erik with a wrench in his hand. "Why didn't you tell me you were going to fix things today, Mom? I could've helped."

"It wasn't much of a fix, buddy," Erik said. "Just tightened up a hose."

"Did you see my spider back there?"

"No."

"I think he moved out," Nora said. She tried to wrap her brain around what it actually meant that Erik turned down the coaching job.

"He's gone?" Danny was incredulous. He peered behind the washer.

"I think he took off right after we saw him that night," Nora said. *Yup, right down the toilet.* "I haven't seen him since."

Danny acted dejected for about five seconds. Then he punched Zach in the ribs and looked up at Erik. "That's him," he said proudly.

Zach looked up at Erik. "He's taller than *my* dad." Zach just kept staring up at him.

"So did you two need something, sweetie?" Nora asked.

Danny shifted from foot to foot. "I need to whisper it."

Nora tousled his hair and bent low so her head brushed against his.

"Zach wants to meet Erik 'cause he might be my new dad," Danny said in a whisper loud enough for the people in the next block to hear.

Nora knew by the expression on Erik's face that he heard every word. Her face flamed.

"Danny, Erik is a friend. That's all." She took him by the shoulders and turned him toward the doorway. "You two go outside and play."

He didn't budge. "But, Mom—" He moved closer to Erik.

"Go on now." She gave him a little shove and he walked from the room, head hanging down. *If anything more went wrong in her life, she was moving to a deserted island.*

She looked at Erik, her face on fire. "I'm sorry. Remember how I told you he thinks every available man is a potential father? He doesn't understand that the guys may not think it's as good an idea as he does."

"No problem." He bent to put the back on the washer again and began to tighten the screws.

The doorbell chimed faintly in the distance and she headed upstairs, grateful for the escape. "I'll be right back." By the time she reached the front hall, Keegan was already in the house, and he and Suzanne were in a heated discussion. Nora hurried toward them, her stomach roiling.

"Can you two take this conversation elsewhere?" she asked.

"Hi, Nora," Keegan said.

Suzanne grabbed him by the arm. "I'm Nora!"

"What?"

"Just play along...or you're not getting the ring." She made a face. "As if you deserve it."

"The etiquette ladies say you have to give it back," he retorted.

"Like you know anything about etiquette," Suzanne muttered.

"At least I know you're supposed to give the ring back."

"And I'm giving it to you as long as we're clear. You get the ring back and that's all you get," Suzanne said.

Nora felt like a Ping-Pong ball bouncing between the two of them. "Go talk about this out—"

"All set!" Erik rounded the corner from the kitchen. "Good as new."

Nora thought her brain might pop this very instant. "Erik," she said. "You remember Keegan?"

The two men shook hands.

Keegan rocked back on his heels and appraised Erik. "I was working with the band at your mother's party. The one that you took—" he paused and looked from Nora to Suzanne "—Suzanne to."

"Yeah. Good to see you again," Erik said.

Keegan put an arm around the real Suzanne and pulled her close. "Nora and I used to be engaged. Now we're just good friends."

Oh, for Pete's sake, he was laying this on a little too thick. If Erik had any brains at all—and of course he did—he was going to think something was out of whack here.

Suzanne twisted out from under Keegan's arm and began to pull him toward the door. "Keegie, hon, let's finish this conversation a little later."

"I really think we should finish it now." He resisted her pull.

"We have a guest here right now," she said in a perfect hostess voice. She tried to drag him onto the porch. "How about you go drive around and I'll give you a call when I'm free to talk?"

"How about I take Erik driving with me?" he said.

An asylum. She lived in an asylum. "Nora," Nora said through gritted teeth. "Why don't you just get that *thing* for him?" She looked at Keegan. "And then you and Nora are even, right?" She glared at him until he nodded agreement.

Nora leaned over and whispered to Erik, "He wants the engagement ring back."

Erik nodded as though insanity like this was just a normal occurrence in his life.

Suzanne dashed upstairs and was back a minute later, her fist tightly closed. "With this ring…I keep the tickets."

"Yeah. So give it to me."

She held out her hand and uncurled her fingers to reveal a big solitaire diamond in a thick gold setting. Keegan picked the ring up, held it to the light and watched it sparkle. His lips curled back in a sort of feral grin.

How could Suzanne have ever liked this guy?

"This baby's worth ten thousand big ones. Thank you, ladies. Sayonara." Keegan shoved the ring in his pocket and sauntered out the front door.

Suzanne slammed the door behind him. "Good riddance. Enjoy your ten percent."

Nora gave Erik an apologetic smile. "It usually isn't so chaotic around here."

"That's okay." He looked from Nora to Suzanne and back again. "You know, I think

I'm finally beginning to see a bit of a difference between you two."

Suzanne almost choked. "People say that all the time and then they keep getting us mixed up. So don't be surprised if you're wrong again later." She grimaced at Nora. "Right?"

"She's right." *And we're both liars.*

He grinned. "Okay. Anybody here up for lunch? I'll buy."

Suzanne shook her head. "Not me. I'm exhausted. I just got home from—" she froze for a moment "—the—Laundromat."

Nora gaped at her.

"Because…" Suzanne gulped. "The washer, you know wasn't working." She made circles in the air with one finger. "What was wrong with the washer again?"

"A loose water hose," Nora said.

"No wonder my clothes weren't getting clean, probably not enough water was getting into the machine."

Nora felt the blood drain from her head. *Stop, Suzanne. Know when to stop.*

"So anyway," Suzanne said. "I got everything clean at the Laundromat…but like I said, it was exhausting." She lifted her suitcase from behind the chair where Nora had tried to hide it. "Oh, here are my clean clothes," she said. "Suitcases work so much better than laundry baskets, don't you think? Clothes stay so neatly folded in them…. I'll just go upstairs and put everything away and rest for a while. I feel like I've been running all day."

Nora was dumbfounded by her sister's performance. She couldn't have made Nora seem any more of an idiot if she'd tried. What must Erik think of the woman he just hired to run the sports medicine rehab center?

He turned to her. "Well? You want to catch some lunch? With Danny?"

She just looked at him. Sometimes when you took too long to act, life forced your hand. Like right now. It was time to tell the truth whether Suzanne had figured out how to tell Camille or not. For whatever reason, Erik had decided to stay in San Francisco. And he had just given her the perfect opportunity to tell all.

"Danny's at the neighbor's…."

"Don't worry about Danny, I'll be here," Suzanne said as she headed for the staircase.

Nora smiled through the fear that was beginning to fill her. "Okay." Her heart started to pound. "How about if we go to Margo's Bistro?" she said. "It's close enough to walk and the food is great." *And when all hell breaks loose after I tell you the truth, I'll have Margo to hold me up.*

"Works for me," he said.

"Have fun. See you later, Erik." Suzanne ascended the staircase, suitcase bumping on nearly every step.

When she was gone, Erik shook his head. "Wow. That's a different Nora than I've ever seen at work."

"Funny," Nora said. "That's a different Nora than I've ever seen at home, either."

CHAPTER FOURTEEN

"SO, DID I HEAR YOU RIGHT? You turned down the job?" Suzanne asked him as they walked to the bistro. The sun was almost directly overhead, the day unbelievably fresh.

He nodded, pleased she had brought it up again. The subject had gotten lost in the chaos at her house and he'd begun to think it didn't make any difference to her. "Got a pretty good reality check from my partners and—" There was no need to tell her about his mother's input.

"So they convinced you the rehab center was a better career choice?"

He stopped and turned to look at her. A wave of longing swept through him. "Something like that," he said.

She watched him, her gorgeous eyes full of question. And he knew that if he touched her now, he would never let go of her again. His heart sped up. He felt like he was at the top of an untried ski run, ready to hurl himself down without any idea of what lay ahead.

Shoving the fear away, he pushed off. He took her by the shoulders and bent to cover her mouth with his. She leaned into him and he drew her closer, kissing her more thoroughly than he'd ever kissed anyone in the middle of the day, in the middle of the sidewalk.

He looked at her as they pulled apart, watched her eyes slowly open and he drew a breath. He brushed a thumb across her lips and touched her cheek. He wanted to bury his head in her hair and kiss the nape of her neck, wanted to feel her beneath him again, loving him until they both were sated.

Then he wanted to lie in bed with her and talk until morning was just few hours away and they fell asleep wrapped in each other's arms.

And after that he wanted to do it all over again.

How had he gone all these years without knowing this feeling?

NORA WANTED TO WEEP. His eyes were so blue, the light in them so warm…and the sun was glinting in his dark hair… And his face, damn, but she wanted to drown in his face.

Oh, God, she could lose him today.

The pain that seared through her at the thought was almost unbearable.

He slung an arm around her shoulders and they walked the rest of the way to the bistro like that. His arm around her, her arm around him, their bodies touching from shoulder to hip, their every step taking her closer to her moment of truth.

Once inside the bistro, Nora introduced Erik to Margo. She could tell by Margo's expression that her friend knew something was up. Nora ordered chicken salad on a croissant, Erik got roast beef with horseradish on harvest wheat. The room seemed overly bright today, the usually warm colors harsh. And every detail felt like it was being etched in her memory.

"I'd better grab a table," she said looking around. "We're here at high noon on a Saturday."

She made her way through the crowded room and set her purse on a table near the front window. Then she sat down, her stomach churning, as she waited for Erik to join her.

Unbidden, her thoughts went to Kevin. Theirs had been a relationship of trust. They'd been friends first, lovers later. They'd been able to talk about everything, openly, knew they could always speak their mind and that they would accept one another, regardless. They had lived trust. She knew how important it was to a relationship. And yet, she had let this lie go on and on with Erik.

She saw him coming across the room and her stomach jumped at the sight of him, all dark hair and blue eyes and grin happy to see her.

Happy to see Suzanne.

Here he was beginning a relationship based on trust. And here she was, lying every step of the way.

She couldn't bear the thought of how those eyes would look at her once she told him how long she had been deceiving him. She couldn't bear the thought that, as soon as she told him the truth, the trust would be gone.

He set their food on the table and took the seat across from her. God only knew how she was going to eat anything with her stomach as nauseous as this.

Out of sheer nervousness, she picked up her sandwich and took a bite. That was one way to avoid talking—keep your mouth full. She chewed slowly, then swallowed and the food stuck partway down her throat. She tried to swallow again and it moved just slightly. *Oh, great.* She reached for her lemonade, feeling like her eyes were bugging out of her head.

"Are you okay?" Erik asked, alarmed. He set down his own sandwich and started to stand.

She nodded and took a big swallow of lemonade. Today was bad enough already—no way were they going to be doing the Heimlich maneuver, too. The lump of food dropped the rest of the way to her stomach and landed with a thud. No more food—not until she got the truth out.

"You sure you're okay?"

"Yeah. I've got something to tell you."

He looked at her expectantly and she pushed forward through her fear. "Remember when your mother called to get personal shopping help for you?" The blood pounded in her ears. "She called when Suzanne was off on a cruise through the Inside Passage. Up in Alaska."

His brow furrowed.

"You see, Suzanne was engaged to Keegan—"

"I thought Nora was engaged to Keegan."

She shook her head. "Suzanne was. And Keegan ended the engagement, so Suzanne traded in their honeymoon tickets for an earlier cruise and took off with a friend."

He frowned. "I think I'm confused."

"You won't be much longer. Suzanne was on that cruise when her largest client—Camille Lamont—called and asked her to do a job for her son, Erik." Her voice felt far away, like someone else was talking, not her. "Suzanne was afraid that if she didn't do the job, she might lose Camille's business." Nora looked away, unable to meet his eyes when she said this next thing. "So, I did the job for her."

She brought her gaze back to him and waited, hoping beyond hope that he would laugh, that he would think it was just a silly prank and forgive her right away.

"You…did the job?" He cocked his head. "So you're…Nora?"

She nodded.

He set his sandwich down on his plate and sat back in his chair. "You're Nora? I've been meeting with, seeing, Nora all this time?"

She couldn't speak for the lump in her throat.

"I…and Nora…" He squinted at her. "At the ski resort?"

She nodded again.

He said nothing for a very long moment. "Why didn't you tell me?"

She swallowed hard. "Suzanne didn't want to lose the account. And I didn't want her to lose it. Once she can support herself, she'll be able to move into her own place."

"I get that. But it's been a while since our first meeting. Why didn't you say something when you and I… when things began to happen between us?" Erik sounded like he was trying to understand and a glimmer of hope formed in Nora's heart.

"I tried." Her voice quivered. "I planned to tell you when we went skiing, but then you said you were taking that new job... And I was going to tell you on Friday when I ran into you at the rehab space, but Andy was there—"

The expression on his face made her stop. He didn't believe her.

"Whose son is Danny—Suzanne's or yours?"

"Mine. It was my husband who died—not Suzanne's." She fought to keep her voice from breaking. "I'm sorry, Erik. I never meant it to go this far. I wanted to end it. I just couldn't figure out when...or how."

"You should have ended it before it began." His eyes narrowed. "Wait a minute. Was this about getting the director job in the new clinic?"

She shook her head vehemently. "No. I was afraid to tell you because I didn't want you to think it *was* about the job."

"Really. Did it cross your mind at all that maybe you owed me the truth before the interview?"

"I was afraid you might— I wanted you to judge me in the interview as Nora Clark, physical therapist. Not as the person who had been—" her voice dropped almost to a whisper "—deceiving you. And then, when you said you were going to be coaching, somehow it seemed like, if you were going to be gone, would it really matter if you knew?"

"Would it really matter?"

"I don't mean it like that." She didn't think things could go any worse than they were going right now.

"What *do* you mean it like?" His voice was cold.

She looked down. "Erik, you don't know how sorry I am. I wish I'd never agreed to help Suzanne. Is there anything I can do to fix it?"

He shoved aside the plate holding his half-eaten sandwich. "Let's see, you've been lying to me about who you are since the day we met. Have had numerous opportunities to tell me what's going on and chose not to. Knew that I shouldn't even have been interviewing you if I was *sleeping with you.* And the only real reason you have for keeping the lie going is that you wanted to get the job based on your own merits."

She could tell by his movements he was getting close to standing up and walking out of her life. "Erik—"

"Merits that I have a little trouble seeing right

now." He shoved his chair back and stood, bending forward slightly to rest both his hands on the table and lean toward her. "Frankly, I don't see that there's anything you can do to fix it." He straightened and turned at the same moment, his arm inadvertently knocking her purse to the floor. Everything inside spilled out in a mess—Chap Stick, change, hairbrush, Tampax, old grocery lists, movie ticket stubs and a hundred other things she had shoved in her purse at one time or another and never bothered to clean out.

She stared in mortification at the synopsis of her life strewn across the floor, then dropped to her knees and began to grab things and shove them in her purse. She glanced at the people at the other tables, but everyone seemed oblivious to the drama unfolding nearby.

"Sorry." Erik knelt to help, picking up items and handing them to her. After a moment, he stopped, a wrinkled sheet of paper in his hand, his expression one of total disbelief. "What the hell is this? *Perfect Dad Possibilities?*"

She could have sworn time stopped. Nothing moved, all she could hear was a buzzing in her ears. She wanted to say something, but could think of absolutely nothing that wouldn't sound like another lie. After all, how many people kept lists titled, *Perfect Dad Possibilities* in their purse? How could she have forgotten to get rid of it? She reached for the paper. He held it back from her and headed out the door.

Nora shoved the rest of her things in her purse and followed him outside just in time to hear him read aloud, "Athletic, likes kids, patient, reads bedtime stories, good income." He looked at her in disgust. "I guess it wasn't all about getting the job, huh? So that's why Danny introduced me to Zach as his new dad."

"That list was a joke, something my coffee group did because Danny was so fixated on getting a father." She closed her eyes at how pathetic she sounded—like a pathological liar. "I told you about that," she said desperately.

He ignored her. "Let me just run through this multipurpose scam you had going and make sure I have it right. Find a well-heeled guy to marry, get a father for your kid in the process… Oh, and land yourself the job you want. All by impersonating your sister."

She touched his arm and he shook her off. "I know what it looks like," she said. "But, I swear to you, the women I meet for coffee thought it would be a good thing to do since Danny wanted a dad." *She sounded pitiful.*

"An easy way to narrow the field," he said. "I rest my case."

"It was just a funny exercise—"

"Cut your losses, Suz— Nora. I've known plenty of women just like you. Sometimes it's better not to say anything at all." He crumpled the paper into a ball and tossed it in the trash can by the door before striding away.

Numbness overtook her. She didn't know why she'd expected any other response from him—had known in her heart that he wouldn't take it well. That's why she kept putting off telling him the truth. But him finding the daddy list was the worst twist of all. As pain welled up in her chest, she turned and went back into the bistro.

Margo met her at the door. "I left Sandy in charge—it's too crowded for us to talk in there right now," she said. "Let's walk to the corner."

In a halting voice, Nora recounted everything that had transpired the past week. "He asked me not to tell anyone about the coaching job until it was official. So I didn't. But now, Margo, he's decided not to take it. *He's staying in San Francisco.* And, I've blown it completely."

"I think you probably have."

"Oh, thanks for the support."

Margo gave her a hug. "Well, no. We knew

you were getting in too deep with the charade. But him finding that stupid daddy list… I really think there's only one thing to do—"

"He already said it. *Cut my losses.*"

"No. Go after him," Margo said.

"Are you kidding? I've told the truth—he didn't believe me. I've said my apologies—he didn't care. I do have some level of pride. There are limits to how low I'll sink."

Margo took hold of Nora's shoulders and faced her. "You made decisions these past weeks—to move forward, to take a chance again. You and Erik found something together. You can't just let it go. *Go after him.*"

"No. I can't handle any more pain." Nora took a step away from her friend. "I'm not putting myself out there to get hurt even worse." She wanted to go home, to be with her son, to wrap herself in her little family again and forget that she'd let her heart out of its cage for a while. "Thanks. I'll talk to you later."

She turned and headed for home, telling herself that, as much as it hurt, she had done the right thing. Oh, but God, to lose him, to lose the chance at love again. An overwhelming ache welled up inside her and the tears started to flow.

Fifteen minutes later, she let herself into the

house. As much as she didn't want to talk about her conversation with Erik, she had to tell Suzanne pretty soon so her sister could call Camille Lamont. And lose the account. After the conversation she'd just had with Erik, Nora had no hope at all that Suzanne would be able to keep working for Camille.

She dropped down onto the couch, kicked her feet up onto the coffee table and listened to the top-40 music playing on the radio upstairs. The afternoon sun filtered through the mini-blinds, casting bright white stripes on the rug. She closed her eyes. Before another five minutes passed, Suzanne came bouncing down the stairs, stopping when she spotted Nora. "Hey. I didn't hear you come in."

"Danny still at Zach's?"

"Yeah. He came home for while, moping about that Erik thing you said to him. So I tried to distract him and asked if he'd found any other new dad candidates lately—"

"Don't! I just gave him a talk about *not* doing that," Nora said.

"Let me finish… He told me that one of these days you were going to meet someone and fall in love and then he'd get a new dad."

"That's what I said to him a few days ago."

"So, then he went over to his Spider-Man

calendar and started pointing at the dates and asking if I knew which one was *one of these days*."

Nora blew out her breath. "At least he's sort of getting it. Too bad, *one of these days* isn't ever going to include Erik." Her eyes filled with tears again. "I told him the truth at lunch."

"I figured you would—"

"Oh, and did I mention that this morning, as he was fixing the washer, he said he'd decided against taking the coaching job?" She pulled her feet off the coffee table and sat up.

"Ohmigod. Stay tuned, the story is changing hourly." Suzanne threw herself onto the couch next to Nora. "How'd he take it when you told him?"

Nora let out a sharp laugh. "He's furious. Thinks it was all about getting the job and finding a rich husband." Unable to sit still any longer, she stood and wandered across the room. "My purse spilled and he found this chart that my coffee group made at Margo's one Thursday…listing all the eligible men I know and their attributes for fatherhood."

"You did that?" Suzanne's voice rose a notch.

"Not me. They did it. All because of Danny's obsession with getting a dad." She rolled her eyes.

"Ohmigod—nails in the coffin. Why don't you tell him *I* made the list and you had nothing to do with it?"

"Too late. Anyway, I'm done with this lying/changing places thing." She stared dejectedly out the window. "Margo thinks I should have gone after him when he left."

"And say what?"

She frowned. "Tell him how I feel. Beg forgiveness—again. Don't let a good thing get away. You know, that sort of stuff."

"Maybe you should."

"No. He knows where I live. The decisions are all his now—he's the one who has to decide if I'm worth forgiving." Nora sat on the couch again, dropped her head down onto one hand and started to cry.

Suzanne pulled her into her arms. "It'll work out. Really. Remember what Grampa used to say? It's always darkest before the storm."

"Dawn," Nora said.

"Dawn?"

"It's always darkest before the *dawn*. Grampa always got it wrong."

"No wonder it never made any sense."

Nora let out a half laugh, half sob. "I finally decided to let go, move forward, say goodbye. I finally decided to risk again and I got exactly what I was afraid of getting—a broken heart. And I've got no one to blame but me."

"And me," Suzanne said quietly. "You can blame me."

Nora rested her head on her sister's shoulder. "Yeah. But I love you anyway." She closed her eyes and mentally relived the last couple of weeks. Every possible *what-if?* popped into her mind. What if she'd never changed places with Suzanne? What if she'd actually told Erik the truth when they went skiing? What if she hadn't applied for the rehab center job? What if he hadn't found the daddy list?

But no matter how she looked at it, nothing ever changed the fact that all those things had happened—and there was no way out for her now. Erik thought she wanted a new job, a father for her son and a rich husband. And if the roles were reversed, she had to admit, she'd think the same thing.

It was too late for what-ifs. She had already lost any hope of having Erik's respect, his friendship, *his love.* She opened her eyes and looked at her sister. "Don't you want to call Camille?"

"I already did. I figured you'd tell everything at lunch, so I called Camille while you were gone."

"Did you lose the account?"

Suzanne shook her head. "It was the weirdest conversation. I asked if I could meet with her to explain some recent developments and she said something to the effect that, *these things happen,* and I should stop by tomorrow morning."

"That's not weird. She just didn't know the truth yet because Erik was still with me at the bistro."

"Wanna bet? She asked me to bring you along."

CHAPTER FIFTEEN

Erik stood at the top of a double black diamond ski run on Mammoth Mountain and took in the view that stretched out in front of him—snow-capped mountains, evergreens, early morning sun sparkling on fresh powder and all of it framed by an endless blue sky.

For the first time in his life he couldn't appreciate it. All he could feel was anger, betrayal…and loss.

This mountain was the place that was almost more home than home to him. He'd driven half the night thinking that just being here would ease the pain. And it wasn't working.

He'd felt like this once before—like he'd been hit in the stomach with a front-end loader and couldn't catch his breath. That had been fifteen years ago when he'd blown out his knees. Then, his whole world had been torn out from under him. Skiing had always been what grounded him, gave him a place to belong.

And then suddenly it was gone and he was facing more than a year of recuperation—and then decisions. What should he do if he couldn't be a world-class skier? The pain of so suddenly losing something he loved came back to him almost as fresh as if it had just happened.

Yesterday he'd planned to tell Suzanne—Nora—that she was the main reason he had turned down the coaching job. But once she'd unloaded her bombshell—and then he'd found that damn list—he'd only wanted to get as far away from her as possible. His mother had been wrong—giving up Suzanne didn't mean he was giving up some great chance for happiness.

Oh, hell. His mother was expecting them for dinner tonight. He pulled his cell phone out of the inner pocket of his ski jacket and punched in her number, relieved when it kicked into voice mail and he didn't have to talk to her.

"Hey, Mom, just wanted to let you know I'm out at Mammoth for the holiday weekend—so don't expect me for dinner tonight. As for all that shit you said the other day, I think there's merit to hanging on to your own identity." He paused. "Speaking of identities, you might want to have a little talk with your personal shopper about hers."

He clicked off the phone, shoved it back in

his pocket and set off down the mountain. All his life, he'd been able to rely on skiing to clear his head. He'd take off alone, immerse himself in what he loved, push himself to his limits. Today would be no different. By the end of the day, he was confident that skiing would refocus his mind on what was really important. This mountain would take away the betrayal.

By late afternoon, though, he had to admit that what had always worked for him in the past was no longer working. Being alone only seemed to make him dwell on Suzanne all the more. He wanted to talk to someone—and he didn't know anyone here. In the middle of riding the chairlift, during the usual small talk about the great weather and where you were from and what the best runs were, he suddenly found himself starting to tell strangers about Suzanne.

He reined himself in a couple of times, then finally gave in and told the whole sordid story to a gray-haired grandmotherly woman sharing his chairlift. He couldn't help thinking that he'd become one of those people who tell the intimate details of their life to a stranger on the bus thinking they'll never see that person again. And then later discover they were telling their deepest secrets to their new gossipy next-door neighbor.

With his luck, someone would figure out he was Erik Morgan, former Olympic skier, and the story would end up in the tabloids. Either that, or he'd learn later he was telling his woes to one of Suzanne's—Nora's—relatives.

And even those possibilities didn't shut him up.

"I don't blame you for being mad. I would be," the woman said.

Erik felt vindicated. He watched the skiers flying down the hill below him as the chairlift chugged toward the top.

"But what does it gain you?" she asked. "Stay mad and all you have is your anger for company. Doesn't sound like fun to me."

There was some logic there. "But don't you think all this lying says something about her character? How could I trust her again?"

"It also says something about her loyalty that she would agree to do something so ridiculous to help her sister," the woman pointed out.

"What about that list of prospective fathers?" He shifted his ski poles to his other hand.

She laughed. "Be flattered. Sounds to me like you made the short list of men she thought she could like."

This wasn't exactly the sympathy he was hoping to find. As they neared the disembark point, the woman sat forward a bit on the seat and Erik suddenly felt like he still didn't have an answer.

"But doesn't this speak to trust?" he pressed.

"Maybe. But she did eventually tell you the truth. If I heard the story right, she told you at a point when she had a lot more to lose than she had to gain. That speaks to something, too. Integrity."

They stood and pushed away from the lift. "Good luck," she called as she skied off to one of the intermediate runs.

Good luck. Yeah, he needed it. He'd just given up the chance to coach the U.S. ski team. He was integrally involved in creating a new sports medicine rehab center. And he'd been taken for a ride by a woman he was now going to have to work with on a daily basis.

No damn way. Something was going to have to change with that situation. He'd talk to his partners when he got back.

How had he not noticed the difference between the two women?

Now that he knew the truth, he'd be able to tell the two apart at a glance.

He shook his head. Amazing. He'd come here to forget about Suzanne—Nora—and instead, he'd been fixated on her all day. The more he tried to push her away, the more she seemed to take over his thoughts.

And then there was Danny. He really liked her son, had already promised to take him skiing again. That wasn't going to happen now. He hated that he was going to be the one to disappoint the kid, hoped Danny wasn't too hurt. But he didn't see he had any other choice.

He stretched his back a little. With the seven-hour drive, he'd arrived late last night—and not slept all that well once he was here. He'd been taking treacherous runs all day—Hangman's Hollow, Cornice Bowl. It was probably time to call it quits. This was when skiing got dangerous—at the end of the day with tired muscles.

Well, dangerous for average skiers anyway. He took a breath, pulled his goggles down and set off down Dragon's Back.

AFTER A FITFUL night's sleep, an anxiety-ridden morning and continuous prayers to St. Jude complete with promises to never do wrong again, *ever,* Nora sat perched in a chair in Camille Lamont's very formal living room and waited for someone to say something about why she and Suzanne were there.

Camille was the picture of graciousness, making small talk and offering them iced tea. Nora's hands shook so much she couldn't even pick up her glass. *Get on with it,* she mentally urged her sister and Camille.

Then, as if the telepathic message had, for once, gotten through, Suzanne began to lay out everything they'd done and why they'd done it. She did a nice job of explaining her mental devastation after Keegan cancelled the wedding, and how she needed to get away to regroup and how she'd thought Nora would take over as personal shopper for only one meeting. "Two at the most."

"Oh, girls," Camille said. "I suspected you switched places when I saw Nora at Erik's the first night."

Nora blanched.

Suzanne choked on her iced tea.

They both gaped at Camille.

"You did?" Suzanne asked.

Nora couldn't believe it. All this effort to keep it a secret so Suzanne didn't lose the account and the woman knew anyway?

Camille nodded. "Give me some credit for knowing who my personal shopper is. I reminded Nora—Suzanne—of something I told her when she and Keegan first broke up. That sometimes the right person is standing in front of you and you don't know it until you clear away the debris."

Suzanne frowned. "Did you say that to me?"

"No." Camille serenely sipped her iced tea. "But even knowing that, I wasn't absolutely certain you'd switched places until Erik told me at the party that Suzanne had a son. And, of course, I knew she didn't. I had no idea what you two were up to…but Erik seemed so taken by Nora, I thought it worth letting alone."

At the mention of the connection between Erik and Nora, Suzanne nodded at Nora as though she should step in and say something. *Absolutely not,* Nora thought. She took a long, long drink of her iced tea as if to tell her sister, *you're not dragging me into another thing.*

But the silence went on so long, Nora finally gave a mental huff and said, "You pretty much know the rest—" at the exact same time Suzanne said, "It sort of snowballed—"

Nora stopped and let Suzanne have the lead.

"Erik and Nora seemed to really hit it off and then he was asking her out and Nora wasn't quite sure just what to do," Suzanne said. "Because it's been a long time. I mean, she's been a widow now five years, and, I, for one, was really happy she had met someone, so we just didn't know how to get the truth out without jeopardizing their—" she smiled at Nora "—budding relationship."

Nora stared at her sister. Was it really necessary to tell his mother all this? "We were just friends, really," she hastily interjected.

"I think it was more than just friends for my son." Camille's voice had the self-assurance of a woman who knew far more than she was letting on.

Nora blushed. "Well, maybe a bit more. But it's over—I told Erik everything yesterday so you don't have to worry about him not knowing the truth anymore." Saying the words out loud seemed to put such a finality on it all. Profound sadness filled her and she just wanted to go home.

"And how did he take it?"

"Not very well," Suzanne said quickly.

Nora felt her expression freeze as her sister chattered brightly on.

"He might have taken it better except he found a list that Nora's coffee group made." Suzanne described the daddy list and how it came to be. "So, when Erik found that, things went from bad to worse. It pretty much sealed everything because he thought all Nora wanted was a rich husband and a father for Danny."

Blabber, blabber, blabberhead. Nora clenched her teeth together. When would her sister ever learn to keep her mouth shut?

"That explains why he's gone skiing to Mammoth," Camille said. "He does that when he needs to clear his mind. I wasn't sure what sent him there this time." She sipped her iced tea. After a minute she said, "I suppose that's all we need to discuss then."

Suzanne cleared her throat and sat up straighter. "I would like to say how sorry I am that I just didn't tell you I was gone on a cruise. And how sorry I am that I asked Nora to take my place—"

"Apologies accepted."

Suzanne's face brightened. "And I would really appreciate a second chance…to keep working with you."

"That goes without saying," Camille said.

"Oh! Thank you! I'll make sure that I find the best of everything for—"

"You always do." Camille turned to Nora. "Have you ever been to Mammoth, dear?"

"Oh, sure, years ago. We've both been there," Suzanne said cheerfully.

Nora jumped to her feet and took her sister by the arm. "Not for a long time, though. Thanks so much for everything. We'll just get going, then." She gave Suzanne a tug and drew her out of the room before her sister could say any more.

Suzanne was positively giddy as she backed

her car out of Camille's driveway. "St. Jude has been working overtime for us. Look at today. I get to keep Camille Lamont as a client. You know where Erik is. Could we ask for more?"

"Could you ever shut up?" Nora asked. "Did you have to tell Camille everything?"

"I didn't tell her *everything*." Suzanne tossed her head. "Anyway, I'm beginning to think Margo had the right idea about Erik. Go after him. Now that you know he's at Mammoth, go up there...recreate what you two had last weekend. I'll babysit Danny."

"Are you crazy? I'm not chasing him to the ski resort."

"Why do you think his mother told us where he is?"

"She was making conversation," Nora said.

"She *wants* you to follow him there!"

"And do what? Wrap myself in Saran Wrap and knock on his door? Because that's about the only way he's going to let me in his room."

"Now there's an idea—"

Nora blew out her breath. "Don't be dumb. I'm just showing you how ridiculous you are."

"I think you should go—"

"Stop, Suzanne. Just stop. I don't even know who I am anymore. And I'm not sure I like what I think I've become. I know for a fact that

Erik doesn't. *And I'm not chasing him to a ski resort.*" Pain started to roll through her again and she made a chopping motion with one hand. "Don't bring it up again."

They parked in front of the house and Nora jumped out of the car and hurried up the walk alone. Danny and the babysitter were making chalk drawings on the driveway. "Ashley, I'll run over with your money in a little bit," she called.

She took the stairs two at a time and went into her bedroom, putting her back against the door to shut it. Anger fought with sadness inside her. She'd tried to move on, she really had. She'd met a guy who was kind, and sweet and fun. Who wasn't afraid to say what he meant, who went after what he wanted…who took risks. It had been a long time since she'd let herself take any risks at all. And she missed it.

She went to the window and pushed aside the curtain to watch her son using a stick to slay a blue chalk-drawn fire-breathing dragon on the driveway. "It happened just like I said it would, Danny," she said softly. "I met someone and we felt a connection. And I fell in love." She drew a shaky breath. "But I blew it."

She thought about her conversation with Erik, how she said she'd wanted him to judge her in the interview on her own merits—and not be influenced by knowing she had been lying to him.

Except, one of the most important traits she could bring to the job was integrity. And she'd displayed a shocking lack of it. Even her decision to finally tell the truth was too little, too late.

Erik believed she kept the truth from him in order to become director of the new clinic. Maybe he was right—things had gotten so complicated these past couple of weeks, she didn't know up from down anymore. All she knew for certain was that she'd pulled back from telling him the truth on the ski trip because he was going after a coaching job that would take him everywhere else in the world but here. When he'd told her of his plans, the pain had been so strong she'd mentally run away, unable to face how much more it might hurt if he learned the truth and rejected her outright.

She'd told Margo she was going to quit running. Then she'd run herself into the biggest mess of her life. She'd gotten the job she wanted—under pretty dubious circumstances. She knew full well that if Erik had known about all her lies before the interview, the job would likely never have been offered to her.

She'd run to avoid pain. And she got pain

anyway. Losing him had been nothing compared to knowing that he thought the worst of her, that he believed she had no integrity. This was an ache so deep it made her soul hurt.

She'd told Erik who she really was. But that alone didn't take the tilt out of her life. In order to do that, she had to right one last wrong. She had to show him that she hadn't kept lying just to become the rehab center director. There was really only one way to do it—she had to refuse the job. And she had to do it now.

She drew a long slow breath and exhaled, more calm than she'd been in days. No one would be in the office on the three-day Memorial weekend—least of all the head administrator. But she could leave him a message turning down the job and Erik could fill in all the gory details for him on Tuesday.

She went downstairs to get the phone book out of the kitchen drawer. Suzanne sat at the table eating a bowl of Elephant Tracks ice cream.

"Do me a favor. Be quiet during my call," Nora said. She ran a finger down the long row of phone numbers for the hospital, searching for a listing for the head administrator. "I don't need any chaos in the background."

Suzanne made a face. "Why would I do that? Who are you calling anyway?"

"Just don't, okay?"

"Fine." Suzanne shoved a spoonful of ice cream in her mouth.

When she didn't find the listing she wanted, Nora called the main number and asked to be connected. As soon as voice mail kicked in, she left her message; with each word she spoke, the weight on her heart lifted a little more.

Suzanne's jaw dropped wide-open and she waved her spoon in the air, obviously fighting to hold back the chaos that wanted to burst out of her.

As soon as Nora hung up, Suzanne exploded. "You quit the job? You've only had it two days! It was everything you wanted to do!"

"Yeah. But it's too mixed-up. If Erik had known the truth about who I was, I doubt I would have even gotten an interview, let alone the job." She shook her head, the sadness inside her almost overwhelming. "He thinks the worst of me and I can't live with that. Jobs are a dime a dozen. But there's only one him. And even if I can't have him, what he believes about me is more important than any job." She pulled a spoon from the drawer and took a scoop of ice cream from her sister's bowl.

Suzanne didn't answer for a minute. Then she said, "You can have the rest of my ice cream."

"Now what?" Nora asked.

"Nothing. I just remembered some shopping I forgot to do for a client." She looked at the clock on the microwave. "Geez, and look what time it is already. I'm gonna take off. Won't be back until late. Okay?"

"Fine by me." More than fine actually. Her life had been in turmoil since Suzanne got home yesterday, and a few hours without her would be peace on earth.

ERIK WATCHED THE FOX ten o'clock news as he lay on the bed in his hotel room, his swollen right knee packed in ice. Been here, done this... Damn, he probably aggravated the cartilage he tore when he blew out his knee fifteen years ago. He couldn't be sure until he had an MRI, but, having seen plenty of these in the office, and having had the experience himself, he was fairly confident of his diagnosis. At least it wasn't like when he was twenty-two—then he'd also had multiple fractures and torn ligaments.

He shook his head. He knew better than to keep skiing tired. But he'd kept going...forcing his muscles beyond fatigue in an effort to keep his brain from thinking about Suzanne. *Nora.*

Leave it to a woman to screw up his life.

If he was right about this injury, he'd probably need arthoscopic surgery to fix it. Then it would be six, eight weeks before he was fully up to speed again. He clenched a fist. He'd been counting on working round the clock to keep him so busy he would forget all about Nora. Now that would be impossible.

He sucked in a breath. *Forget all about Nora.* The thought brought an actual pain to his chest. This was ridiculous.

He pointed the clicker at the TV and flipped through the channels, looking for something other than Nora and his knee to occupy his thoughts.

A firm rap sounded at the door and he frowned. He wasn't expecting anyone, hadn't ordered room service. What the hell did the maid want at this time of night?

He pushed himself to his feet, limped to the door and yanked it open.

Suzanne stood in the hall outside his door.

"What do you want, Suzanne?"

"Oh, good," she said. "You *can* tell the difference. I thought I might have just wasted seven hours driving here." She pushed past him into the room. "Or, God forbid, I would have to impersonate Nora and seduce you."

CHAPTER SIXTEEN

HE SHUT THE DOOR and limped after her. "What the hell are you doing here? It's ten o'clock on a Sunday night."

"Don't I know it. I've been driving since three. And I might ask you the same thing—what the hell are you doing here?" She sank onto an upholstered chair in the corner.

He sat on the bed and elevated his right leg again, gently setting the ice pack back on his knee. "I'm skiing. Your turn."

"I'm coming after you."

"One sister was enough, thanks," he said. "You might, however, consider going after my mother, because when she finds out what the two of you pulled, it just may mean the end of—"

"She already knows."

"She does?"

"She doesn't care," Suzanne said smugly.

"She doesn't?" He was shocked.

Suzanne shook her head. "Apparently she's

known the truth since the first meeting Nora had with you."

She knew? His mom was in on the scam, too? "No way. She would have said something."

"She saw a glimmer of attraction between you and Nora and figured it was worth waiting to find out what might be there."

So his mother had been matchmaking even when he thought there wasn't a snowball's chance in hell of her doing it again? No wonder she'd given that little speech a few days ago. He scowled at Suzanne. "Which still doesn't explain why you're here."

"What did you do to yourself?" She pointed at his knee.

"Probably tore the meniscus—cartilage. I'll know better once I have an MRI."

"You going to be laid up for a while?" she asked.

"Could be. So why are you here?"

"I'd love to explain, but I'm a little parched." She went to the desk and lifted the lid on the ice bucket. "I see you have plenty of ice."

He gestured at his knee. "I kind of have a need for it."

"Have you got anything to drink?"

"Check the bar. Underneath."

Suzanne took a bottle of Snapple and a bag of peanuts from the bar. "Anything for you?"

"Yeah, give me one of those, too—mix some vodka in it. And while you're at it, don't forget to tell me why you're here."

"I think that's called a Snapple Spike," she said as she mixed it up. Once she handed him the drink, she settled into the chair again. "So, why am I here?" she repeated. She took a long drink. "Huh. Well, it really seemed like a good idea when I started out. Now, I don't know. Nora thinks I'm shopping for clients." She gave a light, easy laugh. "On a Sunday night." She took another sip of Snapple, then tore open the bag of peanuts. Her voice grew serious. "Actually, I thought it might be helpful if you heard the truth from the person who started it all."

"You might have phoned," he said. "Save a little time, gas."

"Too impersonal. You need to understand that this whole switch was my idea," she said. "I was afraid if I wasn't available to help your mom, I would lose her account to someone else."

He frowned. *Heard this already.* "You know, Suzanne, I don't really care—"

"You don't get to say that until you've heard the whole story—not after I just drove seven hours to tell it. If, when you've heard the whole story, you still want to say *I don't really care,* then I will get in my car and drive seven hours back to San Francisco and we'll never speak of this again. Agreed?" She raised her eyebrows at him.

He was taken aback. So this was the real Suzanne. "Okay."

"Now, where was I?" Suzanne said. "Oh, yeah. Nora really, really didn't want to take my place. But I begged her. I convinced her it would only be for one or two meetings." She popped a handful of peanuts in her mouth and chewed thoughtfully. "Of course, then your mother had to ask her to speak at the garden club. And you had to ask her to the party. And skiing…"

"Are you saying I'm partially responsible for this?"

"Well, yeah, in a way. Don't you think?" she said.

No. He hadn't thought of it that way at all. But he was starting to understand how Nora got sucked into impersonating her sister in the first place.

"Anyway, then she ran into Keegan, who knew she wasn't me, and started blackmailing her with the information—"

"What?" He hadn't heard a word about blackmail.

"Well, not quite blackmail. That's a whole other story about the cruise tickets and the engagement ring—we can talk about that later. The thing was, Nora agreed to do the personal shopping thing for you—and then you and your mother kept asking her to do stuff and she couldn't figure out how to say no."

"She wanted to say no?" He sat up straighter on the bed, tweaking his swollen knee in the process. He winced against the pain.

Suzanne laughed in a tinkling sort of way. "Not to you. But certainly to your mother."

Oh, well, that was okay. He wanted to say no to his mother a lot, too.

"But then you got under her skin—in more ways than one," Suzanne continued.

"I did?" A warmth started in his chest.

"Yeah. You don't know this…but Nora and her husband had a really good marriage. She pretty much figured she'd never love again. And then you came along." She screwed up her face. "Not that she's in love with you. I mean, she hasn't said that to me or anything. She could be, I suppose, but I don't know. Anyway…there was the potential…"

The potential? He knew all about the po-

tential. He'd given up coaching the *A* team for
the potential.

Suzanne finished off her peanuts and went to
the cabinet to grab a bag of Cheetos. "She
decided she was going to tell you the truth on
that ski trip. But then you…*did it*…and right
after that you told her you were going to take
this all-year, around-the-world coaching job."
She shook her head. "Not the best bedside
manner, doc, if I do say so myself."

"I told her I wanted to keep seeing her."

"Sorry, but after first saying you aren't
going to be around for four years, telling a
woman you still want to see her feels a lot
like, 'Thanks for the good time, I'll call you
when I'm horny again.'"

He stared at her. How had he ever thought Nora
was Suzanne? "But that's not what it was about."

"Like I said, work on that bedside manner."
Suzanne walked across the room eating Cheetos.
"So she didn't tell you on the ski trip. But after
she got the job, she couldn't stand the lying and
she was going to tell you when she saw you in
the rehab center but your partner was there."

"She said that her washer was broken."

"Get a clue. Do you really think she was
walking around up there crying about her
washing machine?"

He hadn't given it much thought before now. "Probably not."

She gestured with her bottle of Snapple. "As for that daddy list? It really was *nothing*. Did you even check out who was on it? It was a joke. One name was the guy who pushes the coffee cart at the hospital. And half of the other names she didn't even know—they were just guys the women in her coffee group threw on the list. Women do silly things like that—usually when they're sixteen, not in their thirties—but it doesn't mean *anything*."

She sat on the edge of the bed near him. "Anyway, she's sort of devastated that you don't believe her."

"She got the job she wanted. So all is not lost," he said with more bite than he intended. He took a swallow of his drink.

"That's why I'm here. You're right. She got the job of her dreams," Suzanne said quietly. "And this afternoon, she turned it down."

What kind of game were these two playing? "What?"

"She called the top guy at the hospital this afternoon and said she didn't want the job."

He twisted his head to look directly at her. "He's not even in today—"

"She left a message on his voice mail."

"But— She was really sick of doing hospital physical therapy. You should have seen her enthusiasm for this new clinic." He struggled to find the logic in what Suzanne was telling him.

"I saw it. That's why I'm here. She turned it down because of you. Because she wanted to prove that everything she'd done wasn't about getting the job."

"Oh, hell." He drank some more. "She's the best person for the job, the most qualified. She gets the vision we have for it. She's the perfect fit to run the place—"

"Well, she's not going to," Suzanne said matter-of-factly.

"What that woman needs is—"

"What she needs is for you to accept her apology and tell her you still want her in the job. Even then, I'm not sure she'll take it."

This is why he didn't get involved with women—they were so damn difficult. He grabbed his cell phone from the table next to the bed and dialed Nora's number. Voice mail kicked in and he shut it off. "Where is she?"

Suzanne shook her head. "At this time of night? Probably at home—just not answering."

"Great. She's the best person for the job and we're going to lose her." Twenty minutes ago he wanted to fire her; now all he could think of was how to make her stay. "Do you have any idea how incredible this center is going to be?"

Suzanne shook her head. "But then, this isn't my field. If you want to talk shopping, though, I could hold my own—"

"It's the kind of place most docs dream of. It was for me anyway. My partners and I have been after the hospital to do this for a long time." He dialed Nora's home again, once more reaching voice mail.

"I'm not sure she'll pick up for anyone," Suzanne said. "She might even be in bed already."

"Hell." He tossed down the rest of his Snapple Spike. "Come on, we're driving back." He took the ice bag off his knee and swung his legs over the side of the bed, exhaling sharply as he stood. "My right leg is out of commission—you'll have to do the driving."

"Maybe you should go to an emergency room—"

"Nope. I'm pretty sure I know what's wrong. And if I'm right, I know what doctor I want to see." He snapped his fingers. "Let's go, it's a long drive."

Suzanne gave him a patronizing look from her seat on the bed. "I know it is. I just made it. And now you want me to turn around and go back? Fourteen hours in a row?" She popped some Cheetos in her mouth and licked the orange off her fingers.

"I'd drive if I could."

"Boy, oh, boy, you are going to owe me big."

He threw back his head and laughed, wincing as the motion put him off balance a little and sent renewed pain shooting through his knee. "All this might do is make us even." He hobbled to the closet, pulled out his duffel bag and proceeded to the bathroom to get his stuff. "Okay, I'm ready. Grab my skis. And get us some of those Cokes out of the refrigerator—the caffeinated ones so we can stay awake."

Fifteen minutes later they were on the highway headed toward San Francisco, Suzanne driving and Erik stretched out in the backseat so he could keep his leg up.

"Estimated arrival time. 6:00 a.m.," Suzanne said. "Wake up merry sunshine."

"We can do better than that. With no one on the road, you can just lay on the gas."

She snorted. "And you'll pay the speeding ticket?"

"The pleasure will be all mine." He shifted in the seat to try to make his knee more comfortable.

Suzanne tossed a glance over her shoulder. "Maybe we should stop at a hospital first. At least you could get some pain meds."

"I can write my own damn prescription if I want. Just drive. I took some over-the-counter stuff right before you arrived."

She did that laugh of hers again. "Okay, you're the expert."

They engaged in small talk for a while, then settled in, listening to the radio, the black road rolling out in front of them, the miles passing as slowly as the hours. He didn't want Suzanne to fall asleep, and he didn't want to fall asleep and leave her on her own, so every now and then, they'd engage in some discussion or another, then let it lapse.

He closed his eyes and let his thoughts drift. He couldn't believe Nora had turned down the job. Not only was it the kind of work she wanted to do, but she truly was the best person for it. Which made it important that she didn't turn it down for the wrong reasons.

Sure, she'd lied to him about who she was. But after listening to her sister for the last hour, he had a complete understanding of how she'd gotten roped into the whole fiasco. Suzanne was a lot like his mother—a steam roller on a mission.

He almost laughed out loud then, remembering how, when he'd first met Suzanne—Nora, actually—he'd thought she didn't seem like the kind of personal shopper his mother would hire. Now that he'd met the real Suzanne, he saw that she and Mom were a perfect match.

In the big picture, there really was no harm done by the sister switch—it didn't affect how she would do her job. And now that he'd decided to stay, he was more determined than ever to make the new center the best possible. Nora Clark as the director would ensure that. She was right for the job.

She was right for him.

He jerked upright, opened his eyes and looked at Suzanne. "Did you just say something?"

She shook her head. "I thought you were asleep."

"No…just dozing." Hell, was that just in his brain? What did it mean?

By the time they reached San Francisco, his knee was throbbing, he was tired and his patience was at an end.

Suzanne pulled into the driveway. "I'm thinking Nora might not be happy I drove out to Mammoth and talked to you. So here's my plan."

"Five-thirty in the morning and we have to follow a plan?"

She nodded. "I'll go in and get into my pajamas. You wait out here a few minutes, then ring the bell. I'll answer the door and tell Nora you're here. That way she'll think I just got out of bed...and never know I had anything to do with it."

Five-thirty in the morning and she was concocting schemes? When he got the chance he was going to profusely apologize to Nora for ever doubting her. No wonder she agreed to take Suzanne's place—he would have, too, if it meant she'd move out of his house. "Okay," he said.

"Then—"

"There's more?"

"Well, yeah." She put the car into Park and shut off the lights. "There's no way you could know she quit the job. She only left the guy a voice mail—and he sure didn't go into work this afternoon and track you down at the ski hill to tell you. You have to find some other reason for being here and then get *Nora* to tell you she quit."

"Some other reason for stopping by at the crack of dawn? Hell, that should be easy."

Suzanne ran to the back door as he limped to the front and waited in the darkness. After a few minutes, he pushed the bell. His knee ached and his head wasn't far behind. When Suzanne didn't answer, he knocked on the door, then pounded with his fist. "Plan's working well, Suzanne," he muttered.

He rang the bell and pounded again. If she didn't get the door soon, one of the neighbors would probably call the police.

Finally, the porch light flipped on and the door opened. He blinked several times to adjust to the sudden brightness.

Nora. She stood in the doorway in short pajamas, her hair mussed, her eyes heavily lidded and sultry, her face flushed from sleep.

He wanted to kiss her.

"Erik?"

"Nora." *Leave it to a woman to screw up his life.*

"Do you know what time it is?" she asked.

Where the hell was Suzanne? "Ah, yeah. It's around five…thirty."

"What are you doing?" Her face was a picture of total confusion and he wanted to kiss her again.

"I hurt my knee. Can I come in?"

She hesitated just long enough that he thought for a minute she was going to say no. Then she gave him a strange look and stepped back to let him inside.

Suzanne bounded down the stairs. "Oh, Erik!" she said gleefully. "How nice to see you.

I was upstairs. In bed. Sleeping. Soundly." She raised her voice a notch. *"Very soundly."*

"Can I sit down?" Erik held up his ice pack.

"How'd you do it?" Nora asked.

"Skiing."

She winced and led the way to the living room, stopping to flip on a lamp to its lowest setting. Slowly, favoring his bad knee, he sat on one end of the couch and put his legs up. From the kitchen came the sound of pans clanking together and water running.

"She sure is energetic for this time of day," Nora muttered. "So why are you here?"

"My knee. It's killing me. I can't sleep. I'm not sure—think I might have torn the cartilage again." He hoped he sounded convincing—at least everything he said was true.

She pushed her hair back from her face and frowned at him, then stepped to the window to look outside. "You drove back from the ski hill in the middle of the night? Where's your car?"

Suzanne stepped into the room just then. "I'm making coffee," she said brightly. "And some of those refrigerated cinnamon rolls. I know how everyone gets hungry in the middle of the night."

"Tinkle tinkle, sister, isn't gonna cut it. Where's his car?" Nora repeated.

"How should I know? I just got up," Suzanne said. "I've been sleeping for hours."

"I took a cab."

Nora turned to face him. "From Mammoth? That must have cost a fortune."

"What's money?" He was starting to get a good sense of how easy it was to get sucked into a big charade.

Nora bit her lower lip as she mulled over his words and he was hit by a realization so hard, it almost took away his breath. When he was with Nora, he had a team. Just the two of them in one boat, rowing in the same direction. He inhaled slowly. *He hadn't come here because she was right for the job. He'd come here because she was right for him.*

THE SIMPLE NEARNESS of him made her weak. She tried to still the racing of her heart and stay detached. "So you've come about your knee? In the middle of the night?"

He nodded. "I've been to the best doc I know and he ordered up physical therapy. I didn't want to wait another minute and have it stiffen up."

"What doc?"

He grinned and his blue eyes sparkled. "Me. So I've come to the best physical therapist I know to get some help. The person who's going to head up the new sports medicine rehab center."

"At five-thirty in the morning." She broke eye contact. She didn't want to touch him, didn't want to feel the warmth of his skin under her hands, didn't want to be close enough to smell his aftershave…didn't want to feel the pain in her heart.

"Humor me. Just check it over…."

"Fine. Lay back." As soon as he was flat on his back, she did a manual test to check for a cartilage tear in the knee—a test that was impossible for anyone to do on themselves. Taking hold of his right leg, she brought it up into a full bent position, rotated the foot inward, then straightened the leg again. She didn't hear any clicking. "Any pain with that?" she asked as professionally as possible.

He looked awestruck. "No. Quick, do it the other way."

She repeated the test, rotating the foot outward this time.

He pushed himself up on his elbows and grinned at her again, looking so cute she could hardly stand it.

"No pain. No tear," he said. "Nora, you are truly a gifted therapist."

She laughed. "It probably swelled so badly because your knee was compromised already."

She sat on the edge of the coffee table and touched her fingers to the big scar that ran down his knee and shin. He'd really done a number on himself. Multiple scars surrounded that main one, so many that his knee looked like a jigsaw puzzle. For a moment, she could almost feel the pain he must have experienced fifteen years ago when he blew out his knee, how the loss of skiing must have devastated him. She touched the scars again, then began to gently work the muscles.

Erik let his head drop back against the couch and closed his eyes. After a minute he said, "Maybe a little higher."

She moved her fingers up onto his strong, solid quad muscle and wished he would kiss her. "There?"

"Yeah, that's good," he said, eyes still closed.

A moment later he said, "Maybe a little more on the inside."

She eyed him suspiciously and slipped her fingers onto his inner thigh. He sucked in a breath.

"Does that hurt?"

"Ah…no." Erik opened his eyes. "You can't turn down the job at the clinic," he said.

"Word gets around fast." She moved her hands away.

"You are far and away the best person for the job," he said.

"No, I'm not. I let the ends justify the means. I should have told you the truth a long time ago, but I rationalized everything." Out of need to do something, she began to work his knee again.

"Rationalization is sort of funny," he said. "I completely rationalized that giving up my career in order to coach was a good thing to do. I thought being part of the team would make me whole." He rubbed a hand across his jaw. "Only a funny thing happened on Friday afternoon. I realized there was something else that made me more whole than being part of the ski team."

She looked up at him, at his eyes watching her with intensity.

"You," he said.

This wasn't happening. It was five in the morning and she had to be dreaming. She wanted to say something but couldn't find the words. Finally she whispered, "What?"

"You. You make me whole."

A contentment filled her, the sensation that comes after waiting for something and wanting it so badly and thinking it will never happen. And then it does. She felt a quiet joy, a gentle relief, like a sigh, like an exhale of breath that one can't hold in because life is so good and moments like these are so rare. A knot formed in her throat.

"I realized then I didn't want to spend years on the road, years getting up at dawn and going to bed at midnight…and never having you. I realized that when I'm with you, I have a team." He smiled wryly. "I was going to tell you Saturday. But then all that other stuff got in the way." He grasped her by the arms and pulled her toward him, until their faces were inches apart. "Stay."

"With the clinic?" she asked.

"With the clinic. With me."

Tears sprang to her eyes.

"I love you," he said. "Will you stay?"

She nodded and leaned into him, kissed him then let herself sink into him. And all the tension of the past three weeks left her.

"Hey, everyone, here's the sweet rolls, hot from the oven. Who wants coff—" Suzanne sang out from the doorway.

They broke apart and turned to look at her.

"Am I interrupting something?" she asked innocently.

"A meeting. We're working on the business plan for the new sports medicine rehab center," Erik said.

Suzanne chortled. "That's just what I thought. I so knew that fourteen-hour drive would be worth it."

"What?" Nora looked from one to the other. "What fourteen-hour drive?"

"Oh, nothing," Suzanne said.

"You went to Mammoth today," Nora said.

"Someone needed to get the train back on the tracks." Suzanne bit into a cinnamon roll.

"I feel like I've been set up," Nora said.

"Join the club. Your sister has a way about her. Next thing you know, you're in so deep you can't find your way out," Erik said.

Nora rolled her eyes. "Don't I know it. It's light and easy laughter, tinkle tinkle. Works every time." She gave her own version of Suzanne's signature laugh.

A child's giggle echoed it from the stairway.

Nora turned. Danny was sitting on the top step, grinning.

"I think that's my cue to call it a night," Suzanne said heading for the stairs. "Come on, urchin, back to bed with you."

Erik bent to kiss Nora once more. "And my cue to pick up right where we left off."

* * * * *

A new member joins the
Thursday night Singles With Kids group!
Derrick Cavenaugh is a single dad struggling
to raise his two daughters—and sometimes
he needs a little help....

Look for Derrick's story
ALL-AMERICAN FATHER
by Anna DeStefano (SR#1410) next month
wherever Harlequin books are sold!

Turn the page for a sneak peek....

CHAPTER ONE

"Nice job, Cavenaugh." Derrick's senior partner slapped him on the shoulder as they left the conference room behind.

"Thanks, Spencer." Derrick replied with the expected hint of nonchalance. "I'll have the merger portfolio ready for Reynolds-Allied to sign by the end of the month."

It felt good to be in control of something.

Anything.

Contract law wasn't as sexy as the professional football career he and his old man had envisioned for his life. But being on top of his game during the morning's high-stakes negotiations felt better than the sweetest touchdown pass. Since returning to San Francisco a year ago, work was the only place he wasn't failing on a daily basis. Where his—God, he hated the word—*potential* wasn't being wasted.

"You're coming to the homecoming game in a couple of weeks, right?" Spencer Hastings's declarative questions usually pinned you where you didn't want to be. And the man held in the palm of his hands the promotion to junior partner Derrick had been busting his butt for. "You'll make everyone's night by showing up."

"I…" Derrick's legacy as Western High's biggest alumni football star had secured him a spot at the firm of Hastings-Chase-Whitney. But he was a chronic no-show at as many social events as he could get away with. Especially the alumni ones, where there would be little business to be done, and too much of what he was supposed to have become, but wasn't, slapping him in the face. "I'll have to find a sitter for Leslie and Savannah."

"Nonsense." Hastings gave his shoulder a firmer slap. The elevator rushed them to the ground floor. "Bring the kids along. Everyone would love to see your family."

Derrick tried to picture his twelve- and nine-year-old, already resentful of the time his job stole from them, listening to Daddy relive glory days with a bunch of people they didn't know. In under half an hour, he'd have a Power Puff Girl-sized mutiny on his hands.

Zam.

Pow!

Dad, we wanna go. Now!

"I'll see what I can do." He flashed the golden-boy grin that always smoothed things over. "My oldest has a science project she's working on and—"

His BlackBerry chirped.

He sifted through his overflowing briefcase as they emerged through revolving doors onto the bustling sidewalk.

"Derrick Cavenaugh."

"Mr. Cavenaugh, this is Detective Oaks with the Atherton PD. I'm at the Stop Right on the corner of Elm and Matteson. I have your daughter, Leslie, here. There's been an incident and the owner intends to press charges...."

Derrick pasted on a panic-free expression, while his insides churned up the take-out sushi he'd gulped down for lunch. Hastings kept his gaze politely focused on the shuffle of business people streaming by. But Derrick could feel the other man's interest, as the cop summed up Leslie's latest contribution to his plunge into single-parent insanity.

His oldest, so brainy and so beautiful, had apparently skipped out of school early again, with her sights firmly set on adding a conviction for petty larceny to her middle school resume.

* * * * *

Turn the page for a sneak preview of
IF I'D NEVER KNOWN YOUR LOVE
by
Georgia Bockoven

From the brand-new series
Harlequin Everlasting Love
Every great love has a story to tell.™

One year, five months and four days missing

There's no way for you to know this, Evan, but I haven't written to you for a few months. Actually, it's been almost a year. I had a hard time picking up a pen once more after we paid the second ransom and then received a letter saying it wasn't enough. I was so sure you were coming home that I took the kids along to Bogotá so they could fly home with you and me, something I swore I'd never do. I've fallen in love with Colombia and the people who've opened their hearts to me. But fear is a constant companion when I'm there. I won't ever expose our children to that kind of danger again.

I'm at a loss over what to do anymore, Evan. I've begged and pleaded and thrown temper tantrums with every official I can corner both here and at home. They've been incredibly tolerant and understanding, but in the end as ineffectual as the rest of us.

I try to imagine what your life is like now, what you do every day, what you're wearing, what you eat. I want to believe that the people who have you are misguided yet kind, that they treat you well. It's how I survive day to day. To think of you being mistreated hurts too much. If I picture you locked away somewhere and suffering, a weight descends on me that makes it almost impossible to get out of bed in the morning.

Your captors surely know you by now. They have to recognize what a good man you are. I imagine you working with their children, telling them that you have children, too, showing them the pictures you carry in your wallet. Can't the men who have you understand how much your children miss you? How can it not matter to them?

How can they keep you away from us all this time? Over and over, we've done what they asked. Are they oblivious to the depth of their cruelty? What kind of people are they that they don't care?

I used to keep a calendar beside our bed next to the peach rose you picked for me before you left. Every night I marked another day, counting how many you'd been gone. I don't do that any longer. I don't want to be reminded of all the days we'll never get back.

When I can't sleep at night, I tell you about my day. I imagine you hearing me and smiling over the details that make up my life now. I never tell you how defeated I feel at moments or how hard I work to hide it from everyone for fear they will see it as a reason to stop believing you are coming home to us.

And I couldn't tell you about the lump I found in my breast and how difficult it was going through all the tests without you here to lean on. The lump was benign—the process reaching that diagnosis utterly terrifying. I couldn't stop thinking about what would happen to Shelly and Jason if something happened to me.

We need you to come home.

I'm worn down with missing you.

I'm going to read this tomorrow and will

probably tear it up or burn it in the fireplace. I don't want you to get the idea I ever doubted what I was doing to free you or thought the work a burden. I would gladly spend the rest of my life at it, even if, in the end, we only had one day together.

You are my life, Evan.

I will love you forever.

* * * * *

Don't miss this deeply moving Harlequin Everlasting Love story about a woman's struggle to bring back her kidnapped husband from Colombia and her turmoil over
whether to let go, finally, and welcome another man into her life.

IF I'D NEVER KNOWN YOUR LOVE by Georgia Bockoven is available March 27, 2007.

And also look for THE NIGHT WE MET by Tara Taylor Quinn, a story about finding love when you least expect it.

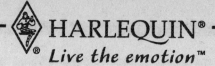

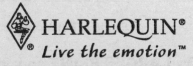

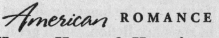
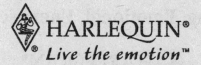

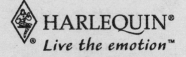

Harlequin® Historical
Historical Romantic Adventure!

Imagine a time of chivalrous knights and unconventional ladies, roguish rakes and impetuous heiresses, rugged cowboys and spirited frontierswomen—these rich and vivid tales will capture your imagination!

Harlequin Historical . . . they're too good to miss!

HHDIR06